JUST HIS ASSISTANT

A SWEET ROMANTIC COMEDY

SOUTHERN ROOTS SWEET ROMCOM
BOOK 3

ELANA JOHNSON

feel-good fiction

CHAPTER ONE

JESSIE

When my alarm goes off, I groan and roll over to silence it. It's been the longest, worst week of my life—but also the very best—and it's only Friday morning. It's almost October in Carolina now, and that means it's not exactly light at five-thirty in the morning.

I'm not one-hundred percent awake. But I will be, because my boss and I are meeting this morning to go over the open house happening tomorrow. It's my first open house—this week has been stuffed full of firsts for me—and I want to get it right.

There's very little that's gone right this week, other than the fact that I keep showing up—on time, thank you, thank you. I wasn't late for my interview last week either. I have the text from Lance Byers to prove it, though I've never told him that.

He still hired me, and I'm still one-thousand-percent

determined to figure out the real estate business. "Don't be one of those people," I sleep-mutter to myself. I once dated a guy who said stupid stuff like, "One hundred and ten percent, Jess," for everything. It grated against my nerves then, and now *I'm* using the nonsensical figure.

There's only one hundred in a percentage. Anything above that just makes no sense.

I roll over and sit up, taking a moment to stretch left and right. The bed my uncle has provided for me is very much appreciated, but it is not very much comfortable. I've also put on about twenty pounds since arriving in Charleston six months ago. All that sitting on Alec's couch with his parrot on my shoulder and eating the delectable food in his fridge hasn't exactly added to my physical fitness.

I don't care though, despite the looks Uncle Jack gives me when I butter my cornbread muffins in the morning. If he doesn't want me to eat them, why does he have his chef make them every dang day?

Because he can, I tell myself as I finally stand. I go through my morning routine, which includes complete skin and hair care, carefully inserting my contacts, doing my makeup, and the careful selection of clothing. Lance told me yesterday that I wear too much red, and I could only stand there in my very crimson dress and stare at him.

He'd sighed—a sound I have memorized after only four days of working with him—and gone back into his office. His has a door and walls—windows on two of those too—while mine doesn't. I just sit at a desk that faces his office, the wall across the hall to my right, and a huge bank of copy machines on my left.

If someone uses the machines, they can't actually see me, because there's a six-foot divider there. Still, when those things heat up, that hot air just comes right around the divider. I've said nothing to anyone about it, because we're Southern, and we understand heat.

A woman named Olive sits at the front podium-desk most of the time, and if the wall with the giant F&F wasn't behind her work area, I'd be able to see the front door and her desk too. As it is, though, I'm pretty isolated at my desk. I have a great view of a clock though—and Lance's door.

That's the most important part. I'm his assistant, and apparently that means I'm supposed to be able to read his mind. Somehow. He even said on the first day, *Jessica, I need you to anticipate my needs and have things ready for me.*

"Anticipate his needs." I scoff. I know what men need, and that's constant fuel for their egos. At least all of the men I've ever known or dated, with one rare exception in my best friend, Alec Ward.

Alec does like being the best though, and people constantly praise his food, myself included. So he probably has plenty of fuel for his ego. He also struck the jackpot when he got his job at Saucebilities, because they're now the top-rated catering service in Charleston, and he's about to get engaged to the owner and his boss, Tara.

I smile just thinking about the two of them, which is such a different reaction than what I'd been doing only a week ago. I carefully paint the pink lipstick onto my lips, pressing to really seal it in. I have permanent lip staining, but it requires some touch-ups from time to time. Lance gives me a *up-down-check-out-in-a-non-sexual-way* look every single time he sees me, and I know if I don't meet his requirements, he won't hesitate to tell me.

I finish up with my makeup and shimmy into a chestnut brown leather skirt I've borrowed from Tara. She said I could keep it, because she literally wears the same thing to work every single day and it doesn't fit her anymore. But it feels like charity to me. I don't need to be given clothes.

I go back into my bedroom and open the closet. I adore clothes, and I've kept all of mine that I brought from Beaufort when I left. Some of them I can't wear anymore due to that fourscore increase in poundage, but I can't get rid of them. Fabrics and patterns inspire me, and I reach out to touch an off-white dress with bright butterflies on it.

It makes me feel like I can spread my wings and fly too, and a smile moves through my soul. I could probably let out the dress and still wear it, though I'm not attending charity luncheons or non-profit fundraisers anymore.

No part of me yearns for that past life, with all the fake

smiles, false eyelashes, and phony friendships. No, thank you. Not for me.

A wave of loneliness washes over me, and I close the closet. "It's Friday," I say. "You're only working half the day. You can do this." I started listening to affirmation podcasts a couple of months ago, and I do feel better about myself and life in general.

I also know I won't only work half the day, because everything that Lance knows how to do instinctively, I don't. I have to learn it, and that takes twice as long. But I only have to be in his presence until lunchtime. Thankfully.

After that, Callie, one of my only friends here in Charleston, said she'd come over and help me institute a filing system. Right now, the precarious stacks of folders on my desk aren't really getting the job done right. Lance even eyed them yesterday like they were giant slime balls that might attack him next time he strode past my desk to use the restroom.

Honestly, the man is a like a big, black fly in a perfectly pretty glass of lemonade. He's the party-crasher. The killer of fun. He probably laughs when babies cry—that's how surly the man is.

I remind myself that he's in the top five real estate agents in terms of sales in the whole state of South Carolina, and I'm very lucky to be learning from him. "Very, very lucky," I tell myself as I leave my bedroom and head into the main part of the house. Hopefully, it'll still be too early for Uncle Jack or my cousin Rufus to be out and about.

They're about as insufferable as the hundred-degree temperatures on a Carolina Sunday, and I'm *this-close* to being able to move out. I need my own freedom, and in any spare time I have, I've been looking at apartments around the city.

The trouble is, everything is more than I can afford. I'm almost hoping Alec will get his plan together to propose to Tara, and then I can ask if I can sublet his apartment from him. He'll probably let me, and I can even say I'll take care of Peaches for him when I'm not at work.

The cornbread muffins sit on the kitchen counter, but I don't see any evidence of nearby humans. However, as I split and butter a muffin, footsteps approach. I know the sound of shiny, leather shoes that have literally never seen the outside of this mansion. They belong to Uncle Jack.

"There you are," Uncle Jack says in that ultra-smooth voice of his. It's like he polishes his voice box in one of those rock tumblers before using it. He swoops his medium brown hair to the side just-so, and I've never seen him with an ounce of stubble. Not even a half-ounce.

Where else would I be? I wonder, but I say, "Here I am. Good morning, Uncle Jack." I step over to him and give him a kiss on both cheeks. I am a proper Southerner, after all, and I've been taught to respect my elders no matter what.

No matter that he tried to set me up with someone

fourteen years older than me. No matter that Rufus keeps bringing home these little weasels for dinner, as if it's an accident they're all dressed up in designer suits and silk ties.

I may be from a rich family, but I'm not stupid.

"Thanks for always getting these muffins," I say, slathering on more butter though it's a little heavy-handed, even for me. I smile and take a big bite, immediately regretting it. Way too much butter, and I didn't think that was even something that could happen. Still, I chew through the slippery butter-muffin in my mouth like it's the best thing I've ever tasted.

My uncle gives me a terse smile, which is actually a step up from his tight ones. "I'm glad you like them." He reaches for the coffee pot and frowns. "Oh, brother. Wesley didn't make this in the last hour." He looks around as if his personal assistant will be hovering there, waiting for his approval on the brew.

"I have to go," I say, because the last thing I need is a display of Uncle Jack's money. We get it, he's got money. Enough to have a personal assistant make his coffee and a personal chef cater all of his meals. Enough to have a shed full of cars and motorcycles. Enough for a pool, a theater room, and that prison-like library.

Big freaking deal. BFD, as I like to say. Tons of people have money, and it doesn't make them special, just like it doesn't make Uncle Jack better than anyone else.

Outside, my sedan sticks out like a whore in church on

Sunday, but I smile at her. I've nicknamed her Lucy, because Lucille Ball is a personal heroine of mine. She opened doors for women in comedy no one had before, and she was the first female to head a production studio.

Mama hates my idolization of Lucille Ball, but she's not here in Charleston, and I don't have to answer to her anymore. I get behind the wheel and pat it. "All right, Luce. Just to work and back today, I swear."

Sometimes we go all over town—or at least to Alec's—but since I'll spend the day at the agency and I have that open house tomorrow, I have no detours planned today.

She starts up on the second try, and her engine seems to chug along pretty nicely. I ease away from the front of the house and along the graveled drive until it turns into hard-packed dirt. Uncle Jack lives on the outskirts of the suburbs of Charleston, in a town called Sugar Creek. Barely in Sugar Creek, which is where Callie lives. Live*d*. She moved in with Dawson, who's in another small town kissing up against Charleston—Cottonhill.

Lucy and I go down the road, really gaining some momentum when we hit the road that leads into a more populated area of town. The downtown area of Sugar Creek is straight out of the historical South, and I love every old brick and all the crumbling façades.

Lucy doesn't seem to love the quaint buildings as much as I do, and she starts to sputter just as I go through the single stoplight. I ease her over right in front of the bakery, noting the steam starting to rise from the hood.

"That's not good." I get out of the car and stand on the sidewalk. I've seen people open the hoods of their cars, but I'm wearing a silky white blouse with orange trim on the sleeves to signal my support of autumn arriving. A single smudge will ruin the entire outfit.

This might be the end of Lucille Ball the Camry, but I still have to get to work. Callie doesn't own a car, and she and Dawson go to their downtown office together.

Lance lives in Cider Cove, and while it's not exactly on the way through Sugar Creek, it *is* on the way into the city. Since I left over two hours before I need to be at work, surely he'll still be home.

I pull out my phone, who I've named Missy Rings-A-Lot, though she doesn't, and tap when I see I've gotten a text from him. *Confirm that you've received the Hudson docs.*

"Would it kill him to say please?" I mutter to myself, and I tap on his name to call him. I'm sure I got the docs, and I can just tell him I did and then check my email. I mean, do people not get emails these days?

"Jessie," he says. "You got the docs?"

"Yes," I say. "But actually, Mister Byers, I'm calling for a favor."

"A...favor?" he asks as if he doesn't know the meaning of the word.

"Yes," I say, lifting my free hand to my mouth to bite the thumbnail. "My car broke down in Sugar Creek, right in front of the bakery." I turn and look at the building, which already has a line out the door. "I was wondering if you could stop by and pick me up on the way to the office. I can get a Carry home."

Why I can't get a Carry there, I'm not sure. Maybe because my bank account has seventeen dollars in it, and I tell myself in a stern voice, *no maple bacon doughnut for you, Jess* as the scent of the treat reaches my nose.

"Fine," Lance says as if I've asked him to rip off his arm and feed it to his dog. "I'll be there in an hour."

"Thank you," I say, my voice small and tinny. The call ends, and I face my nemesis: the bakery. A maple bacon bar won't be seventeen dollars, but I figure I better go take care of my money situation before treating myself to a second, fat-filled pastry that morning. After all, I do now have an hour to kill.

CHAPTER TWO

LANCE

I SEE MY ASSISTANT, JESSICA DUNAWAY—JESSIE, SHE'S asked me to call her—sitting on a bench, her blonde hair reflecting the morning sunshine in so many haloes of gold light. I clench my fingers around the steering wheel, because I have a soft spot for blondes.

Scratch that. I have no soft spots anymore. When my fiancée left Charleston with my diamond ring on her finger, everything turned hard. My heart is hard. My chest always feels stuffed full of concrete, so my lungs can't really get enough air. I've been pouring myself into the treadmill and the gym since Hadley's departure, so my muscles are hard too.

Life, in general, has been hard for me lately.

I flip on my blinker and ease up to the curb in a spot several yards down from where Jessie sits with an older gentleman. She pinches off a piece of doughnut and tips her head back as she laughs. I can't hear her, as I've got my windows up and the AC blowing. Watching the two of them feels like a scene from a peaceful movie, and I long for the easier days of this year, when everything seemed to be going my way.

A doughnut sounds amazing, and I get out of my truck and walk down the street in my casual Friday clothes—a black pair of slacks and a light blue button-up shirt. I'm wearing a red and white checkered tie that my mom gave me for my birthday at the beginning of the year, and I feel patriotic and put-together at the same time.

Jessie's wearing a gorgeous silk blouse that looks like God Himself reached down and touched it, making it glow white. Dark orange strips of fabric rim the sleeves, a very subtle nod to the calendar, which is almost to October. She's paired that with a brown leather skirt, and I lick my lips and swallow the sudden extra saliva in my mouth.

It's because of the mini pecan pie on the bench beside Jessie. Yeah, that's it. It's not because she's the type of woman that ticks every single box I've ever thought of when it comes to a girlfriend.

I'm not dating for a while. I need to figure out where I went wrong with Hadley, and where we deviated. I hadn't even known it, and that unsettles me the most.

I'm cursing Dawson's name when Jessie turns toward me. I'd told him I couldn't hire her, but my two previous assistants hadn't even lasted a week. Not even long enough for his wife and secretary—who's seriously one of the best

in the city—to come train them. She's coming this afternoon, though Jessie wasn't the one to tell me.

Callie told me, because she said I better have
Cayenne's there for lunch, and plenty of Skittles to help
her get through the Friday afternoon at the real estate
agency. I'd promised her she'd have it all, and I'm actually
pretty proud of Jessie that she's made it through this whole
week.

She has no idea what she's doing, but she tries. I can
tell that much.

"Mister Byers," she says, rising to her feet. "I got this
for you." She collects the miniature pecan pie and extends
it toward me, as well as a friendly, if professional, smile.

I simply stare at it as I take it from her. "Thank you."

"Is this your sweetheart?" the older gentleman asks, his
voice raspy like sandpaper over rough wood.

"Oh, no," she says waving her hand. She darts a look at
him, back to me, and then to him. "He's my boss."

"She's just my assistant," I say, smiling at the older
man. My heart pounces through my chest, and I hate that.
I feel like I'm falling for a minute, and then I look at Jessie
again. "Should we get going?"

"Yes," she says. "I'm sorry you had to go out of your
way. I'll use a Carry from now on." She tucks her hair
behind her ear, but the thick lock just flops right back out.
Her hair isn't quite long enough to tuck and have it stay,
and I smile at the rebellious curls.

"It's fine," I say. "You'll have to deal with Cha-Cha's

hair, though I did try to brush it off." I had, but only for a second at a stoplight on the way here, when I'd thought about it.

"Cha-Cha?" she asks, looking at me with those big, beautiful blue eyes.

"My dog," I say. "She's a corgi, and she's shedding her summer coat to grow her winter one." I open the passenger door for Jessie, because I'm not a complete ogre. I'm just on a female fast. I also don't mention that I open the door for Cha-Cha, and that I have to lift the stubby-legged pup onto the seat so she can ride up front with me.

"Interesting name," Jessie says with a smile and a glint in her eye that says she really thinks it's silly.

"I didn't name her," I say as she slides by me and gets in the truck. Her skirt pulls up as she steps up onto the runner, and I stare at the extra thigh I can see. My whole body flushes, and I feel like I'm sinking in quicksand. Everything is moving quickly around me, but I'm stuck moving at sloth-speed.

That's why I don't realize Jessie is stumbling before she's falling backward. All I have time to do is open my arms in a wide splay and catch her as she hits me. I grunt and fall to my knees, but that's as far as I have to go.

I'm touching so many inappropriate things, but I can't let go of her. Her body shakes even as she says, "I'm so sorry. My heel slipped."

I can't speak, so I just steady her as she gets to her feet, trembling all the while. She brushes her hands down the front of her body with her back to me, and after several long seconds, she turns to face me.

Bright pink patches decorate her cheeks, and she extends her hand toward me. "Did you rip your pants?"

"I'm sure it's fine," I say as I take her hand, not that I need her help to get up. I do need help with something else—my erratic heartbeat and the way my hands now have muscle memory of the feel of her body against them.

I manage to stand up, and I glance down at my slacks. Sure enough, there's a rip in the knee on my left leg. Jessie sucks in a breath and starts to apologize again.

"Stop it," I say, and I don't mean to sound so much like a scoundrel. I sigh when our eyes meet and hers are filled with anxiety. "I'm sorry," I say. "I didn't mean to bark that. I'm just...tired of listening to you apologize. It's not necessary."

The expression in her eyes changes to one of defiance, and she nods just once, barely any movement at all.

"Ready to try again?" I ask when I realize we're just standing there staring at one another on the sidewalk.

"Do you need to go home and change?" she asks.

"No," I say. "I have extra clothes in the office." I indicate the truck. "I'll help you up this time."

"My heel just slipped," she says again, turning. This time, she does grab onto the bar just inside the truck, and I put my hand on her hip to balance her. She doesn't flinch, and my skin tingles though I'm really just touching the leather on her skirt.

She makes it into the passenger seat, and I close her door for her. I go around the front of the truck, straightening my sunglasses and wishing I could straighten out my thoughts and my pulse. Well, maybe not my pulse. A straight heartbeat indicates death, and I don't want to be dead.

I just don't want to be duped again.

I get behind the wheel and cast a quick glance at Jessie. As I buckle my seatbelt, I say, "All good?"

"Yes, sir," she says. We ease away from the curb, and she clears her throat. "Who named your dog if you didn't?"

Everything tightens again, and I work to release it, the way I've been learning to do in therapy. "My ex-fiancée." It's my turn to clear my throat. "The first one."

"Oh." Jessie adjusts her purse and grabs the pecan pie as it starts to slide. "How many have you had?"

"Just two," I say, though that's a lot of fiancées, in my opinion. Especially if you can't get them to become wives.

"Ever been married?"

"No," I say. "You?" I'm not sure why I ask. Seems like the right thing to do. Someone asks you how you are, you answer and then ask them how they are. Right?

"No, sir," she says. "Never been engaged either, much to my mama's disappointment."

"Yes, well, it's not all that fun to tell your mama that your fiancée has called off the wedding either." I'm aware of how dark my voice comes out, but I don't know how to lighten it. Hadley left four months ago, and I feel like I should be further along than I am. The truth is, I have good days and bad days. Some days where I think I'm going to be okay, and I could probably, definitely, take a new woman to dinner. Some days where I think I'll never figure out who I am and what I want, and getting it is never going to happen.

Today is kind of in the middle, to be honest.

"I'm sure it's not," Jessie says. "I'm sorry, Lance."

"Jessie," I say in a warning voice.

"Oh, sugar honey iced tea," she says. "I apologized again. I'm sor—" She clamps her mouth shut and claps one hand over it. She isn't one of those women with fake nails and fake eyelashes and a fake chest. I know, as I basically just felt her up while she fell backward.

I smile and look away from her before I drive us right off the road. I need to get us back on safe ground, and there's nothing safer for me than work. "All right," I say, maybe adding on a little thickness to my Southern accent. "What did you think of the Hudson docs?"

"Oh, uh, I thought they looked good," she says, and I hide my smile. She has no idea what the Hudson docs even are, and in all honesty, I shouldn't expect her to.

So teach her, I think but that's very dangerous ground. If I start to teach her, that means I care about her, and I absolutely, cannot—*will not*—start to care about Jessie Dunaway as more than just my assistant.

But I do want to have a good, competent assistant. I

sigh as I turn toward her. "It was a letter of intent to purchase," I say. "Shiela Hudson wants that riverfront property I showed her a couple of weeks ago, and she doesn't want anyone to slide in an offer before she can get hers in."

Jessie turns toward me, and she looks like she's ready to soak up every single thing I say. "Okay," she says. "Is there an acronym for that?"

I grin at her. "Yes, Jessie. LOI."

"LOI," she repeats, plucking her phone from her purse and starting to type a note into it. "Got it. Was there anything else in the docs?"

I like that she's eager to learn, and I shake my head. "Not in that email."

"Yes, sir," she says, going back to her phone as I continue the drive toward the downtown agency. I tell myself that telling her about a letter of intent was not an attempt to get closer to her. It wasn't flirting, because that would be pathetic with a capital P.

It was just me being...nice. Yes, I do know how to be nice, and I'm proud of myself for achieving it so early in the morning.

CHAPTER THREE

JESSIE

MY BRAIN IS FULL OF ACRONYMS AND WORDS LIKE "closing docs" and "escrow lost" as I get out of Lance's enormous truck. He has a front spot near Finley & Frank, because he's a managing partner. I didn't realize that until Wednesday, but luckily, I only managed to wedge my toes into my mouth before I figured it out.

There's nothing wrong with my leather skirt as I follow him up the sidewalk, but I keep brushing at it anyway. He's the one with the rip in his pants, though his stride is sure and even. Everything about the man comes across that way, and I can't help giving him a smile as he opens the door, pauses, and waits for me to go through first.

Southern gentleman, enters my mind, but I quickly try to banish it. I can't even imagine what Mama will do if I text her and say I have my eye set on a successful, good-looking real estate agent in Charleston. She'd probably look them all up and text me their pictures one at a time, gauging how fast I respond to determine which one it is.

That brings a small smile to my face, and I greet Olive with it as Lance and I approach the front desk.

"Mister Byers," she says, sliding a red folder onto the countertop. That's for me, and I know what's in it. I may have only been at the agency for four days, but I know red folders are Lance's important documents for the day. It's my job to make sure he sees them, signs them, and gets them out to wherever they go by five o'clock.

The pressure behind my eyes double, and I glance at Lance, literally seeing red.

"You have a conference call in fifteen minutes," Olive continues seamlessly. I wonder if my voice sounds that polished and professional, and I highly doubt it. I'm a little nasally on the best of days, though I've never had anyone complain about the timbre of my voice.

Except Mama, of course. The woman can complain about how much money she has in the bank, as if it's some great burden she carries alone. I mentally roll my eyes while sliding the red folder off the counter and into my hands.

Olive reaches for something on the lower desk. "And this message came in for you." She looks up, clear worry in her eyes. She hands the slip of paper to Lance, and while I have fast eyes, they're not that fast.

Lance frowns at the paper, fists it, and tosses it onto

the counter. "Tell her not to call again, should she choose to do so."

"Sir," Olive says.

"Olive," Lance warns. He doesn't slide his eyes toward me at all. It's like I'm not even there. "Send the call through with Kyle when it comes in. Jessie."

"Mm hm, yes," I say, though I'm not sure why. Perhaps to remind myself—and everyone else—that I'm in the room.

"I need all the Hudson docs before the call."

"Yes, sir," I say, not even sure what that entails.

He does give me a look this time, and I nod like I'll have it all in hand. No problem. Yes, sir. I really want to grab that tiny wad of paper and find out what the message was that made him go from pecan-tartlet-happy to stormcloud-over-a-picnic grouchy in less than a second.

He walks past me and toward his office, and Olive's eyes round. "Lance," she says, but he just keeps going. "You have a problem..."

He enters his office and closes the door without turning or looking back.

"...with your pants," Olive says. She trains her wide eyes on me, and I simply give her a smile.

"I like these cat's eye glasses," I say, indicating hers. "The purple is amazing too."

"He had holes in his pants."

I brush at my leather skirt unconsciously. My feet

shift. "Uh, yes. Lucille Ball broke down this morning, you know?"

Olive's surprise turns to confusion.

"She's my car," I say quickly. "Lance—Mister Byers—had to give me a ride to work. He has this huge truck, and I maybe couldn't quite get in it. My skirt is a smidge tight." I laugh like me falling backward into Lance's arms is the funniest thing since Bette Harold came to town and charmed us all with her Southern stand-up comedy.

In truth, pure humiliation still rifles through me.

"Why does he drive that huge truck anyway?" I ask, glancing toward the frosted glass in his door. Lance Byers, ABR, ALC stare back at me in gold. *Gold.* I don't think I've ever seen my name in gold. Maybe blue gel pen, when I was fourteen.

"Lance bought the truck a month or two ago," Olive says, her eyes dropping back to her desk. She shuffles things around like she's suddenly very busy and can't talk to me. She's always been kind to me around the office, and I don't want that to change. "He said he needed it to move furniture, stage homes, that kind of thing."

"Makes sense," I say brightly, and that brings Olive's eyes back to mine. Surprised again. Probably at the level of enthusiasm I just displayed for why someone would buy a truck.

"Okay," I say with a laugh that sounds nervous. "I have a lot of docs to print." It'll take me the twelve minutes I have before the conference call just to figure out which docs to print, and I see some yelling in my future.

I glance at the tiny, wadded phone message, and Olive swipes it off the counter. I turn on my heel like I've joined the marching band and dash down the hall and around the bank of copiers to my desk.

I need twelve months to sort through everything here, but I take a deep breath and focus. Hudson docs. I only need to find and print all the Hudson docs.

I open my email, because I know Lance sent me something about the account today, and everything I need is probably there.

The top email reads *Here are all the Hudson docs. One copy each, please.*

It's from Lance, and the black, bold letters stare me in the face. My heart begins to pound like a jackrabbit jumping away from a fox, and I have no idea what to do with that please.

Please?

"Jessie," someone says, and I flinch away from my staring contest with my computer screen.

"Yes." I clear my throat and look up. Right into Lance's baby blues. I jump to my feet. "Yes."

"I don't hear the printer whirring," he says, knocking twice on the edge of my desk. "Right now, please."

"Yes, sir," I say for probably the tenth time that morning. I tell myself it's not an apology, and I hurry to get his email open and the docs printing. Eight minutes later, I take them into him, along with his red folder of must-do's for the day and hand everything to him.

As I turn to leave, he says, "I need you in here for the call."

I stall, the first part of his sentence every woman's dream. *I need you.* I can imagine him saying it right before he lowers his head and kisses me. My face flushes, and I nearly trip over my own feet as I turn back to him.

"You do?"

He looks up from the red folder, his pen still scratching out his signature. "You want to learn real estate, don't you?"

My mouth gapes like a fish out of water. *Blub, blub.* "I'm sorry?" Mama would've turned British and used, "Pardon?" but I can only stare with my fish-lips flapping.

Lance gives me a sly smile, as if he can see through my clothes to my underwear underneath. "We're not apologizing, remember? Go get your laptop and get back in here. Once the door closes and the call starts, the offer expires."

I stand there for another moment, and then I fly back to my desk, collect my laptop, a yellow legal pad, and a black pen. I'm at his door when Olive's voice comes over his intercom. "Mister Byers, I have Kyle Corison on the phone."

"Great," Lance says. "Send him over." He sets aside the items in the red folder and nods to me. "Close the door, Jess."

I do, wondering if I've confined myself to a lion's den

or a day at Disney World. Right now, with the look of determination on Lance's face, it's a toss-up.

———

"I BROUGHT REINFORCEMENTS," Callie Houser says as she sails into the real estate office. I turn from the counter, where I've been going over a scheduling thing with Olive.

A smile pops onto my face at the sight of her. She is just so pretty, and so kind, and so dang smart. I tell myself I'm smart too—I've just never had the opportunity to prove it to anyone quite the way Callie has.

She holds three to-go cups of coffee in a carrier, the branding for Legacy Brew evident. As she sets them on the counter, and we all reach for a cup, I say, "You're a lifesaver."

"And right on time," Olive says, taking the cup marked with caramel. "Are you sure you don't need a new job?"

Callie giggles and shakes her head. "I like working with my husband."

"Yeah?" Olive asks dubiously. "Because I'd kill mine if I had to do that." She grins, takes a sip of her hot drink, and settles back into her chair. I switch my smile from her to Callie.

"Come on back," I say, inhaling the earthy, strong scent of the coffee Callie's brought for me. It's just after lunchtime, but Callie never comes empty-handed.

Besides, for what she's going to be teaching me, I'm going to need the caffeine buzz.

I step around the wall with all its fancy lighting on the ampersand between the Finely and the Frank, and move past the copiers. One of them is shooting papers the color of canaries into the tray, but no one's there babysitting it. The *chunk-chunk-chunk* at lightning speed makes me wince, and I take a long draw of my coffee before I even round my desk.

"Wow," Callie says—more like yells—above the shockingly loud copier. She eyes it like it might turn into a wolverine and attack at any moment. I've done the same, so I get the feeling. No, I've eyed it like I have a pitchfork in my trunk I know how to stab with really well. I don't, but the thought of going after that copier until it's last replication wheezes into the tray has crossed my mind a time or two.

Or twenty-nine.

Callie stalls at the corner of my desk, pure horror entering her expression. If the copier doesn't kill her this afternoon, it looks like the manila folders and stacks of paper on my desk might do the job. "What is going on here?" she asks, her voice getting punctuated with the *chunk-cha-ch-cha-chunk* of paper hitting the tray and falling into the pile.

"This is my desk," I say, pushing aside a box of paper clips to make room for my cappuccino.

"No." Callie shakes her head as if I've committed some

sort of assistant assassination. Her lips press into a tight line. "No wonder Lance glares at you all day."

I did tell her that, but I'm not sure what my desk has to do with it.

I indicate the huge pile of folders nearest her hip. "Those came right there in that spot. I *inherited* this mess."

Callie sighs—or it looks like she does. I can't actually hear her above the copier—and sets her drink on top of the folders. "Honey, you *inherit* diamonds and estates. Files, you shred or put in a drawer." She smiles at me in a kind way, and I want to scream *help* at her.

Help me, I beg silently instead.

Callie must be really good at reading minds—or maybe women's faces with wide I'm-trapped-in-the-headlights eyes—because she continues around the desk and says, "Okay. This is what we're going to do."

She proceeds to walk me through making piles. Shred. To-file. Working documents. Current clients. To-do daily. To-do this week.

Somewhere in there, the copier finishes clunky-chunking, and at the end of a couple of hours, we have the trio of filing cabinets in my space labeled and organized. She feeds another file into the shredder, the sound of it doing about the same to my nerves.

My desk looks like Marie Kondo has shown up, and it currently holds two trays Callie's labeled with *Daily* and *Weekly*. They're empty, which makes me feel so accomplished.

She perches on the edge of my desk and finishes her coffee. Mine's long gone, and my head pounds in a way I haven't felt in a while. I used to get these types of headaches whenever Mama would say, "I've asked Stan to make us a nice dinner tonight."

That was code for, "I've asked a man twice your age to come eat with us in the hopes of marrying you off."

Happiness accompanies the freedom I feel as I collapse into my desk chair. "Lance is going to be so impressed."

Callie smiles and reaches into her purse to pluck out a bag of Byrd's cookies. She had those all this time and didn't get them out? I eye her like she's just escaped from prison and wants a ride somewhere.

"He does like things neat and nice," she says.

"Ninety-degree Lance is what I call him," I say, taking an offering gingersnap with a smile. I immediately want to suck the words back into my mouth. Callie's friends with Lance, and I shouldn't be bad-mouthing my boss.

Callie tips her head back and laughs, a reaction I wasn't expecting. It sends relief through me, and she offers me a handful of candy. I let her sprinkle some Skittles into my palm while she finishes giggling, and then she looks over her shoulder toward Lance's closed door.

"He only has this now," she says, a somber quality entering her voice.

"This?"

"The real estate firm," Callie says, meeting my eye again. "Hasn't he told you?"

Lance and I have spent very little time discussing personal things, so I just shake my head. "I don't need to know."

"His fiancée—"

"She said she doesn't need to know, Cal."

Callie jumps, nearly going pretzel as she twists to look at Lance behind her. I didn't see him ninja-up on us either, and I too leap to my feet. I adjust my skirt and run my fingers through my hair, as if I care what the blond god thinks about my looks. We've just spent hours getting dirty and sweaty, and I don't.

I do *not*.

Lance wears a look of complete disapproval on his face and nods to my phone. "I've called you four times. Why is your phone on silent?"

CHAPTER FOUR

LANCE

I'm seriously second-guessing my decision to teach Jessie anything about real estate. Maybe third-guessing. Fourth and fifth-guessing as Callie launches into a lecture about how she's spent all afternoon in my copier-infested office helping my assistant, and I have no right to glare at her with the force of gravity.

I do, actually, as she was about to tell my assistant personal things she has no right to tell. I simply roll my eyes and step toward my desk. "Come on, Cha-Cha." My corgi waits at my calf, as usual, and we go into the office.

"You brought your dog," Jessie says, her heels following me into the office. "Hello, sweetie. Oh, yes, you're so sweet, aren't you?" She crouches down and puts her face right next to Cha-Cha's. The corgi goes into Bliss with a capital B and gives me a look that says she wishes I would pay this much attention to her.

I give her an eye roll too, because it's not like I haven't walked her, fed her, given her fifteen body rubs that day, and then fed her bites of my hamburger as I ate lunch. Not only that, but she got to ride in the truck, the window down, and her funny face out into the wind as she sniffed all the smells of the city.

Jess looks up at me, and I lean against my desk. She straightens, her easiness with the dog disappearing as she smooths her clothes. "What are you doing here? I thought you were taking this afternoon off?"

I sigh, my lips almost fluttering the way a displeased horse's would. I manage to pull back on the ferocity of the sigh before then, thankfully. The last thing I need to do is turn into an equine in front of my pretty assistant.

She's just your assistant, I tell myself sternly. It doesn't matter what she looks like, as long as she gets the job done.

"A prospective new client called," I say.

"Did you see my desk?" Her eyes light up then, the way my soul did when the call had come in from Thurston Meadows. I have plenty of clients, and far too many to take on another one right now, especially one as articulate and sharp-tongued as Mr. Meadows.

But my mind had immediately seized upon Jessie, and then all kinds of trains had swarmed, all of them crashing and derailing and creating complete chaos in my head. For some reason, out of all the thoughts in my head, I'd plucked out the one that told me to call Jess and find out if she wanted to take on a client of her own.

"I did not," I say.

"Come see." She gestures for me to follow her, and since Cha-Cha doesn't seem to care that she's on a leash and has been *my* dog for six years as she follows the energetic Jess back into the hallway, I go too.

She brandishes both hands toward it now, indicating where Callie has sat behind the computer. "Ta-da!"

The surface of it can actually be seen, and surprise fills me. "Wow," I say, not wanting to be rude.

"We filed everything," Jess says in a rush. "Shredded stuff you don't need and kept all of our other clients in the cabinets." She indicates those as if I've never seen one before. Her face glows, and I find I want to know so much more about her than I currently do.

"Callie set me up with two trays—things I need to accomplish that day, and things I need to finish by the end of the week."

"And," Callie practically yells, pinning me with her bright blue eyes. I hate it when she looks at me like that. She puts both palms against the desk and pushes herself to a stand as if she needs her hands to do so. She looks around innocently, as if really searching for something. "There's no Cayenne's here, and it's well past lunchtime."

I give her a smile, because she really is an amazing woman. Dawson's the luckiest man in the world to have been tamed by her—plus, he got her all the way to the altar, something I haven't been able to do with anyone.

I glance at my oversized watch. "Ten minutes," I say. "It'll be here in ten minutes."

"Why are you here?" Jess asks me again, coming to my side. She looks up at me, and I can't have her doing that. The scent of her perfume follows the direction of her gaze and goes right into my nose.

The flowery, soft scent addles my mind, and I blink at her. "Uh, a new client called." I clear my throat. "I can't take them on, but I don't want to turn them down."

Jessie blinks at me. Blink-blink-blink. Her eyelashes are really long, and then her perfectly pink lips curve up. I can't even form thoughts.

Her mouth moves, but I'm not sure what she says. My phone rings, and I jolt with the buzzing in my pocket and the jazzy, snapping pop-music that indicates it's Dawson on the other end of the line.

"Is that your ringtone?" Callie asks with a snicker.

I pull out the phone to silence it. I answer the call and say, "I'll call you back in five minutes," and hang up before Dawson can say a word. He knows his wife is here; he knows I'm not working this afternoon; he probably wants to hit the rec center and play basketball or pickleball.

Callie's face is turning bright red, and I look from her to Jess, whose grin is now a mile wide. "What?" I demand.

"I'm pretty sure that was Britney Spears," she says. "No?"

Embarrassment shoots through me, and I pray Dawson never calls me again. Unfortunately, his ringtone fills the air again, the high-pitched tones of *Oops, I Did It Again* making me cringe.

I want to throw the phone in the shredder and escape the state, but I stand there, holding my ground. "I happen to like pop music," I say.

Callie bursts out laughing, as does Jessie, but I don't care. I can see the irony of liking Britney Spears when I'm this polished, buttoned-up version of my step-father, the man who knew more about real estate and the market in South Carolina than anyone who'd ever lived. I've never seen him wear a shirt without a collar, and while he has a lot of admirable qualities that I've worked hard to emulate, he definitely needs to relax in the clothing department.

I start to chuckle despite myself, and blast Dawson from here to Mars, he calls me *again*. This time, fearing he's suffering from a shark bite alone, I hum along to the Britney Spears song for a measure or two before answering his call with, "What?"

"You hang up on me?"

"I said I'd call you back in five minutes," I say.

"No, you answered, and then promptly hung up."

"Okay," I say, deciding not to argue with him. "What's going on?"

"Do you need five minutes?"

Callie and Jess probably do to get over the stupid-laughter they're still in the throes of, but I turn away and say, "No, what's up?"

"I need a second pair of eyes on an ad campaign," he says. "I figure you're not doing anything this afternoon..."

I glance over my shoulder, then refocus out the window in my office. "All right," I say, pulling a page from his wife's book. "But I want Alec's steak bites with blue cheese for dinner, so you better make a call the moment we hang up."

"Steak bites with blue cheese," Dawson repeats. "I'll get him to make those asparagus things with the bacon too."

"Vegetables?" I grin at the sunshine through the window, starting to feel slightly like myself again. He comes and goes, and while he's here, he doesn't stay for long. The moment the call ends, the shelled, hollowed-out version of myself that I've become will return.

"Don't tell anyone," Dawson says with a laugh. "Especially not Callie." His voice turns hard and all traces of laughter disappear. "If she knows I actually like vegetables, it'll be all I hear about for weeks."

Voices beyond my office door distract me, and I turn that way to see the man wearing a Cayenne's shirt turn the corner. Perfect.

"I need twenty minutes," I tell him. "Your office?"

"See you soon."

The call ends, and Jess fills the doorway. "A new client called?"

"Yes." I take a deep breath, knowing there's one more delivery, and I'd like to get out of here before the rainbow screams start. "I can't take on a full client. I was thinking... you could take the lead. I'll advise you."

Her blue eyes round, and those pink lips nearly undo me for a second time today as she asks, "Take the lead?"

"Candygram!" a man yells, and then he appears directly behind Jessie. She turns, and we both stare at the man wearing the colors of ROY G BIV from head to toe and bearing not just one case of the rainbow-colored candy that Callie loves so much. Not simply two. But six.

"Skittles for days!" he announces as if royalty has arrived.

A shriek fills the air, and I can't help grinning again. I step closer to Jessie, pressing in close behind her. "I told her I'd make sure she had her Cayenne's and her Skittles."

"You delivered," she says.

"She helped you?"

"So much," Jess says, turning toward me slightly. Our faces are far too close together for a man on a female-fast. The thoughts—biscuits and gravy, my thoughts. They're Thoughts with a capital T, and none of them support my current dietary habits.

"I'm glad," grinds through my throat, and then Cha-Cha joins her surprisingly loud barks to the shrieking and hugging Callie's doing in the hallway.

"Lance," she yells. "Get out here."

"We'll talk more about the client at the open house," I say. "Okay?"

"Sure," she says, and I might need to get my eyesight

checked, because it sure looks like she swallows before she ducks her head and vacates the doorway.

————

"THE ORANGE IS TOO BRIGHT," I say the instant Dawson pulls out the mocks.

"I knew it." He sighs and runs his hand down his face. "Fred thought it would make it all pop."

"All it does is give me a headache," I say, though that's because those train-thoughts have been crashing into my skull for hours now. "And then go—wow, that's a lot of orange." I lift the soda I stopped to get to my mouth and take a long pull on the straw. The carbonation and caffeine should help me through this evening. Cha-Cha collapses in the corner of Dawson's office, clearly worn out from all the shrieking and patting that happened at the agency.

I give her a smile and look back at the mock. "Everything else looks good. Maybe the word 'occasion' is a little too small."

"Yep," Dawson says. "What else?" He sits back down at his desk and starts to type. The keyboard is one of those gaming ones, and it makes horrible clacking sounds as his fingers practically assault the keys.

"The green outline on the bird needs to go," I say.

"Mm hm."

"Maybe a light blue instead of the orange."

"You don't think that will make the darker blue words less...amazing?"

"Perhaps," I say. "You'll have to see."

"Next?"

I tilt my head to the side, as if I'm really thinking hard. "The colors on this are so wonky."

"That's their business," Dawson says. "Keep going."

"I'm thinking of asking my assistant to dinner," I say.

"Okay, and—" Dawson cuts off, and so does the typing. "What?"

"Yeah," I say with a huge sigh. "I think you go back to the drawing board on this." I look at him and stoop for my dog's leash. "I have to go."

"You can't go," Dawson says as Cha-Cha gets to her feet.

"Come on, Chachy."

"Lance," Dawson says.

"I don't want to talk about it." I walk out of his office as he calls, "But the steak bites aren't here yet."

I keep going, and Dawson runs after me. He beats me to the door and presses against it with his palm. "You're not leaving until the food comes. Now get back in my office and start talking." His dark eyes give me zero room for negotiation, and I'm a pro at such things.

"I don't want to talk about it."

"Yeah, well, I don't care. I have a secretary that became my wife. I have some experience with this. Now get going."

He's not going to budge on this, so I turn around my corgi and head back into his office. Maybe if I give him a few details, he can help me figure out how to handle Jess at the open house tomorrow in a way that doesn't make me look or sound like a complete fool.

CHAPTER FIVE

JESSIE

I LEAN AGAINST THE LIVE OAK, FEELING THE HUNDRED years of its life flowing through me. That's probably really the pink drink I'm sipping, as I read an article once about how pink things make us feel better. Not just pink things, specifically drinks.

So instead of the buttery corn muffins I usually eat in the morning, today, I asked Wesley to make me a strawberry banana smoothie. He did, and I finish the dregs of it next to the live oak.

Lance hasn't shown up yet, and I remind myself that I came out to the road at least forty-five minutes before our agreed-upon time. I didn't want him to have to drive down the dirt lane, past all the billions of live oaks, the emerald green grass, to the columned mansion. I don't need that drama in my life. At least not with Lance.

The image of him comes up in my brain, even when I

try to push him out. That blond hair that he keeps so perfect. Those blue eyes. I swear sometimes they can cut through icebergs, and sometimes they look like they could radiate sunshine the way the sky does.

He's strong, and tall, and I shiver when I think about him stepping so close to me in the doorway of his office yesterday. It had taken every ounce of my willpower not to sag into him and just let some of his body warmth sink into mine when we touched.

My mouth curves when I think about his horrible ties. Well, the ties themselves aren't horrible. They're actually quite expensive. He just doesn't know how to make them match anything he's wearing. I wonder, not for the first time, if he's colorblind, but I've heard him ask for blue folders and the other day, when someone needed to sign something, he said, "Sign on all the red flags."

Of course, I'd put the flags on, and Lance could've been guessing. He doesn't seem like the type to guess at much of anything, IDT. I don't think. I've only known him for a couple of weeks, but nope, he's not a guesser.

I raise my cup to my lips again, though the smoothie is mostly gone. I suck the straw anyway, getting a little hint of the pink.

A horn honks, and I jam the straw straight up and into the roof of my mouth. A curse flies from my lips at the same time Lance says, "Sorry, I thought you saw me."

I drop the cup, because I don't want to take it with me to the open house. The taste of blood touches my tongue, and my hand moves to my mouth to see how bad it is. Why do we do that? I know I'm bleeding. Why do I have to see it too?

I step away from the tree, annoyed with myself for letting my thoughts—fantasies, if I'm being honest—run away from me. I was so distracted thinking about Lance's eyes, and his silly ties, and what I think about him.

"It's fine." I take a professional step, whatever that means, toward him, the rumble of the truck engine now filling my ears. The stupid things betrayed me, and I tell myself to focus today. I have to, because Lance spent a large part of last night texting me about what we needed to talk about today before the open house. Then I need my game face for the event.

I'm not going to fall getting into Mammoth Truck. *Not today, Satan*, I think as I reach for the door handle. "Thanks for coming to pick me up," I say as I open the door. Lance hasn't gotten out of the truck, and he smiles at me from behind the steering wheel. I've ditched the heels for today's event, and I step up onto the runners of the truck in my ballet flats. They go amazingly well with a black denim skirt with chunky buttons down the front, none of which are the same shape or size. Some are made of wood, some metal, one even a bright turquoise.

I pull the skirt straight and glance over to Lance, catching him eyeing the skirt. "I like that skirt," he says, and the words sound like he put them through a meat grinder first.

I look at it again. "Thanks." I take in his clothes too—khaki slacks, mint green polo, no tie. "I've never seen you without a collared shirt and tie."

"It's the weekend," he says.

"You look very nice," I say, facing forward again.

He clears his throat, doesn't say thank you, and puts Mammoth in drive. "You got your paycheck okay?"

Relief punches me, though it's a good question, with an even better answer. "Yes, thank you," I say. Now any maple bacon doughnuts I buy won't be what costs me a twenty-dollar overdraft fee.

"What ever happened with your car?" he asks.

I wave my hand. "Oh, my cousin went and got it. He took it to a shop for me." I make it sound like the repairs for Lucille Ball won't take long and will be no big deal, but the truth is, Lucy might be on her last leg. Her final breath. I ignore the pinch in my chest, reminding myself that it's just a car.

She's not just a car to me, and I clench my fingers together, wishing I had a pencil in my hand.

"You live with your cousin, then?" Lance doesn't look at me as he asks.

"Yes," I say, my voice turning a little more guarded. "And my uncle."

He nods and doesn't say anything else.

"You live alone?" I ask, immediately regretting it. Of course he lives alone. The absence of two fiancées is my first clue.

"No," he says, almost a bark. "There's Cha-Cha."

"Oh, right." I flash him a smile that feels way too tight along the edges. My fingers wind around one another, and I hate it.

"Nervous?"

"Yes," I say. "I've never done an open house, and you haven't said one word about taking on clients of my own." A surge of word vomit rises up my throat, and I can't swallow fast enough. Last time this happened, I left Beaufort and haven't been back.

"I can't take on clients of my own, Lance. The very idea is preposterous."

"Sure, you can."

"I don't even know what half the acronyms mean." My hand gestures wildly also of its own accord. "The ones I do are only because I've been studying at night." My chest heaves wildly, and let me tell you, that's not a good look for me.

"Jess," he says, and I like how he uses my nickname. Almost like we're friends. Almost like we could be more.

I don't stop, however. Because he's lost his ever-loving mind if he thinks I can take on a client, even with him at my side. "I could never have printed off all the docs you needed for that meeting yesterday. I didn't even know how to file the folders sitting on my desk until Callie showed up."

She'd gripped me by the shoulders after Lance had hugged her and said she was very welcome for the six cases of Skittles he'd bought for her. And all that chicken, which I had eaten with her after he'd left to go help Dawson with something.

She'd told me I could do this job.

She'd made me promise not to quit until at least a month had gone by.

I'd believed her then, but now? Sitting in Mammoth with some horrible pop song on the radio? I don't believe her.

"Jess," he says again.

"No," I say. "Don't *Jess* me. We all have strengths, and one of mine is not LOIs, or—or FSBO or FMV or any of the Fs!" I take a deep breath, my throat so dry. I need more pink to drink.

"Are you done?" he asks.

I take another breath and blow it out slowly. "Yes."

He makes a right turn, and magically, the house that we're showing that day appears on the right. I haven't kept very good track of the time or the turns. He pulls down the street and parks in front of a house two down from ours and throws Mammoth into park.

"Why don't you have a place of your own?" he asks.

I'm so tired from my outburst that I just reach up and touch the corner of my eye. I've done my makeup to perfection today, and I'm not going to ruin it by arguing with my boss. Or crying. That would be akin to returning to Beaufort and telling Mama to "make a nice dinner."

"Because, Lance," I say. "I'm poor. I don't have enough

money to get a place of my own." I look over to him and add, "Yet," in a loud voice. I remind myself that I'm Jessie Dunaway, and I don't need to do anything to impress Lance, except keep the to-do basket empty by getting all my work done.

He gives me a small smile and nods. "You'll get there, Jess." He exhales and reaches for his seatbelt. "Come on. I suppose we better go see how things look inside. The Morgans left a few weeks ago."

He slides from Mammoth and opens the back door while I'm still caught in the jaws of the seatbelt. I press the button, and still, it doesn't release the clasp. Lance gathers the things he's brought, and the back door slams.

I'm still wrestling with the seatbelt, my heartbeat flapping against the back of my tongue when Lance opens my door. "What are you doing?"

"I'm trapped," I say. "Mammoth won't release the stupid buckle."

"I think it's the catch you need to release," Lance says, those blue eyes sparkling like clear water on an even clearer day.

"Really?" I snap at him.

"What's Mammoth?"

More humiliation drives through me. "I, uh, named your truck Mammoth."

Lance chuckles and bends to set the basket he's holding on the ground. "Let me help you."

"You have a very large truck."

"Mm." He leans over me, and I press my back into the seat, though every cell in my body urges me to wrap my arms around him and take a deep breath of his cologne, the rain-crisp scent of his body wash, and the cottony freshness in that perfect polo.

"Mammoth is brand new," he says, the warmth of his chest flowing right over my lap. "I can't believe he has a flaw already." He's totally making fun of me, but I can't get my voice to work right now.

Thankfully, Lance struggles with the stubborn seatbelt too. He grunts as he puts quite a bit of pressure on my hip. "I've almost got it."

"It's fine," I say. "I can try it."

He pulls on the shoulder part of the belt, which tightens the strap across my lap, which makes my breath suck right in. "Lance," I say.

"I've almost got it." He grunts again, and this time when he pulls and the belt doesn't release, the back of his wrist flies up toward the ceiling of the truck. He makes a terrible groaning sound, and still the seatbelt stays clasped.

Now his breath heaves, and his eyes meet mine. The moment lengthens, and I wonder what he'd do if I took his face in both of my hands and kissed him.

"How hard is it to replace a seatbelt?" he asks.

"I have no idea." I blink, and I see myself stuck in this beast of a truck forever. Lance will have to bring me my meals, and somehow, I'll have to figure out how to take care of my business. Hairdressers will have to come to Mammoth to cut my hair, and I'll die in this skirt.

At least it's cute, and I glance down at the buttons. They bring me back to reality, as does the very distinct flicking, metallic snick of a pocketknife opening.

"I guess I'll find out," Lance says, and the next thing I know, he starts sawing at the belt that goes across my shoulder. When that one releases, he works at the one near my hip. Finally, he steps back and offers me his hand.

"I'm sorry," I say.

"Not apologizing," he says, his lips quirking up. "Though the number of problems you've had with... Mammoth is making me rethink giving you a ride again."

I put my hand in his and manage to get out of the truck without making a fool of myself. He picks up the basket, and I say, "Aren't you Little Red Riding Hood?"

He chuckles and flips open the top. "Just a few things that make open houses go better."

I spy chocolate chip cookie dough, the kind that comes in a chub. "We're baking cookies?"

"Yes," he says. "It makes people think of what after school will be like with their kids."

"Wow." We move down the sidewalk together, and if I could just slip my arm though his, and we escaped into the woods, it would be a picnic. A date.

My mouth turns dry again, making swallowing very difficult.

"What else have you got in there?"

"Candles," he says. "Everyone loves candles, and they set the mood. It's very homey."

"Sure," I say. "Is this what you do in your spare time? Put together picnic baskets to take to open houses?"

"No," he he says. "I run. Play basketball with Dawson. Eat Alec's food. What do you do?"

I feel his eyes on me, but I don't look at him. The little white brick house we're showing today is on our left, and I can't tear my eyes from the apple green door. "Maybe I should buy this place," I say.

"You don't answer very many of my questions," he says.

"I do too." I pause when we reach the sidewalk leading from the road to the front door. "In my spare time, I design clothes."

His mouth drops open, and I pluck the basket from his hand and leave him standing on the sidewalk. "I'll get the cookies started," I say, because while I'm not a great cook, I know how to put rounded spoonfuls of already-made cookie dough on a tray and slide it in the oven.

CHAPTER SIX

LANCE

Nothing has gone right since I cut Jessie loose from "Mammoth." First, I can't get my pulse to freaking stop leaping around like a ridiculous frog. I can even hear the ribbiting in my ears somehow.

The house wasn't in great shape when I followed Jessie to the front door and unlocked it so we could go inside. Everything smelled musty, and someone had left a window open, and we'd spent thirty minutes cleaning up dust and dirt that had been blown inside over the past couple of weeks.

She'd put the cookie dough in the oven, and that had improved things. Several people had come through the house—also good. But I have ears like a hawk, and I've heard them all say a version of the same thing.

There's too many different types of flooring.

The Morgans are going to have to do a carpet allowance

or something if they want to sell this house. I've told them that before, but they wanted to try one more open house.

Finally, the last potential buyer leaves, and I close the front door in one of the most ghastly colors of green that exists on Earth. Jess had gushed over it, and she'd hung the wreath I'd brought in the picnic basket while I'd been up to my elbows in cleaner.

"All right," Jess says, handing me the picnic basket with the wreath and any trash we've created. "That was actually fun."

"You're good at talking to people about nothing," I say, meaning it as a compliment.

She smiles at me, and now that the adrenaline of the event has worn off, I can see how tired she is. I want to ask her about the clothes she designs. I've seen her wear some interesting things, but I don't usually comment on my assistants' clothes. I did tell her not to wear so much red, and she hasn't worn the color again.

Her blouse today is a light sky blue, and it makes her eyes brighter somehow. Right now, they hook into me and make me think I've said something wrong.

"I think that was a compliment," she says.

"It was." I open the de-wreathed door and hold it for her to go first. "Did you design your skirt?"

"No," she says. "I mean, kind of."

"Kind of? What does that mean?"

"I sewed on new buttons," she says. "That's all." She

marches away from me and down the steps, and I stand in the doorway, wondering how many more things are going to go wrong today.

I follow her, my determination to renew my female-fast much easier when she's not fluttering her eyelashes at me. Dawson told me to see how today went and give myself another couple of nights of sleep before saying or doing anything. I'd told him that I hadn't done anything. No invitations to dinner. No hand-holding. No indication of interest whatsoever.

It's what happens to a man's head on the inside that messes us all up. Dawson told me to try to make sure I have my head on straight first.

An image of her gazing into the distance next to that tree fills my mind, but it's not nearly as good as the one I have right in front of me at the moment. Jessie Dunaway walking away from me in that dark skirt, her hips swinging side to side.

I hurry after her, wondering if she's said something else I've missed while I've been standing there in a stupor. "You had to have the eye for the buttons," I say, catching her.

"I collected them over several months," she says.

I don't know what I did wrong, but I let her keep her silence all the way down to the truck. I open the door for her, and the ruined seatbelt stares us both in the face. "Need help?"

"Not yours." Jessie steps past me and gets in the truck just fine.

I frown at her, but she doesn't look at me. She also doesn't have anything else to do, as she can't fiddle with the seatbelt. It hangs like a limp noodle near the door, and the other straps have been laid over the console.

"What did I do?"

"What did you do?" Jessie whips her attention toward me. I actually fall back a step with the danger in her expression. "You have not said thank you one time for what I did back there. You made sure everyone who walked through the door knew I wasn't the agent in charge. You ate the last cookie, right as I was reaching for it. And then, you stood there on your phone while I went around and cleaned up."

I blink at her, sure that's not true. I'd gotten an email that had come from the interest form on the website for Finley & Frank. I had to answer it.

"I'll get you a cookie," I say.

"Don't you dare," she says in a hiss. "Please take me home." She comes right at me, and I back up again. "In fact, I'll call a Carry."

"You don't have to do that."

She pulls in a breath, and I like this version of Jess. The part of her that is a little bit wild. A little bit out of control. A little bit uncensored. She's been so buttoned up with me, and I like riling her up—too much.

"I'm sorry," I say. "I didn't realize I was doing any of those things."

"You haven't said a word about having me take the lead with anyone, which means you don't think I can do it."

"You said you couldn't do it."

"Lance," she barks.

"What?"

"You're arrogant. You're too good-looking for your own good. And your shoes don't match your clothes *at all*." She slides those eyes down to my feet and back, and I do the same with my gaze.

"My shoes?" I look at the red loafers. "I like these shoes."

"They look like clown shoes," she says. "They don't go with khaki and mint, not even slightly."

My mind whirs. "Mint?"

"And your ties never match."

"Hey, now," I say, lifting my eyes to hers. "My ties match."

"Not once," she says. "In five days. Not even one time, honey."

I don't know what to do from here. I've always thought I looked good, but now my confidence is shaken. My houses don't usually sit on the market for this long either. I host one open house, and I have five offers by evening.

I don't think anyone will call today.

My phone rings, and mercifully, it's not Dawson. It is,

unfortunately, my sister. Her ringtone isn't that much better, and Jess actually starts to sing along with the Justin Bieber song before I can swipe Ruth to voicemail.

"I'm sorry," I say again. "I didn't mean to treat you as inferior. I didn't know my shoes came from Clowns-R-Us."

Jess folds her arms.

I search my brain for what else she said, and it's incredibly difficult with that hip cocked and all. "Thank you for all you did today. I think you're smart enough to learn how to take on clients of your own."

Really smart and really pretty, my mind screams at me.

Jess visibly softens, her arms unclenching. She nods.

"You're not going to quit, are you?"

"You seem worried about that."

"I am worried about that."

"Why? Because you're such a beast to all of your assistants? You told me it was their incompetence that made you go through them so fast."

I lift my chin. "I'm not in a super-great place right now."

"Why's that?"

"I'd rather not talk about it without a lot more cookies between us."

Jess narrows her eyes at me and studies my face. "Okay," she says slowly. "But not the gross kind with all those preservatives. *Homemade* cookies."

"You just complained about how I ate the last cookie."

"Seriously?"

I hold my hands up in surrender. "You want cookies? Let's go get some cookies."

She nods like *dang right you'll get me some cookies,* spins on her heel, and gets back in my truck.

———

I GLANCE up toward my open office door as voices come my way. Our way. I glance at Jess, who's also twisting that way. The voices go by instead of coming in, and she focuses on me again. Today, she's wearing a pair of big, square glasses that make her even sexier than without them. I've chosen not to comment on her wardrobe choices anymore, because she clearly has the upper hand.

I've brought no less than six neckties for her approval, and she looks back at the neckwear on my desk. She glances back to me, and I feel naked in front of her. This can't be this hard. I'm wearing a pair of black slacks and a light pink shirt.

"Let me see the shoes," she says.

I work hard not to roll my eyes as I step out from behind the desk. This is the third day we've done this, and I remind myself that I asked her to help me. I don't want to be walking around Charleston looking like a fool. The fact that I've done so for so many years brings heat to my face as it is.

"They're just shoes," I say.

"No," she says. "Those are Beckett Simonon's." Her

eyes travel back to mine, hers getting a little wider. "Tan, I believe."

I look back at the shoes. "They're loafers."

"Bite your tongue," Jess says playfully. At least I think she's teasing me. When I meet her gaze again, she's smiling at me in a way that's less assistant and more friendly. Definitely teasing. For some reason, I smile back at her too.

"If you want...loafers that go with anything, you need to get the brown ones of these," she says, turning her attention to the ties on the desk. "Or the Bordeaux would work too. You chose tan, which means they have a ton of red and a ton of orange in them."

"I'm wearing orange shoes?" I lift one foot as if I can't see down the length of my body. "They look tan to me."

"No blues or purples with reds and oranges," Jess says as if I haven't spoken. "You want more reds, oranges, or..." She whaps a tie against my chest. "With that pink shirt, I'd go brown."

I put my hand over the tie before it can fall from my chest. She releases the tie and smiles at me as if she's just climbed Mount Everest. I look at the tie, and it's the ugliest one I brought. In fact, I only brought it as a joke.

"This isn't right," I say, my brain not quite computing.

"It's right," she says. "Put it on, and then you promised me you'd tell me about some rent-to-own options."

I make some grunting noise that elk probably do when they see a female elk they like. I can't believe it, but I tie on the neckwear she's selected and look longingly at the others on the desk. "Are you sure...?" I begin, but her icy blue eyes slice me into silence. "Fine."

I round my desk, my red-orange clown shoes getting caught on the leg on the far side. I stumble but catch myself with one hand against the top of the desk. Will nothing go right today? It's Wednesday, and we've always gotten along just fine. Today, however, Wednesday seems to be After Me, with a capital A and M.

"All right," I say, breathing out over the top of the words. "Rent-to-own."

"You can't just walk in there," Olive says, her voice on the outer edge of panic. Both Jess and I look toward the open doorway again. A woman has indeed just walked into my office. She's wearing similar professional clothes to Jess—skirt, blouse, ballet flats. Her midnight black hair has been piled on top of her head in a bun, and she too sports a pair of glasses on her face. Hers are small, though, and I like Jess's way better.

"Can I help you?" I ask.

"Sorry, sir," Olive says, squeezing into the room too. "She insisted."

"It's fine," I say, though Jess shoots a dagger in my direction. She says I'm a little ADHD, to which I scoffed and then moved onto the next subject. I can focus. I haven't been able to stop thinking about her, for example. Tell me that's not some serious attention dedication, not a deficit.

I still don't know what to do about all of the thoughts.

Dawson called me on Sunday, but I didn't know what to tell him. The open house hadn't gone great. Jess had been upset with me. We'd eaten far too many cookies. I dropped her off by the live oak. The end.

She's been helping me with my ties for three days, and I've promised her I'd help her find somewhere to rent so she can move out of her uncle's house—and we're still working toward her taking the lead with clients.

Unfortunately, another new one hasn't come our way. The email I got on Saturday was a dead-end, and the guy I was going to originally train her with was a no-show yesterday afternoon.

"Yes, this is Lance Byers," Jess says, slapping her palm on my desk. I blink, because I've zoned out a little bit.

Mm hm. Yep, I'm Lance Byers. I stand, as Jess has, and look past her to the dark-haired woman.

"I filled out your interest form," she says. "No one called."

My brow furrows. "Oh." I jiggle the mouse to wake my computer. I apparently haven't even gotten that far this morning. "When did you fill out the form?"

"Last night."

"Last night?" Jess asks. "Before or after business hours?"

"When I got home," the woman says.

"Mister Byers is very busy," Olive says, and I nod to that.

"I normally get a notification when someone fills out

the interest form," I say. "I didn't get one last night." I check my work inbox. It's stuffed to the gills with emails, but none of them are from the interest form.

I glance over to the woman and find her rolling her eyes. I don't like her, and I don't want to work with her. Jess steps in front of me. "Are you looking to buy or sell?"

"Buy," she says. "I'm in this awful situation, and I need to get out of it."

"Mm, yes," Jess says. "I understand that." She throws me a smile. "I'm sure we can help you."

I've only worked with her for a week and a half, but I know that sparkle in those baby blues. She wants to take the lead with this client. I look at the other woman again, noting that Olive has left the office. I'll probably have to go talk to her too, just to make sure she knows she didn't do anything wrong.

"Jess," I say. "We're really busy right now." That's my gentle, compassionate way of trying to tell her that we don't want this woman as a client. She has Problem written all over her, all of the letters in caps. I give her a professional smile that my sister has told me looks like I need to use the bathroom really bad. "Sorry."

"We're not that busy," Jess says through her teeth. Her smile hasn't slipped a bit.

"Yes," I insist, thinking of the note Olive tried to give me the other day. I don't need clients who just cause problems. There are plenty of others out there to be had, and

I'm not working for my was-gonna-be-mother-in-law, even if she does have money.

"We have all of our clients here," I continued. "A new place we're trying to find. All the problems with the carpet, and then the trees."

One of our properties—I'm not sure when I started grouping Jess and I together—had two trees blown over in Monday's windstorm. And the Morgans agreed to the carpet allowance, but *they* want to replace the carpet and then do another open house.

"How long have you two been together?" the woman asks, slicing her gaze between me and Jess.

I open my mouth to protest. Jess and I are not together. She's just my assistant.

But Jess gives a little giggle and says, "It's still very new." She moves forward and actually reaches out and touches the woman's glasses. "I love these. Mine might be too big."

"They look great with your short hair."

I have no idea what world I've just been dropped into, and all I can do is stare.

"What's your name?" Jess asks, reaching for the legal pad she was about to take rent-to-own notes on.

"Sabrina Shadows. I'm a lawyer at Farmer, Buhler, and Cason."

"You're kidding," Jess says, plenty of gasp in the words. "I know someone who works there."

"Yeah?" Sabrina looks like she might pin Jess to the ground if she says the wrong name. "Who?"

I actually move around the desk so I can assist Jess in her soon-to-be wrestling match with this Shadows woman. She is definitely a problem, and I'm going to have to tell Jess how to read a person before taking them on as a client.

"Jason Finch?" Jessie guesses.

Sabrina—who was one stiff wind away from a hurricane already—goes to a full Category Five in less than a breath. "Oh, yeah," she says with plenty of bite. "I know Mister Finch."

"We went out once," Jess says. "Trust me, that was all it took." She laughs and shakes her head.

"Must've been a while ago," Sabrina says, tossing me another look. "You two seem to get along well. I'll admit, I'm not sure about working with a boyfriend-girlfriend pair."

"We're—" I start to say, but Jess overrides me with "Completely professional on the job, Miss Shadows." She steps even further into her, causing the dark woman who matches her name to turn around. "Why don't you come out to our assistant's desk, and I'll get some info from you? Lance has a conference call in about twenty-four seconds."

She practically yells that last part, and I follow them to the doorway. Olive stands at the end of her desk, her eyes wide. She's worked for Finley & Frank long enough to know what to do, and precisely twenty-four seconds later,

she says, "Mister Byers? I'm transferring over that...confer-
ence call."

Jess meets my eye from behind her desk, so many
emotions there I can't name them all. Pleading, sure. Play-
fulness, maybe. I can't quite tell if there's any desire or if
that's just wishful thinking on my part.

"Mister Byers?" Olive chirps again, and I wave to her.
I disappear back inside my office and close the door. Then
I start to pace like a caged tiger, wondering what Sabrina
saw between Jess and I to think we're dating.

If a perfect stranger can see whatever is between us,
can everyone else?

CHAPTER SEVEN

JESSIE

I haven't had to employ such fakery in a long time, and I'm surprised at how easily I can smile, nod, and get Sabrina Shadows to agree to let me find her some houses to look at. In all, the conversation takes about fifteen minutes, and that's only because I then asked the lawyer about her skirt.

"I got it online," she says, looking down at the patchwork of patterns. "It's from that design show."

"Cutting the Cloth?" I ask, my whole soul lighting up. "I love that show."

Sabrina smiles as wide as the sea. "I do too. Thursday night is my favorite night of the week."

"Same." I stand, noting that Lance's door is now closed. Sabrina gets to her feet too, and I walk her toward the exit, telling her I'll be in touch later that day or for sure tomorrow morning with a few things she might want to look at.

"Really?" she asks. "That soon?"

I swallow, thinking I've made a horrible mistake by saying I can look at listings and find some for her. She gave me what she's looking for. Square footage, bedrooms, bathrooms, yard. Air conditioning. The glint in her eye when she said that was fierce.

I've never sat in with Lance when he goes over things with a new client, but how hard can it be?

"We'll see what's out there," I say. "I know of a great little white-brick house we have. They're putting new carpet in it this week." I've never been happier to have ridden in an enormous truck I'd had to be cut out of to go to an open house than I am in that moment.

"Okay," Sabrina says. "You have my number."

"That I do." We reach the double glass doors, and out she goes. I breathe a sigh of relief, my breath fogging up the glass in front of my face. "What in the world are you doing?"

Sabrina Shadows is smart. Like, lawyer-smart, not just regular-person-smart. She's going to see right through me in a matter of seconds the moment I start showing her houses. At the same time, she thought Lance and I were dating, and I can't help wondering why that had been so obvious to her.

I turn around and meet Olive's eyes above the chest-high counter. She's seated, so I can only see her from the nose up. I approach, more nervous than when I showed up for my interview. "Was Lance mad?"

"I have no idea," Olive says. "She's going to be a client?"

"I think so," I say. I didn't get her to sign any paperwork, because Lance only signs contracts with sellers. Buyers are free to use different agents to find them their dream house. Miss Rings-A-Lot snaps and crackles, and I pull it from my pocket.

"It's him," I say, lifting my eyes back to Olive's. She lifts a bowl toward me, and it holds Hi-Chews. I take a grape one and a grapefruit one—the two most superior flavors of Hi-Chew—and turn to face the frosted glass in his office door.

Those gold letters.

I picture him in that brown paisley tie and his light pink shirt, and my knees go a little weak. *Game face*, I tell myself as I take the first step.

Somehow, I rap on the door and open it at the same time. Lance stands at his window, gazing out. He turns toward me as if someone had slowed time to half speed. Then it freezes all the way, and I see him for what he is.

A god among men.

So terribly good-looking. So tall. So talented and strong and discerning.

He sees everything when he looks at me, and the only thing I have going for me is that I've opted for a bright blue blouse today after learning that he graduated from Auburn, whose colors are blue and orange.

A fashion nightmare for everyday wear, but for the runway or for haute couture, orange and blue would be fabulous. The beginnings of a dress start to form in my mind, and I wish I had a pencil and my sketch pad.

Instead, I have the gorgeous, grumpy, going-to-train-me-now Lance Byers staring holes into my face.

I step inside, breaking the time-warp between us, and close the door delicately behind me. "So she wants me to show her some houses," I say. "I'm going to need your help."

"I don't think you should take her on as a client."

I tilt my head to the side. "Why?"

"She's trouble," he says. "With a capital T."

I smile at him, because what an adorable thing to say. "Mister Byers," I say. "Do you think I can't handle a little trouble?" Heck, I'm craving it right now.

"You realize she thought we were dating," he says.

I sober and nod. "Yes," I say. "She did mention that a couple of times."

He moves over to his desk and perches on the edge of it. "Why do you think she thought that?"

I shrug, suddenly too nervous to get any closer to him. "IDK."

"IDK?"

Everyone knows what that acronym means, don't they? "I don't know."

"Did you tell her we weren't?" He gestures as if he's trying to swat away flies. "You know? Dating?"

"No," I say slowly. "It didn't come up while she was telling me how many bedrooms she wanted."

"Jessie," he says, the word full of frustration.

"Lance, just listen." I fly toward him now, my hands doing things my brain hasn't told them to do. I pat his tie so it'll lay flat, and wow, the man has muscles in his abs. I reach up to straighten his tie, though it's perfectly knotted around his throat. "She showed up. She's the first one who has, and you don't want her as a client anyway."

Lance holds very, very still and glares down his nose at me. "You don't either, trust me."

"But maybe I do," I say. "You promised to teach me real estate, and I can learn it. I can. But I need a client."

"You're not a licensed agent," he says. "At Finley and Frank, we only employ licensed agents."

"You'll be the agent of record," I say. "Come on, Lance. So we have to pretend to date a little. Is that the worst thing imaginable?" WTI, as I always say. I have a few of them, which doesn't make one "the worst," but I keep that to myself for now.

"You can help me find an apartment *and* teach me how to sell a house to Miss Shadows." I don't beg him by adding a really pathetic *please* on the end of the statement, but it hangs in the air between us anyway.

He softens, though he keeps his hands in his pockets. My hips are practically burning for how badly I want him to put his hands there. "I can't say no to you. This is ridiculous though."

"So it's not the worst thing imaginable." I back up, grinning and gesturing between us. "Me and you dating."

"No," he bites out. "It's not the worst thing imaginable."

"Yeah," I say. "You wearing that sky blue tie with those shoes definitely is, though."

"Come *on*," he says, though a small smile appears on his very strong lips. Kissable lips. With horror, I realize I might have crossed some imaginary line with him. He straightens and goes around his desk, adding, "We're going to need some rules."

"Rules?"

He takes his seat, and so do I. Our morning is starting all over again, just an hour later than it should be. "Yeah, Jess," he says. "Fake dating rules."

I pick up my yellow pad and pen and write those three words on the top line. I look up at him, my eyes wide behind my non-prescription glasses. "Ready."

"Ready?" he repeats, surprise dancing across his face.

"What's your first fake dating rule?"

"I'm not going first." He folds his arms and stares me down. "You name one."

"I've never fake-dated anyone before." I don't tell him it's been quite a while since I've real-dated someone. "You're the one with two fiancées."

A growl comes out of his mouth, and his eyebrows

bunch over those eyes. They'd been shooting blue fire at me before, but now I'm getting punctured with cold ice shards. "That's called real dating."

"Okay," I say. "So in real dating, people hold hands." I scratch it out on my paper. "Doable or not?"

"Doable," he grunts.

"They go to dinner," I say, almost sing-songing the words. "Walk on the beach. Text each other." I look at him, hopeful. "We're already doing that."

"We have not walked on any beaches."

"Why are you so grumpy?" I set down my pad of paper and push up my glasses.

"I'm not," he says. "You want to go to dinner?"

"Sure," I say, grinning at him, not sure why I find teasing him so fun. I'm not usually the giggly, flirty girl.

"Mister Byers," Olive says, intruding into the conversation. "Your step-father is on line three."

"Thank you, Olive," Lance says, his voice turning more professional—deeper, even—with every syllable he says. He reaches for the phone, and then stalls. "We need to talk about—uh—kissing. Kissing rules."

My mind blanks for a second, like I've never kissed anyone before. Then Lance nods, picks up the phone, and says, "Hey, Dad," while I'm still there doing the fish-mouth thing and wonder if Lance likes to kiss fishy faces.

Then I get the heck out of his office, taking my legal pad with a very lame rule about how hand-holding is okay in a fake relationship.

———

"OH, THIS IS A NINE-ONE-ONE SITUATION," Tara Finch says as she arrives at the end of the table. For some reason, my eyes fill with tears at the sight of her. Maybe it's the sight of that pink pastry box she's carrying.

I jump to my feet and hug her. Nope, definitely her.

"What is going on?" she asks, completely dumbfounded. I step back and swipe at my ridiculous tears, nodding at Callie to fill in the silence.

"Jessie has gotten herself...into a...situation with Lance."

Tara swings her ginormous purse off her shoulder and sits on the couch with Callie and me. In front of us is an assortment of all the deliciousness Legacy Brew offers. Coffee cakes made with pumpkin, as is everything this time of year. Million dollar bars. Brownies with marshmallows and walnuts.

Tara sits her box on the coffee table in front of us and opens it. A sigh actually passes my lips at the perfectly decorated sugar cookies.

"Did you make these?" I ask.

"Yep." She beams first at them and then Callie and me. "It was a client's party. These are leftover."

"Just four?" Callie asks, her eyebrows up near her hairline.

"I maybe have more in my freezer at home," Tara says with a grin. "Planning a wedding is hard, you guys." She shakes her head and takes out a delicately decorated daisy. She hands it to me, saying, "But we'll talk about that later. What situation with Lance? Did the ogre fire you?"

I shake my head, sure the flaky cookie is going to be The Thing to make me feel better. I take a bite, and while delicious, it doesn't solve my problem with Lance.

"She led a client to believe that they were dating." Callie accepts a cookie from Tara, which is a good thing, as Tara stills and gasps at the same time.

"You did not," she says. Her dark eyes search my face, and I have no defense. No excuse. No nothing.

"I want to learn real estate," I say, but it sounds like a pathetic excuse wrapped in a tinny voice. "And this lawyer came in, and she didn't like Lance. I could tell. Anyway, he's been saying he'll teach me, but our other clients canceled or didn't show up."

Tara blinks and returns her attention to the cookie box. "Okay, first, breathe." She takes out a rose with dollops of deep red frosting. "Second, how did that lead to you dating him?"

"Fake dating," Callie chimes in.

"Sabrina thought we were dating," I say. "I didn't correct her."

"Sabrina?" Tara asks. "Sabrina who?"

I swallow and set my cookie down. After slumping into the couch behind me, I close my eyes, wishing I can just drift away into the kaleidoscope of colors behind my closed eyelids. "Shadows," I say. "She works at Jason's firm."

"Yes," Tara says. "I've met her. She's a…severe woman."

My eyes pop open, but I can't quite see Tara's face. Her back is still straight, and she's facing the table. "I liked her," I say.

"You like everyone," Tara says, dismissing me. As if liking people is a bad quality. "So what happened?"

"We talked for a minute," I say. "Before his step-dad called. He said holding hands is okay, and he asked me to dinner."

"Wait, whoa," Callie says at the same time Tara chokes. Then she asks, "Like, legit asked you to dinner?"

They both stare at me like I've grown fifteen horns on my head. "Yes," I say. "What is the big deal? It's fake."

"Mmm-nope," Callie says, shaking her head. Her dirty blonde hair swings with the action, and she tucks it behind her ear. "I've known Lance Byers for years. *Years*, Jess. Over a decade. He doesn't date casually. He doesn't do *fake* anything."

I sit up, puzzling through what she's said. "What does that mean?"

"If he asked you out, he asked you out," Tara says, translating Callie-speak for me. She nods, and then speaks slowly. "I think she's right. Lance is…careful. Lance is polished. Buttoned tight. He's serious, but he doesn't take himself too seriously."

She dusts her hands of the cookie crumbs. "He's honestly perfect for you. I should've set you up with him instead of Jason."

Callie coughs, and it distinctly sounds like she says a name.

"Who's Hadley?" I ask.

Callie's bright eyes round, and she shakes her head. "You'll have to ask Lance."

"One of the fiancées?" I guess.

She and Tara nod, but they don't say anything else. Even when I try to get them to tell me more, they won't.

"You'll have to ask Lance," they both say, over and over and over until I want to take a glob of the daisy frosting and stick it in my ears just so I can't hear them talking.

So I say, "Fine. I'll ask him." I'm not sure if I will or not, but if a woman named Hadley is going to be a problem or come between me being able to sell Sabrina Shadows a house, I need to know.

"Did you try on the dress today?" Callie asks, and I whip my attention to Tara.

"You tried on a wedding dress today?" I ask.

"Yes," she says. "No. Maybe? Sort of."

"How do you sort of try on a dress?" Callie asks, shaking her head. Before Tara can answer, another woman joins the party by flopping into the recliner situated at the head of the coffee table.

"Howdy, ladies," Macie Wilheim says. She wears a bright smile and zero makeup, though she does brandish a cup holder filled with fresh coffee in to-go cups. She sets it on the table, nudging over the pecan tartlets a little to do so. "What's going on over here?"

"Tara was telling us about how she sort of tried on a dress today," Callie says, meeting my eye.

I swallow even as she nods at me again. This time, it's real subtle, like *Go on. Tell her. Show her.*

I clear my throat. "Tara," I say. "I'm, well, I like to— design clothes. I wondered if you wanted to look at some of my wedding dress drawings and have one made for you." I cough, because she's only the second person on the planet—whoops, the third, as I did tell Lance I designed clothes in my spare time—who I've told about my sketches.

She'll be the second person to ever see them.

Her eyes round, and she looks past me to Callie, and then over to Macie. "A custom wedding dress?"

I can't tell if she's excited or wants to throw me through the front window for suggesting it. I nod, doubts flying from left to right inside my head. "I'm not any good," I say. "I just thought—"

"She's amazing," Callie says, and I wish she wouldn't. I don't need her to come to my rescue, especially not with Tara. She's not jealous of me anymore, but we had some rough times for a while there. She's engaged to my very best friend in the whole world, and Alec Ward happens to be a man.

So me being in his life...well, it was hard for Tara.

"I want to see some sketches," Tara says, smiling at me. "I'm sure they're good, Jess."

"No obligation," I say, bending to get the sketchbook out of my bag. "But I had the greatest idea for a dress today —right after the whole fake-dating conversation, actually."

"Wait a hot chicken minute," Macie says. "Fake dating? Again?" She shakes her head, her eyes moving along all three of us seated on the couch. "No. Y'all have *got* to stop this."

Callie grins and gestures to Tara. "It worked out for us. We're batting a thousand."

I flip open the sketchbook, and Tara gasps again. "Jess," she says, snatching the book from me without asking. "Yes. Yes, I want this wedding dress." She looks at me with stars for eyes, and all I can do is smile.

CHAPTER EIGHT

LANCE

"COME ON," I GRUMBLED TO CHA-CHA, THOUGH I suspect she's doing the best she can with her short, stubby corgi legs. I can't seem to run fast enough, and I only have two legs. Someone honks, but I just keep going.

No, I'm not abusing my animal. I know I don't have a shirt on despite the near arrival of November. I know what the thermometer says. My blood happens to be boiling, thank you very much.

Holding Jessie's hand.

Ridiculous.

Taking her to dinner.

Preposterous—and I'd canceled via text and spent Wednesday evening lying on my couch, a throw pillow my sister gave me for Christmas last year clutched to my chest. It was downright pathetic. *I'm* downright pathetic.

The fact that I didn't throw that pillow in the trash on December twenty-sixth proves that. I can't tell you what it has on it, other than when Ruth comes by for a visit, she smiles at it.

I jog in place at a stoplight in Cider Cove, where I live. There is neither cider made here, nor a cove nearby. I'm not sure how the town got its name, but I know I like living near the city but not in it. I like being close to the beach but not on it.

I like working with Jess but not dating her?

I shake my head as Cha-Cha positively pants at my feet, and the light turns green. Off we go again, and Cha's nails *tickety-tick-tick* along the asphalt until we get to the other sidewalk.

Someone honks again, and this time I throw up the hand that's not holding Cha-Cha's leash. *I'm fine. Thank you.*

"Hey, bro," someone yells—another male, at least.

I glare as I look to my left. I don't ask the twenty-something practically hanging out of his friend's window anything.

"Did you know you've got company?" He laughs and points behind me. My breath wheezes into my chest as I turn and see not just one woman, but two, three, four, all jogging in my direction.

The light is still green, and more women—*shrimp and grits*, I think. *Those are girls*—round the corner I just did.

The man's laughter rings in my ears, and his buddy floors the accelerator. Tires squeal, and Cha-Cha barks.

Only one of the women in the pack is old enough to be out of high school, and she gives me an up-down look as she approaches. "We've been trying to catch you for a mile," she says, her breath catching like mine.

"Why?" I ask.

"Track team," she says, flying by me. "You should come train with us. I see you running every day."

As teenaged girls—teen girls!—go by me, every one of them wears a smile and a high ponytail. The very last thing on this planet that I need is to run with the girl's track team at the local high school. I can see the scandalous headlines now.

I stand there like a fool, nodding and smiling while mostly naked, until the track team passes me. Then I turn Cha-Cha around, pull my shirt out of the waistband of my shorts and back over my head, and start for home.

Along the way, a jammin' tune by Ariana Grande comes from my phone, which is secured in my bicep holder. Since I'm meticulous about assigning everyone who calls my cell their own ringtone, I already know it's Jess.

Jess.

Jess, Jess, Jess.

What am I going to do about Jess?

I can't ignore her. Despite her obvious lack of real

estate knowledge, she is a good assistant. Dawson told me yesterday afternoon while Callie got her nails done that I like Jess because she's moldable. She'll do anything I say, the moment I say it.

I told him he makes me sound horrible, like some sick puppet-master who only wants his women to be seen and not heard.

Jess certainly isn't that, and I don't mind all of her questions. I also know why she's calling, and I can't let her call go to voicemail without some consequences.

Unfortunately, the straps holding my phone to my arm take more time than I have to undo, and the call does go to my inbox. I quickly get the device out and return her call.

"Hey," she says, a bit of fluster in her voice. "I'm standing on your front porch, and you aren't here."

"Why are you standing on my front porch?" I'm at least two miles from home and currently walking with no intention of picking up my pace again. I pause and turn the other way. Cha-Cha looks up at me with a devilish look in her eye that says she's going to bite my jugular in my sleep if I start running again.

Her tongue lolls out the side of her mouth, and I regret not bringing her traveling water bowl. I'm a bad dog dad, but I'd been in a hurry that morning.

All at once, I realize why I'd been in a hurry. "The apartment showing," I say at the same time Jess does. "Jess, I'm so sorry. I'm on the way home right now."

I start to jog, and let me tell you, running breath into

the phone is so not sexy. I slow to a walk again and pull the phone away from my mouth. My thoughts are all derailed again, the loudest one clanging and chugging at me. *Why do you care if she thinks you're sexy?*

I don't know why, only that I do.

"Are you out running?" she asks.

"Yes."

"Where are you? I'll come get you so you don't have to run home. Unless you're just around the corner."

"I'm not just around the corner," I say. I'm fast, and I could probably be back to my house in fifteen minutes. Then I'll want to shower, change, make coffee... "I'm on the corner of Pine and Main. I have Cha-Cha with me. It would be great if you could come get us."

"Okay," she says. "Lucy can't wait to meet Cha-Cha."

I look up into the sky, noting how gray it is. "You'll let me shower?"

"Do you have time?" she asks. "Don't we have an appointment for the showing?"

I pull my phone away from my face, horrified at the time. Ten-oh-seven. "Yes," I say. "We don't have time." I look down at my running clothes. The thing with exercise apparel for men is that we don't wear it around town.

Women can, sure. They have these cute leggings, and everyone likes seeing women in tight clothes. Even their tank tops have flowers and sexy stripes, and most of the women I see wear stuff like that to the grocery store, the park, everywhere.

Men?

No man wants to wear his ultra-short running shorts and his sweat-stained tank top to an apartment showing. Especially not with the woman he's been crushing on—hard—for the last week.

"Could you get me some clothes?" I ask, immediately regretting the question.

"What?" Jess sounds like I've asked her to blast off to the moon.

"Never mind," I say. "You're what? Five minutes out?"

"Yes," she says. "If that."

"Pine and Main," I say, glancing down the row of shops on the other side of the street. "Five minutes." I hang up and sprint into the road, practically dragging Cha-Cha with me. She barks, but I keep going. There's a department store right in the middle of the block, and Franco's has men's shorts and polos.

"Ma'am," I call to the woman who's just come out of the shop. "I'll give you twenty bucks to stand here with my dog for less than five minutes."

She looks at me like I'm crazy, and right now, she's not far off. "Please," I say, not above begging in this moment. "My girlfriend is on her way to pick me up for an appointment I forgot about. I can't wear this." I gesture to myself as if I'm covered in honey and cat hair and nothing else. "Less than five minutes."

I hand her the leash as her expression softens. "Okay," she says.

"Thank you." I kiss her cheek and dart into the store. I don't have time to try anything on, but I don't need to. I know what size I am, and I'm not here to buy a designer suit that needs alterations.

I yank a blue polo with white stripes and a sailboat on the front of it from a hanger, then grab a pair of khaki shorts in a thirty-eight. I've just swiped my credit card when my phone rings out Ariana again, and the clerk—a middle-aged woman—looks at me with raised eyebrows.

I smile, tell her to keep the receipt, take my twenty bucks in cash-back, and dash for the dressing rooms. "I'm almost ready," I say in lieu of hello. "Are you on the corner?"

"Yes," she says. "There's a cop here who's eyeing me and Lucy."

"That's just because he's never seen a car like her before." Sixty seconds later, I exit the store, exchange the twenty for Cha-Cha, and scramble back across the street.

I tell myself to calm down as I approach Jess and Lucy. Her sedan is a color I can't name—it's not quite beige, but not tan. It's not orange either, but somewhere in the middle of all of that. She's definitely Unique with a capital U, and I pull open the rear passenger door and command Cha-Cha to get in.

The corgi does as Jess twists to look at me. Her eyes widen at my "running attire," and as I slide into the passenger seat, she starts to giggle.

"What?" I ask, swooping my hand through my hair.

I've lost my visor somewhere, and I realize I left all my running clothes in the dressing room at Franco's. I don't envy the person who finds them, but I grin at Jess like I've planned this whole morning.

"You run in a blue-and-white-striped polo?" She reaches over and peels a sticker from my chest. "Hmm, a large blue-and-white-striped-polo."

With a massive grin, she folds the sticker on itself, hands it to me while I'm still trying to think of something to say, puts the car in gear, and eases away from the curb. "I can't believe you forgot about the showing this morning."

"I didn't forget," I say, shoving the size sticker in my new shorts pocket. "I just...got sidetracked."

"Mm hm." She cuts a look at me out of the corner of her eye, and I know that look. Women have given it to me for years.

"I'm not ADHD," I say, giving her a side-eyed look too. She's wearing the most crimson top I've ever seen. I blink, and the shape of her sleeveless blouse burns behind my eyelids. I look fully at her, but the sunlight glints off an enormous gem that sits right at her neckline.

My gaze slips down, and I can imagine cleavage. I grind my voice through my throat and return my eyes to something safer. More appropriate. "I was running my dog."

"To death, apparently," Jess says, glancing in the rear-view mirror. "Poor Chachy."

"Not poor Chachy," I say, though the corgi has already passed out on the backseat. She doesn't even open her eyes when Jess coos at her. "What kind of dog dad would I be if I let my dog get heart disease? Running is good for her."

"Dog dad?" Jess's smile lights up the whole car, dimming the brilliance of the yellow gem resting against her chest. "That's a new adjective for you I haven't thought of yet."

"Yeah?" I look out the passenger window, still a bit breathless from the running, the dashing through the streets, and changing my clothes. Maybe that red shirt. "What adjectives do you use for me?" I swing my attention back to her. "And don't say grumpy or scatterbrained."

I'm neither. I have a lot on my plate. I'm *busy*. My fiancée took my diamond ring and left town. I'm *healing*.

She doesn't know that, I think, and the next thought is the most dangerous one of all.

Then tell her.

I can't do that, not right now. The words sit in a lump halfway up my throat while I wait for Jess to use some adjectives.

"Hard-working," she finally says. "Handy. Honest."

"Those are all H-words," I say, something starting to glow in my chest. "Are we doing them by letter?"

Jess grins at me and follows the directions the computerized voice on her phone tells her to. "Sure," she says. "You go next and say an adjective for me starting with an A."

Attractive pops into my head, but I can't say that. Can I? *Beautiful* is better, and that's a B. She'll get B, and I try to count all the way to G for *gorgeous* or P for *pretty*. I get lost pretty fast inside my own head, and Jess says, "Nothing? You've got nothing for A?"

"Articulate," I say, almost cutting her off.

"Brainy," she says to me, and the game is on.

"Clever."

"Dedicated."

"Easy...going," I say.

Jess shoots me a sharp look. "Nice save, boss."

"I was going to say *easy on the eyes*," I say, shrugging as buckets of embarrassment fill me. "Or *easy to talk to*. Then I thought that was too close to articulate." I glance at her, and she doesn't look like she'll come across the console and rip my face off with her fingernails. "I could go with *enthusiastic*."

She peers up and through the windshield as she eases up on the accelerator. She comes to a stop in front of a duplex, and I recognize it from the listings we looked at on Friday after work. "This is it."

"Yes." I wait for her to get out, but she doesn't. She puts Lucy in park—my word, I'm thinking of her car as a person now—and looks at the duplex. After several seconds of sitting there in silence, I ask, "What are you thinking?"

"It has good curb appeal," she says, turning to look at

me. She wears hope in her eyes, obviously seeking my approval. "Don't you think?"

I grin at her and hold back my chuckles. "That's thinking like a real estate agent," I say. "And today, Jess, you're just you, looking for a place to live." I reach for the door handle. "Come on. Let's go see what it's like inside."

CHAPTER NINE

JESSIE

Fantastic.

Fabulous.

Fit.

Funny.

All F-words that I could've used to describe Lance. I didn't get the chance before we arrived at the apartment, and now my feet are taking me down the sidewalk after him.

He would've gotten G, and I wonder what he would've said for me then.

Gorgeous.

Generous.

Gifted.

Green.

Any of those work. I feel like I'm about to throw up, so

the green fits. I'm also brand-new at this realtor-ing and assisting, so it definitely describes me.

I can admit I want him to use *gorgeous*, and I continue to plot ways to continue the game the moment we're back in the car.

Lance runs his fingers down the front door of the apartment on the left, and my eyes get drawn to the peeling paint too. "We should ask them about this."

"Should we?" I ask.

He twists and looks at me over his shoulder. "Yes, we should."

"There aren't a lot of apartments in my price range," I say. "And the ones that are available go really fast." In fact, this apartment's been up for rent for four days now, and if we don't put in an application today, I'll lose it.

A sour look crosses Lance's face. "That doesn't mean they can't take care of the place."

He can say that, because he has a house. A nice one too, from the look I got on the front porch. He has spectacular curb appeal, what with two skinny, Cindy-Lou-Who pine trees and a bush with lots of knobby branches. The leaves had started to fall on that, but I hadn't seen a single one on the ground.

Lance had probably been up at the crack of dawn to rake them, then paint his front door—which had been a stark white without a single smudge anywhere—and then go for a sixteen-thousand-mile run with his corgi.

"Oh, Cha-Cha," I say, turning back to Lucille Ball. "Is she okay in there?"

"I should get her out," Lance says. The door swings open, and he pushes it with a couple of fingers. "You go inside and look around. I'll be right back." He moves past me, and it's probably my imagination, but it feels like he moves into me, not away from me.

I look up at him, but he's only there for a moment, then he's past me and headed down the sidewalk. I watch him go for a moment, trying to figure out when my pulse started running the hundred-yard dash inside my chest.

I do want to see the apartment without any outside pressure, so I lean forward and peer inside. The first thing I see is a giant deer head on the opposite wall. That will have to go instantly, as I'm not trying to create a backwoods bayou vibe in my first apartment.

That's not even an accurate description, and as I step into the house, I start searching for gator skin or swamp things. That would be more bayou. I'm confusing myself, and I clear my head.

The elk-deer-whatever draws me back to him though. I want to tear it down right now, because the last thing I need is any hoofed animals in my life.

I finally tear my gaze from Elky-Boy to find the living room takes up the space to my left, and the apartment comes furnished. Those aren't in large supply either, which is another reason I should've put in an application on this place yesterday when Lance had found it on his fancy, backdoor realtor listings. Sight unseen.

A couch and a loveseat sit perpendicular to one another, and they look like they're in decent shape. The floor is hardwood, with a rug the color of snail slime—if I'm imagining such a thing to be gray and dull. That will have to go too.

I need color in my life, and I'm actually surprised Lance didn't comment on the color of my shirt this morning. A coffee table fills the living room, and it's actually too much furniture. I'd remove the love seat and the table, and leave the couch, add a cute, bright rug, as well as a tall lamp with a funky shade.

The whole place would look more open and brighter if I did that, and I smile to myself as I notice the big window behind the couch. I'm thinking like a realtor, and I can hardly believe it.

The window needs a curtain, as does the one beneath Elky-Boy, and then my gaze swings toward the kitchen. It sits in the back right corner, and it has all of the essentials. The same flooring runs through the whole space, which is nice, and I nod in approval.

A small dining room table sits in the awkward space between the kitchen and living room, and I'd definitely move that. Or get rid of it. There's no breakfast bar to sip coffee at, but I can buy something like that at a home goods store. Now that my bank account isn't so slim, that is. And maybe not for a while still.

The hallway only takes three steps to move down, and I take in the curtain hanging at the end of it. I reach out like I'll find a dead body behind it, but when I yank it to the side, there's only board games and hand towels.

"So this is the storage system," I murmur. I passed the bathroom on the first step, and there was nothing remarkable about it. I'm definitely going to have to watch some cleaning videos to sanitize this place—if I get it. We're talking sudsy mop heads scrubbing the tub and all the way to the ceiling.

The bedroom is nothing remarkable, and the smell alone tells me a man lives here right now. I don't go inside, because I wouldn't want someone all up in my underwear drawer or seeing what I'd eaten last night from the dregs of what remains on my plate.

Of course, I'd take my dishes down the hall to the kitchen sink. It does only take six steps, for crying out loud. The sink was white at one point in the past, and I remember a video about vinegar that will probably at least eradicate any viruses nacho-man has left behind.

I sigh and turn, having seen all six hundred square feet of the apartment already. It's nothing to write home about —not that I'm in the pen pal mood with Mama—but it would be mine.

A sense of pride starts to creep up my throat, and I take a few steps past the kitchen table to the window Elky guards. There's a small yard in the back, but as autumn is breathing out the last of its life and winter is about to arrive, the grass isn't super green.

Outside, Cha-Cha barks, and Lance says something to her in his bass voice. I can't catch the words, but I do turn back that way. I take a step, but something yanks on my hair. My hand flies to the back of my head, and I feel...antlers.

I suck in a breath and glance up, expecting Elky-Boy to have dropped several feet. It's not him. He lords over me though, and while I'm looking up at the bottom of his mouth, it sure seems like he's laughing at me.

"What is this?" I ask, feeling around behind me. My curls have only gotten more tangles in even more of the horrible, pointy fingers of whatever head was mounted to the wall that I didn't see.

Lance comes through the door, and Cha-Cha beelines for me. Apparently, she's found her second wind, and she launches her thirty-pound body against my legs. "Hey, Chachy," I say, trying to bend down and pat her while keeping my head straight and level.

Since I'm not Go-Go-Gadget, and I actually have a spine, that doesn't really work. In fact, my hair pulls more, and my eyes start to water. Cha-Cha leans her front paws against my knees, keen to get a scrub.

I look up at Lance, who's frozen in the doorway. "Help," I say, and that springs him into motion. He crosses the microscopic apartment in only three strides, and then his hands are in my hair.

Sweet honeyed tea. I'd get my hair stuck in fifteen deer's antlers to have Lance's hands in my hair. Deers? Deer?

I close my eyes as he jostles my glasses, because it's taking everything I have not to sigh and sag into his chest.

"This is insane," he says in a disgruntled voice. My eyes fly open again, and my glasses sit sideways on my face. Our eyes meet, and he adds, "Oops." He tries to fix the glasses, but they're a lost cause.

I want to rip them off and toss them to the side the way heroines do in movies. Then they pull out their ponytails and the man of their dreams pulls them close...and kisses them.

"I'm going to pull it," he says, his deep blue eyes searching mine. "Okay?"

"Okay." I hold as still as possible, and then my scalp is on fire. "Ow," I moan.

But I'm free. I stumble away from the jaws of antler death on the wall and bump right into Lance. His arms do come around me, and the whole world frosts over. I breathe in. He does too.

We breathe out.

"I think it's a jackalope," he whispers, as if the beast is still alive and he's afraid to scare it.

"A what?" I ask, still lost in his eyes.

He chin-nods toward the wall. "Half-rabbit, half... something else."

I turn, and sure enough, a rabbit head has been mounted

to the wall. An antlered rabbit head. A couple of the antlers hold blonde strands, and I reach out and brush them away. They fall to the ground, and I realize Lance hasn't backed up.

Almost at the same time, we move—him backward and me toward the kitchen. He coughs and bends to get Cha-Cha's leash. "Come on, girl," he says. After a healthy pause, he dares to glance at me. "The attacking jackalope notwithstanding, what do you think of the apartment?"

"Hey," a man says, and someone four times as wide as me fills the doorway. He's carrying a case of Coors Light and a plastic grocery sack. "Sorry. I thought you'd be done by now." He comes into the apartment as if he owns the place, because he definitely lives here.

That guy has jackalope written all over him.

"We're done," I say in a VAV—very authoritative voice, the same one I used on Mama when I left Beaufort—and stride toward the exit. I don't breathe until I get outside, and then I suck in a big breath of fresh air.

Lance follows me, but neither of us speak until Cha-Cha is in the back seat and we're buckling our belts.

"I do like the orange tabby cat brick," I say.

"But the paint on the door is peeling," he says.

I nod and knead the steering wheel. "Yeah. Yep. That one's out." I look over to him. "Want to take me to lunch and give me a starts-with-G adjective?"

A smile blooms across his handsome face. "We're actually on F, and it's your turn."

"Fine," I say, feeling flirty and fabulous—both F-words. "I'm going to go with...fit."

"Fit?"

"Yes."

He harrumphs, and I giggle. "Come on," I say. "I just said you were physically attractive."

"You did?"

"Come *on*," I say, full-on flirting now. If he doesn't know it, he's deaf and blind. I even reach up and tuck my curls behind my ear, where they promptly pop out again. I eye him for a moment. "I can even see the ripples in your abs through that shirt."

Lance looks down at his midsection and then over to me, that smile even wider now. "Okay," he says. "My turn." He reaches toward me and takes my right hand from the wheel.

I pull in an audible breath as he tucks his fingers into the spaces between mine. "This is okay, right?" he asks. "I believe our dating handbook had holding hands in the approved column."

I nod, my voice box a tiny jack-in-the-box in the bottom of my stomach.

He sighs and leans his head back. "Good. Okay, for you...G...I'm going to go with genuine."

"Lame," I say, my fingers automatically tightening in his. "You're handsome. That's the H-word I'm going with this time."

"Lame?" he asks, immediately followed by, "Handsome?"

"Yes," I say, bringing up every ounce of bravery I have as I drive one-handed through Cider Cove. "And your correct G-word, Lance, was *gorgeous*."

CHAPTER TEN

LANCE

"Jolly?" I scoff. "I think this game is over." The hostess beams at me with a smile as wide as George Washington's nose on Mount Rushmore, and I incline my chin. "I think they're ready for us."

Thankfully. I don't want to come up with any more adjectives to describe Jess.

Gorgeous, Lance. The G-word you're looking for is gorgeous.

Of course I would've said that if she was my real girlfriend. But she's not. Even though I lost my mind for several minutes there and held her hand. Even though she let me. Even though she spoke to me in that flirty tone I've heard women use before.

So much confusion streams through me. I like this woman, and I can't figure out why. That sounds terrible, because Jessie Dunaway is amazing. She's pretty

—*gorgeous*—witty, and trying so hard. She's a sponge, soaking up everything I tell her.

Right after she told me I should've given her *gorgeous*, she squeezed my hand tightly and told me how she'd thought like a realtor inside the apartment. We'd talked staging and then I'd started swiping to look for more for-rent listings as she drove us to this Mexican restaurant.

There isn't much on the market right now, but I'm determined to find something for Jess that she can afford. She hasn't said much about her living situation, but I can tell she doesn't like it. I have back-channels and friends in the industry I can text, and I'm willing to bet one of my pinkies that I can find her an apartment before it gets listed.

I haven't told her that yet, but I've got it tucked away in my back pocket.

"You don't like jolly?" Jess asks, her voice on Flirt Level High as she follows me and the hostess.

"No," I bark at her. "I'm not Santa or one of his elves."

She peals out a string of laughter that I can admit makes me feel more like a man. As much as I like it, I also hate it.

I'm on a female-fast. That means no women. None.

As I slide into a booth and people descend with chips and salsa and wanting to know my drink order, my phone starts to mimic Justin Bieber. I swipe my sister to voicemail and give Jess a piercing glare. "Not a word."

She mimes zipping her lips closed, though her eyes

sparkle with a teasing glint I normally like. She picks up her menu and so do I, though I've been here plenty of times and know the loaded beef chimichanga is the way to go. I've actually choked on how much meat they can stuff into a tortilla here, and I'm hoping it'll happen again today.

Maybe then, I'll stop saying inappropriate things.

"Has anyone ever told you that you go from hot to cold really fast?" Jess asks, keeping her gaze buried in the menu.

"No." I whip the word toward her. "No one's ever told me that."

"First time for everything." Her eyes flick toward mine, but I look down. Something seethes inside me, and the self-loathing grows in my lungs until I can't breathe.

I slap the menu on the table. "You know what? I dated a woman before you." I cut off, not even quite sure what I'm saying. We're not dating. Jess and I. We're not.

"For a while. Two years or something like that. I was in love with her." My chest heaves, but this is just the pain of stabbing into a really infected wound. Once I get all the words out, I'll feel better. I know I will.

"I bought her this really expensive diamond that took me three months to save for, and you know what? She took it and left Charleston only eight days later." I reach for a chip and dunk it in the salsa almost angrily.

I am angry. I'm angry at Hadley for what she did to me. I'm angry I didn't see her for who she was. I'm angry about how much money I wasted on her. And the time. Blue corn chips and hot salsa, the *time* I lost on my relationship with Hadley.

"So you'll excuse me if I'm a little hot and cold about...this." I push the chip toward her, some of the salsa flying at her and causing her to flinch. I stuff the tortilla chip into my mouth and mash my teeth together like a monster. "I don't even know what *this* is. It's all confusing."

Jess has lowered her menu too. Her eyes are wide as moons now, and those long lashes wave at me as she blink-blinks.

"Hey," a woman chirps. I glare up at her instead of at Jess. "My name is Annika, and I'll be your waitress today. How's the chips and salsa?"

"Fabulous," I say, though it sounds like I said they're laced with arsenic.

Annika blinks too. "Are you ready to order?"

"Yes," I say, though I want to walk out. I just need a minute to breathe, and there's no air in here. "I want the double-beef enchilada, loaded." I hand her the menu and pick up my water glass. The water will taste like dirt, and there's no ice in it. My pineapple daiquiri can't come fast enough. "And a huge Diet Dr. Pepper," I add. "Tons of ice."

"Yes, sir," Annika says, and she's smart—an S-adjective —as she's realized this is not a personal lunch. To make that true, I pull out my phone and start texting a few colleagues in the real estate industry while Jess scrambles to put in her order.

By the time Annika walks away, my texts are sent, and three people have responded that they'll let me know ASAP about any one-bedroom apartment rentals that come up for eight hundred or less. Satisfied that I've made this a business lunch and not a personal one, I shove my phone under my thigh.

Humiliation dive-bombs me the way seagulls do when someone drops bread on the beach. "Listen," I say in a measured voice. "I'm...sorry. I shouldn't have shouted at you about...whatever I just said."

To my great surprise, Jess paints a small smile on her lips. It's pretty and perfect and not even a little bit patronizing. "You don't have to apologize to me," she says. Both of her hands come across the table and cover mine. "I'm so sorry you went through all of that. How...long ago did this happen?"

"Four months," I say. "Give or take." I focus on the tabletop, further embarrassment coursing through my veins like red blood cells are made of it.

"Unbelievable," Jess says. "You're so put together. If that had happened to me, I don't think I'd have left the house yet."

A waiter arrives with our drinks, and I immediately reach for the straw, slipping my hands out from under hers. She pulls her arms back across the table and does the same with her straw. I take a big drink of the sour drink and feel the alcohol take effect immediately. My muscles relax even as my throat burns.

Jess stirs her strawberry smoothie and takes a more delicate sip. "I left Beaufort with whatever I could fit in Lucille Ball after a massive fight with my mama. She's been trying to marry me off for a decade, usually to men twice my age. I'd had enough."

She pauses to set her glass on the table, really studying it. "She cut off my money, and I drove to Charleston a sobbing mess." She shrugs one shoulder like everybody has days like the one she just described, but I don't think they do.

"I'm sorry," I say.

"Are you close with your family?" she asks, looking up at me again.

"Yes," I say. "I mean, my mom and step-dad. My sister and her husband. My biological dad...not so much." I take a moment to think about the man I haven't talked to in a while. How long? At least five years.

"He and my mom divorced when I was only three," I say. "He wasn't around much. Mom remarried only a few years later. My step-dad is my dad."

Jess nods, her smile encouraging now.

"What about you and your dad? He just let you walk out?"

"Well, Daddy spends a lot of time out in the battle-field," she says casually, as if everyone does such a thing. "Mama can be...difficult, and he's been with her a long time. He copes the best way he can." A hint of sadness accompanies the words, but her face brightens only a moment later. "Is the salsa hot?"

I nudge the bowl toward her. "No." I don't know what to say to what she's told me. Despite her obsession with red, on the outside, Jess looks put together. She has cute clothes that fit in the office, and I've never seen her without draping jewelry and plenty of makeup. I would've never thought she was running out of money or that she didn't have stellar relationships with her parents.

She definitely seems like a woman who calls her mother every night after work, and I'm a little jarred—and embarrassed to admit to my judgment—by what really happens behind closed doors.

I clear my throat. "I'm sorry about your mom and dad," I say.

Jess flashes me a smile and takes another chip to swipe through the salsa. "Thank you," she says. She takes a deep breath. "Okay." She blows out the air. "Let's talk about something else."

My phone chimes, and I pull it up to the top of the table. I glance at the text from Rich. "Oh, this is good," I say, flipping the phone around so she can see it. "A friend of mine might have an apartment for you."

Her gasp is probably heard in Mongolia. "You're kidding." She lunges for the phone, which makes me chuckle, and all of the knots in my chest finally untangle all the way.

———

"YES," I say to my sister, Ruth. I glance over my shoulder as if Jess has followed me inside my house. She hasn't. She didn't even get out of Lucille. I press my eyes closed and clench my jaw. I can't believe I'm calling that sedan Lucille Ball.

"She said I was handsome."

Ruth whistles in a super-annoying older sister way. "Wow, Lance."

"Not wow," I say, moving over to my fridge and opening it. I'm not hungry. Jess and I just went to lunch, where the conversation after the initial confession-fest was actually really great. "I'm not dating right now."

"This isn't dating," Ruth says, and it sounds like she has something in her mouth. Probably her paintbrush, as my sister loves to call me while she's painting. She tucks her brush in her mouth, steps back, and tilts her head to examine her work when she's not quite satisfied with it yet. "It's fake dating."

"I'm bad at both," I say, practically slamming the fridge. "Who fake-dates?" Is there a guide for this type of thing?

Like a flash of lightning, I realize that Dawson—my best friend in the whole world—started his relationship with Callie on false ground. "I have to go," I say to my sister.

"No," Ruth shouts. "Don't hang up on me, Lance."

I want to rush out to my truck and get over to Dawson's right now. My muscles bunch and release, tighten for a moment before I almost fall down.

"Lance?"

"I'm still here." My older sister can be so bossy sometimes.

"Listen," she says, and I know I'm not going to like what she says next. The paintbrush has come out of her mouth, and that means she's ready to lash me with her words.

"If you like this woman, you don't need to feel bad about that. If you don't like fake-dating her, then make it real. Just because Hadley hurt you doesn't mean she will."

I hiss at my ex-fiancée's name, but that doesn't slow down Ruth's tongue. "Just because you declared yourself on a female fast doesn't mean you can't break that at any time. You're smart, so figure it out and talk to Jess."

I swallow, because I'm not sure I can open the chambers of my heart only to have them hollowed out again. "Okay," I say anyway.

"Text me after you do."

"Okay."

"Do not just parrot affirmations to me."

"Yes, ma'am," I say, which would cause her to throw a saltshaker at me if we were in person together.

She growls and says, "Lance," in her Mom-voice.

"Can I go now?" I ask, starting to laugh. She hates it

when I treat her like my mother, but then she shouldn't lecture me like I'm her son.

"I'm calling you tomorrow after work," she says. "I expect some action on your end."

"You want to hear about my action?" I ask.

"I'm hanging up now."

"Good thing," I say, chuckling now. The call ends, and I drop my hand to my side. The laughter dies, and I wish my thoughts would. They don't, and instead of rushing out to find Dawson and solidify the fake-dating rules, I head down the hall to shower, as I never did that after my run.

Maybe the rainfall shower head will help my mind align and know what to say to Jess that can take our relationship from fake to real without making me sound or look like a fool.

CHAPTER ELEVEN

JESSIE

"And what?" Tara asks, glancing over to me from her spot in the grass. Her hens cluckle and warble around her, pecking at the feed she's sprayed from her fingers.

"And nothing." I study the blade of grass in my hand. Maybe it will have tiny letters on it that'll tell me how to act at work tomorrow morning. "The conversation moved on. It was a fun lunch. I dropped him off at home."

"He didn't call or text?" Tara walks over, and I scootch over so she can sit on the steps leading up to her deck.

"No," I say, throwing the grass out into the lawn. "We're not dating, Tara. Why would he call or text?"

"You said he expects you to be ready twenty-four-seven," she says.

"Yeah." He has called or texted on evenings and weekends in the past. I mentally command myself not to pull out my phone to check and make sure the volume is all the way up.

Tara says nothing, and her dogs smash themselves between us. As I absently rub Tommy's head, my thoughts can only rotate around one thing: Lance Byers. How he got so completely inside my head I have no idea.

Not only that, but he's my boss. I'm his assistant. I don't want to mess anything up by assuming something with him or doing something that can cost me my job. I need the job, and I like the job, and I want him to teach me about real estate.

What if I kiss him and it goes badly? I could never show my face at Finley & Frank again, and my whole future as the sixth best real estate agent in Carolina will disappear faster than steam.

"You have the rules," Tara says. "You stick to those."

"He held my hand."

"But that's within the rules." Tara's gaze lands on the side of my face. "Right?"

I look at her and shrug. "Yeah."

"Then he didn't break them."

"We weren't in public. No one was around." We were just driving in my car. My stupid fingers twitch as if they need his between them to stay calm.

"Maybe he..." Tara exhales. "I don't know, Jess. I've been there, and I still don't know."

"How did you and Alec take it from not-real to real?"

"He showed up on my doorstep one day and kissed

me," Tara says. "We had a very, um, short talk in between some more kissing about how it wasn't fake." She brushes her hair back off her face just as a male voice calls, "Hello?"

"That's him." She gets to her feet and extends her hand toward me to help me up too. I make the mistake of meeting her gaze. "Just maybe...try to find out if it's real."

"What if it's not?" I ask. And if I try, and Lance is like, *Nope, so sorry. Just assistant-boss from here on out,* then what will I do? Hide behind a wide-brimmed hat and the copiers forever?

I'd have to quit, and I know this way down deep inside. I don't confront problems head-on. I'd rather say nothing and let hurricanes blow by, or I'd rather scream and shout and then run out.

There is no way I could continue to show up for work, day after day, and see Lance if he told me he wasn't interested in me after I'd told him I was interested in him.

"Hey," Alec says, and I turn toward him.

"Not a word," I say out of the corner of my mouth, but I take one look at Alec, and it's obvious he already knows something. Maybe not that Lance and I are having a fake relationship, but at least that I said something to Tara just now.

"What's goin' on out here?" He scans the yard beyond us as Tara and I climb the steps. I let her go ahead, noting how she jogs the last couple of steps to Alec, and how he swoops her into his arms. They love each other so much, and I've never seen Alec so happy.

My heart swells with joy for him, because he's my best friend, and after he lost his inn, I thought he'd be lost forever.

"Hey, Alec," I say, tipping up to kiss his cheek as he lets Tara go.

"What were you two talking about?"

"It was a private conversation."

"Right," Alec says, obviously not caring or believing me. "Something about Lance, maybe?"

"No," I shout, and even I wince with the volume of the word. Who knew two-letters could be so violent? I glare at Tara. "I shouldn't have told you. I didn't realize you'd blab to Alec."

"We're engaged," Alec says while Tara shakes her head.

"I didn't tell him," she says, and Tara has never lied to me. Sure, we had a rocky start, but that's all over now.

I switch my eyes to Alec and then fold my arms and park them across my midsection. He's familiar with this stance, and he sighs. "Dawson may have mentioned something," he says. "Lance told—said—some...thing."

My curiosity flies off the charts. "What did Lance say?"

"I don't know," Alec says. "They've been friends since college. I'm the new guy. I wasn't there."

"New guy," I repeat with a scoff. The chickens have

moved on from the feed in the yard to the pasture that borders it, and I watch them bob around, searching for food. Chickens are funny little creatures, and I bend down to pick up Goose, Tara's second dog.

"Can I take him home with me?" I ask her, knowing she'll say yes.

"Sure," she says.

"I can't." I stroke the canine's head, wishing I could. "My uncle would throw a fit." I set Goose on the ground and sigh. "I'm going to go. Thanks, Tara."

"Anytime," she says, and I start into the house. Alex asks her about me, and why I came over, but Tara says, "She can tell you if she wants to," and I appreciate that so much.

I haven't even moved through Tara's whole house before my phone dings. I pull it from my shorts pocket and see Alec has texted me. *Come for an early breakfast tomorrow. I'll make the bacon and spinach quiche, and you can tell Peaches your secrets. We both miss you.*

Tears spring into my eyes, because my life before I started at Finley & Frank was so easy. No, I had no money. No, I existed with mostly hopelessness—and a parrot who says "bacon pancake" more than any other English words.

But I wasn't confused. I wasn't worried about how to talk to a man. I wasn't scared of losing things I didn't even know I wanted.

Okay, I tell him, and then I silence my phone, noting

that I have no missed calls or texts from the handsome, honest, handy, hard-working Lance Byers.

———

KIND.

My heart rebounds from my feet, where it had fallen when I'd seen my boss's name on the phone screen. I look up, but I'm momentarily blinded as darkness has fallen completely since I retreated to the study to put something on TV.

I didn't put anything on. I'd suffered through dinner with Rufus and Uncle Jack, and that alone can cause a woman to need a nice long winter nap. I'd laid down on the couch and enjoyed the silence, that was what I'd done.

I may have fallen asleep. The jury's still out on that one.

Lance's text has woken me way the heck up. "Kind?" I repeat out loud, suddenly catching up to our alphabet game. I have to sing the alphabet to get to the letter after K —L, by the way—and then I let my phone fall to my lap.

I had great H-words for him, but J was a flop, and I can't let L be lame too. At least if it's not geriatric and mythical, I might be in the clear.

Instead of texting him another adjective, I let my fingers fly across the screen. *Thank you*, I say. *I had a good time yesterday. Did you get your afternoon nap with Cha-Cha?*

He'd said he wanted to shower and sleep when I'd dropped him off. I'd teased him about the size of the chimichanga he'd consumed at the restaurant, and how I'd sleep for a year after eating all of that.

Unfortunately, he says back. *My sister called, so no nap.*

Ruth had called while we were at lunch, but I don't remind him of that. *Oh? What did she have to say?*

I'm not sure if this is a friendly conversation or a flirty one. In the fourteen days since I started at Finley & Frank, Lance's only texts were about documents, clients, or emails he'd sent me.

Do you have an older sister? he asks.

Yes, I tell him.

Then it's like that. He sends a smiling emoji with it. *She likes to boss me around.*

I can't imagine you being anything but the boss, I say, and *that* definitely is flirting. The way I'm smiling tells me that, though Lance can't see me. To me, Lance is a powerhouse. He has the pinstriped suits and the shiny shoes. The boxy shoulders, and every time he enters the office, I imagine paper airplanes made out of Post-It Notes flying around in the tornado his very persona creates.

Everyone bends to his will, including me, and we all secretly want to be let behind that frosted-glass door with the gold lettering on it. I mean, it takes someone special just to have a door with gold lettering on it. A boss.

Are you home? he asks, and my smile slips.

Yes.

Wanna go for a ride?

I immediately look up, as if Lance will be standing outside the study windows. I get instantly transported back to high school, when hearing the *tick-click* of a rock against glass could get my heartbeat spiking up to dangerous levels.

Of course, no one is standing outside, and even if they were, I wouldn't be able to see them. There are thorny rose bushes outside the study besides. And it's pitch-black.

Instead of answering him with my fingers, I call him. "Go for a ride?" I ask when he picks up.

"Yeah," he says casually, as if he hangs out with all of his co-workers on Sunday evenings. "It's cool tonight, and I have a convertible."

Of course he does. I swallow, not sure how to say yes or how to say no. Why is there no easy answer to this question?

"I want to talk about the fake-dating rules," Lance says, his voice almost an octave lower than normal. He clears his throat. "We never got back to them the other day, and I don't think they're complete."

I get to my feet, plenty I could say about how Sabrina isn't expecting to see both of us for a while. Who are we really pretending for? No one else at the office heard me tell Sabrina that we were dating.

"I need to get shoes," I say, scanning myself to make sure I'm dressed. Uncle Jack requires a dress for Sunday dinner, and I certainly can't go meet Lance in my semi-formal gown, even if it is blue.

Why not? a voice whispers in my head. I didn't wear shoes to dinner either, and I decide a joyride with Lance doesn't require footwear. My heart tap dances in my chest as I consider what I'm doing. I'm thirty-four years old and about to sneak out of my uncle's house, shoeless.

"Where are you?" I ask, hitching up my skirt. I can't get down to the live oaks along the road very quickly.

"I just turned down the lane," he says.

"Wait there," I practically yell. "I'll be there in a minute."

"You sure? I can just come up to the house. I live in the South. I know what mansions look like."

Uncle Jack has cameras anyway. If Lance is just sitting there, headlights on, idling, Uncle Jack might send out Donovan, his evening security, to find out why.

"Okay, I say, making a snap decision. "I'm on my way. I'll see you right outside the front doors."

"Sounds good." Lance hangs up, and I dart over to the study door. I tell myself that I'm thirty-four years old and allowed to leave the house after dark.

Then I run on my tippy-toes down the hall and around the corner, my sights set on getting to the front doors without anyone seeing me.

CHAPTER TWELVE

LANCE

I'm sure I'm hallucinating when the double-wide, double-tall front doors of the mansion open. A woman slips out, a beautiful blue ballgown coming with her. With a start, I realize it's Jessie.

I fumble my seatbelt, and by the time I get out of the car, she's already reached the top of the steps. She comes down them in a step-step, step-step-step pattern that makes her more feminine.

I am in so much trouble.

I was all Dawson-prepped to lay out the fake-dating rules. No touching except when Sabrina is around. No one else knows about the false relationship, and I don't need to be holding Jess's hand in her car while she drives us to lunch.

We don't need to be going to breakfast, lunch, or

dinner. No coffee, no stopping by cookie parlors, no nothing.

As I stand at the corner of the convertible, I can only stare. If I met this woman somewhere, I'd try to get her number. First, I'd try to talk to her to see if I like her, then I'd try to get her number. But I already know Jess. I know she's articulate and clever, easy to talk to and genuine. I'd also given her the adjective *intelligent* for the letter I, and then *kind*.

She's all of the above, and drop-dead gorgeous too.

She works for you, I start to chant in my mind. *She works for you. She works for you.*

She reaches the bottom of the steps and says, "Hey, why are you out of the car?"

Because I can't tell Ruth I didn't come around and open the door for a princess, I think. "Let me get the door." I dart around the hood and reach the passenger side of the car just as Jess arrives. She gives me a smile that is only illuminated by the moonlight, and then sinks into the convertible, the top of which is already down.

A flush fills me from top to bottom, and the night suddenly isn't anywhere cool enough for this ride. I actually pull at my collar, which has three buttons undone. If I pull on it anymore, it'll rip down the middle.

I do a deep-knee bend to get into the car, and I take a moment to get comfortable in the capsule-like pod meant for the driver. "Okay?"

"Yes," she says, her seatbelt clicking. "Unless this car

of yours decides not to let me out." She flashes me a smile that only sends a hormonal shock down to my toes.

"I tested the seatbelt before I came over," I say.

"Really?" Jess giggles, and that doesn't help my train of thought. It derails, and I grip the steering wheel like it's a throat, and I can choke it to death. I release my fingers, because I don't want to choke anything to death. Maybe the seatbelt if it doesn't release when it's time for Jess to get out of the convertible.

"I did," I say with a smile. "Clasped and unclasped just fine, about five times."

"Perfect," Jess says, glancing toward the house. "Let's go."

I put the car in gear and go, because I don't need to be told twice. Jess sighs and puts her right hand over the windowsill in the car. "This is so nice," she says. "It really is different than just riding in a car."

"It really is." My throat is so dry, but the convertible is a two-seater and isn't big enough even for cup-holders.

"Restless tonight?" she asks innocently, and I hear her ADHD accusation in the tone. I ignore it and chase the moonlit shadows from the live oaks.

"A little," I admit. I reach the end of the lane and make a right, which doesn't take us back toward the city or into Sugar Creek.

"Where are we going?" she asks.

"The country," I say.

"Is this your car?" she asks.

"Yes," I say. "Sort of. My step-dad and I bought it together, and I keep it here in Charleston. He lives in a fifty-five-plus community in Florida, and they don't have the parking." I glance at her, and she's pushing her hand through her hair.

I have never envied someone's hand so much. I focus on the road, but all I can imagine is myself pushing my hand through Jess's hair while I kiss her.

Jess lets a mile or two go by in silence, and I'm still trying to figure out how to swallow. "You wanted to talk about the fake-dating rules?" Jess prompts just as I ask, "Do you always wear ballgowns on Sunday evenings?"

Jess exhales a long sigh that tells me I'm insufferable—or else the dress is. "My uncle requires a dress for dinner on the weekends," she says. "At least it was only him and Rufus tonight. Last night, he tried to feed someone named Phil and did I mention that there was a light violet gown laying on my bed? Just you know, in case it was my size."

I grin into the night, a measure of relaxation flowing through me. "Let me guess: it was your size."

"Yes, it was," Jess says. "Lucy and I went to get a hamburger, and while I was gone, the gown mysteriously disappeared."

"Did you say anything to your uncle?"

"No," Jess says, her voice as dark as the night. "That's not what we do in my family, Lance. We just stay silent and pretend like nothing happened."

"But he came into your bedroom—twice—without your permission."

"I haven't had privacy for years," Jess says, and she keeps her head turned away from me while she does.

"Jess," I say, but she just shakes her head. My heart pounds against my breastbone. "When you get your own place, you'll have all the privacy you want."

"Yes," she says quietly, but the vastness of the sky seems to trap the emotion in the word and echo it back to me endlessly.

"I heard from Chip too," I say, though her apartment isn't what I was going to talk about with Jess tonight. She finally turns toward me, such hope in her face. "He said he doesn't have anything right now, but he'll let me know if something comes across his desk."

"Thank you, Lance," Jess says, and she reaches over and brushes my hair off my forehead. Time slows to nothing, and I'm surprised I don't drive the convertible into the nearest tree.

I press harder on the accelerator, not quite sure where I am or where I'm taking us. I finally get my voice to say, "I thought we could go up and around Hidden Wood and back into the city from the north."

"Sure," Jess says, as if she doesn't have a care in the world. On the outside, someone meeting her for the first time might think that. I probably did. No, I probably scanned her down to her shoes and found her lacking. I'm sure I frowned at her, and I'm sure I said something about how I'd see how long she could last.

Sometimes I really hate the things that come out of my mouth.

Thankfully, the stars keep us company as I drive, and nothing needs to be said. I know the way, because I've done this drive plenty of times. I'm alert and awake, thanks to the copious amount of coffee I drank at Dawson and Callie's. They're working on a big project with a deadline this Wednesday, and I left them in a mess of samples, advertising banners that had been printed in the wrong color, and vats of take-out.

The lights in Charleston come into view, and Jess pulls in a breath. "Oh, wow," she says. "Look at the city."

"It's beautiful at night," I say, glancing over at her. "You haven't seen it like this?" I hardly recognize the gentle tone coming out of my mouth.

"No," she says, turning and smiling at me. She reaches for my hand, and I happily give it to her. I might be in trouble with this woman, but I decide with her slender fingers in mine that I don't care. If there's trouble to be had, I want it to be with Jess.

"Thanks for inviting me on this drive," she says. "It's exactly what I needed to face the week ahead."

"We don't have a busy week," I say.

"Maybe you don't," she says. "Every day is like navigating a mine field for me."

I chuckle, realizing too late that I shouldn't. I try to

judge how she feels, but I can't quite see her whole expression. "Is it because of me?"

"Let's just say I'm still learning how to anticipate your needs."

"You're the one with all the nonsensical acronyms," I say, grinning. "I've started a list in my phone and everything."

She bursts out laughing and says, "You have not."

"Yes, I have." I'm not sure if I'm flirting or just having a good time. Ruth tells me I'm too proper to flirt, and Dawson says I need to either let go or do up another button and be Aaron Finley to the T. But I don't want to be my step-dad, at least not in that way.

"Tell me one acronym I've used that you didn't know," she challenges.

"NBD," I say instantly. "You texted it to me on Thursday, and I'm still not sure I know what it means."

Jess laughs again, and let me tell you, I want to make her do that every single day of my life. I find myself laughing with her, at least until she says, "Well, what does it mean?"

I cut her a look out of the corner of my eye, the city lights coming closer. "No big deal?"

She beams so brightly she could be the moon. "You got it. That's UGI, BTW."

I blink. "You did not just say all of that."

"Everyone knows what UGI is, Lance. It's like that LOI or the FVM or the CDC."

Laughter soars from my throat. "I'm pretty sure that last on is the Center for Disease Control," I say through my chuckles.

"Laugh it up," she says, though she's laughing too. "In fact, I'm going to make that an acronym too. LIU."

"Oh, we can't have two with L's and I's." I grin at her. "That's just too much."

She shakes her head and readjusts my hand in hers and settles them both on her leg. The orange streetlights come over us, and a new weight settles on my shoulders. Out in the country, I can't feel the pressure, but back in Charleston, it descends with the force of gravity.

She allows me to drive through the city, right along the water, and start for Sugar Creek again. Only a couple of miles from her uncle's house, she says, "You never said anything about the fake-dating rules."

"Mm." I keep my gaze on the road in front of me. How do I tell her I don't want it to be fake? Will she think I'm just rebounding? What if I am?

I come to the lane that leads past all the live oaks to the mansion, and I make the turn. I let the convertible ease to a stop, and I gaze down the straight lane, with all the trees clawing up into the moonlit sky.

"Jess?"

"Yeah?"

I'm going to just say it. If I regret it, I'll survive somehow. "What if I don't want it to be fake?"

Jess turns her head to look at me, but I can't quite meet her gaze. "I..."

"Just say it," I say, because I got to say what I wanted.

"All right." She takes a breath, and one thing about Jess is she doesn't ever clear her throat. I have to work hard not to do it right now myself, but she breathes when she's nervous. I sound like I'm gargling glass.

"I'm scared," she says. "What if it doesn't work out, and we break-up? I need this job, Lance. You're my boss. You said you'd teach me real estate." She pulls in another breath, and I slide my hand out of hers.

"Fair points," I say as evenly as I can. She just friend-zoned me. No, worse. Boss-zoned. The simmering, bubbling anger boils in my stomach. I get the convertible moving again, and neither of us say anything until I pull in front of the wide front steps and marble columns on her uncle's mansion.

"Jess," I say. "I just don't want us to be like your family. We have to be able to talk." I turn my head and look at her. "Okay?"

"Of course," she says, almost in a British accent.

"Okay," I say. "So fake-dating when Sabrina Shadows is around. Otherwise, boss-assistant." I touch my chest on the word *boss* and gesture toward her on *assistant*.

"I'm sorry, Lance."

"Please," I say. "Don't be sorry. It's fine. I'm on my female-fast anyway." I try to give her a smile, but I'm pretty sure it looks like I'm one breath away from eating off her face.

She looks...sad. Hopeful. Upset? Confused? I honestly have no idea. But I know she needs to get out of my car right now before I made a bigger idiot out of myself.

"See you tomorrow," I say, turning to look out the windshield again. Jess gets the hint—and my Southern gentleman act has fled—unbuckles her belt, and gets out of the car. As she tippy-toes back up the steps, I realize she isn't wearing shoes.

A shoeless princess.

I sigh as I drive away and leave her in my rearview mirror. Isn't the prince supposed to rescue the shoeless princess—my word, she's Cinderella—and whisk her away to his castle, where they'll live happily-ever-after?

"Yeah," I mutter to myself as I drive under all those statue-like trees again. They'll probably turn into her carriage drivers to get her to a real royal man. "But Lance, you're no prince."

I'm just a man on a female-fast whose fake girlfriend just told him she doesn't want to try a real relationship in case she then loses her job.

Definitely not a prince.

CHAPTER THIRTEEN

JESSIE

I pick the piece of bacon from the eggy custard Alec has baked to perfection. "I don't know." I pop the bacon in my mouth and do my best not to look at my best friend. I fail at that, just like I'm failing at everything these days.

"What does that even mean?" Alec challenges me. He always has, and I'm not sure why I got up before dawn and left the house to come be interrogated by him. Probably because anything is better than running into Uncle Jack in the morning. And this quiche is fifty-two times better than the corn muffins I like so much.

"Jess," Alec barks at me, and I sigh. My head rolls on my shoulders, almost too heavy for me to hold up.

"It means, Alec," I say, employing my Southern socialite tone. I glare at him, but he simply looks steadily back at me. "That I don't know."

"You like him."

"I mean, yes." I can admit I like Lance. "He's a little..intense sometimes."

"We all are," he says. "Men. You know. It's how we are."

"Daddy's not like that."

"Because your mama is intense enough for both of them," Alec says, a frown appearing between his eyes at the same time a small smile touches his mouth. He sighs, his quiche long gone. "Jess, I just don't get it. The man came to the house last night and took you for a ride. He didn't do that to talk business. He likes you."

"I know that." The words come out of my mouth, but I'm not sure my heart believes it. My brain is still having a hard time catching up to the situation too.

"You held his hand. You touched his face..."

"Are you saying I led him on?"

"I'm saying he probably thought you liked him too." Alec stands and picks up his plate. "Are you going to eat that?'

"Yes," I say, picking up my fork. "You can't take my quiche."

He chuckles, shakes his head, and walks into the kitchen. "I'll box this for you. You can take it to work."

I groan out the word, "Work," then stuff my mouth with more eggs, spinach, and bacon. What am I doing? How am I going to face Lance in just another hour?

I can't.

My first instinct is to fly away. Grow wings and soar up into the sky.

My second is to stay right where I am. I never need to leave Alec's apartment again. I can go back to birdsitting Peaches, who squawked so passionately when I got here that Alec had to cover her just so we could talk. He has a couch; I can sleep there.

My third thought is to grow up and face Lance like a thirty-four year old woman. I can do it. He's my boss, and I want the job. I can do the job. I can learn. I'm smart.

I tell myself all of these things while Alec puts my lunch-quiche in a plastic container and then returns to the table. "Jess." He sits down again. "Here's what I think."

"Here we go," I say, teasing him.

He smiles, but it's fleeting, and I know it's time to be serious. "You don't want to go back to Beaufort, I get that. You finally found a job you like, and honestly, you must be good at it, because Dawson says Lance has fired his last several assistants after only a few days. One was gone by lunchtime on the first day."

I cut off another bite of quiche, my eyes filling with tears. I can't eat. I can't swallow. I can't breathe.

"Honey." Alec covers my fork-holding hand with both of his. "He put himself way out there. I know you like him, and I know you don't want to pretend in front of your client. So don't pretend."

"I don't know how to tell him," I whisper. "I *am*

worried about losing my job." I look at him, silently begging him to understand. To tell me what to do.

"How about you tell him all of that, and make an agreement that he can't fire you if it doesn't work out? That you can only be let go if you mess up—which you won't, Jess. You won't."

His doorbell rings, and no sheet or blanket can contain Peaches when that happens. She starts to imitate it, then screams, "Someone's here. Someone's here. Someone's here," on repeat.

I grin at him and stand up. "You get the door. I'll get Peaches. She misses me so much."

Alec stands too, but instead of going for the door—it's probably Tara or one of the ten-year-old twins down the hall—he takes me into a hug. "Jess," he whispers. "It's time to be that phoenix you've been trying to become." Then he walks away, leaving me in the kitchen while he deals with Peaches and one of the twins.

The boy came to see the bird before he has to go to school, and his mother hovers in the hallway while Peaches does all of her new tricks for him.

"Time to become the phoenix," I tell myself. They're majestic birds, and they can be reborn from ashes. That's what I had to do when I first came to Charleston, and even though I burned everything between Lance and I last night, I can rebuild it this morning. I know I can.

"Bacon pancake!" Peaches yells as I approach. She

takes off from the boy's hand and lands on my shoulder. "Motorbike, I love you!"

I laugh at her, give her a stroke with my pointer finger, and hand her back to Alec.

"Going?" he asks.

I take a breath and square my shoulders. "Yes," I say. "I'm going to fix this."

———

HALF AN HOUR LATER, I greet Olive with a smile. She stands from her anchor-spot in the office and extends a yellow piece of paper toward me. "A message?" I ask, true surprise flowing through me. "For me?"

"Sabrina Shadows called," she says. "Twenty minutes before we opened." She gives me a look that says the same thing Lance told me. Sabrina is Trouble with a capital T.

"Thank you," I say as professionally as I can. I put my leftover quiche in the office break-room fridge and make my way to my desk-copier compound. Happiness flows through me at the sight of the clean desk, the two trays, and my computer. I open my bottom desk drawer and put my purse inside, then pluck the picture frame out I brought that day.

It goes next to my computer, and it shows me with my brother and my sister. I'm the middle child, and Amelia is a few years older than me, and Jonathan is a few years younger. Mama has never called them anything but their full names—I get called Jessica whenever she speaks to me —but I call them Amy and Jon.

They're still in Beaufort, but they're still talking to me too. Amy is blissfully married to a man named Scott Sorenson, who is a decade older than her. She has her own mansion and gardens to maintain, and how she has survived there, I have no idea.

Jon isn't married yet, but Mama has the Southern belles coming all the time. I swear, she hosts balls and parties and dinners just to bring women over for him to pick from. It's almost like those Regency novels and movies, where people's eyes meet from across the room, and though they know nothing about one another, they fall madly in love.

I don't believe in Regency romances, and while I adore ballgowns and tiaras, I would rather never attend another ball.

I glance over to the gold-lettered door. It stands closed, and I have no way of knowing if Lance is in yet. "Of course you do," I mutter to myself, and I glance down at my phone. The clock on it bounces from spot to spot on the screen, and it's not nine a.m. yet.

Which means he's not in.

Lance is nothing if not the most scheduled person alive, and he has four more minutes before he'll come through the double glass doors out front, chat with Olive for a moment, and then move into his office.

I'm expected to be here before him, and I am. I wake

my computer, my heartbeat thumping like a jackrabbit's hind leg. I read my message from Sabrina, but all it says is to please call her at my earliest convenience. I'm feeling rather inconvenient right now, so I put the note in my to-do-today box and check my email.

I know the moment Lance enters, because he's on the phone, and his voice fills the lobby and carries around the corner to my ears. "...absolutely not, Kyle. Sheila Hudson has a letter of intent to purchase, and you will not accept that offer."

I stand, imagining him with those paper airplane Post-Its and his hair waving in the wind. His jacket flaps open to reveal that broad chest, and he'll be wearing a light-colored shirt in violet or pink or yellow, with a tie that doesn't match.

My mouth turns dry at the fantasy in my head.

"I don't care what you told them," Lance says, appearing past the wall and then the copiers. "I know you got that LOI. My assistant confirmed it with you days ago. The offer will be—" He enters his office and slams the door behind him hard enough to make the glass rattle.

My bones do the same thing, and I swallow down anything I've planned to say to him. He didn't even use my name with Kyle, though the other agent knows who I am. I've spoken with him on the phone several times, and we exchange emails like we're pen pals.

I sit back down, but it's more like a stone dropping. My chair has wheels, and it slips. I'm free-falling for a moment, and then my shoes grip the ground, and I manage to keep myself from barreling into the temporary wall behind me. Peter Frank's assistant has a little cubicle there, and I suddenly want to find a shank and tunnel through the beige, carpet-covered partition and escape into her area.

The warden opens his door and looks at me. "I need Sheila Hudson right now," he says, ducking back into his office.

"Yes, sir," I call after him, wishing I was important enough to not have to dial my own calls. At least he didn't slam the door this time. My fingers tremble as I pull up Sheila's number and dial it for Lance.

She answers with a, "Hello, Jessie, darling."

I smile despite the mood in this corner of the agency today. "Howdy, Sheila," I say, really drawing out the Southern syllables. She's from Georgia, and she loves Southern belles. "Mister Byers needs to talk to you about the riverfront property. Can I transfer you over?"

"In a minute," she says sweetly, in her own slow-as-cold-molasses drawl. "You got yourself a boyfriend yet, sweetie?"

"Uh." I pause, because I don't know how to answer this question. With red phoenix wings in my head, I continue with, "Almost, ma'am. Workin' real hard on it." I don't know why I slip into a Texas cowboy accent instead of my born and bred Carolina one, and I press my eyes closed. "Let me transfer you."

The first time I tried to transfer a call from my phone to Lance's, I hung up on the client. The second time, I couldn't get it to leave my headset, and Lance had come out to my desk to take the call, glaring like he'd been born with an exasperated expression on his face and it had been stuck like that forever.

Olive finally took pity on me and taught me how to do it, so the call goes easily from my phone to Lance's, and he answers on the first ring. I hang up, because Sheila is not my client, and I'm just the assistant.

My ears ring, and when I blink, I can't focus on the letters on my computer screen. I won't be able to either—until I talk to Lance. I get up and move around my desk, positioning myself next to his door. I press my back into the wall like I'm a cat burglar about to steal the Queen's jewels, and tilt my head to the side, listening.

"...know that, Miss Hudson," he says, his tone placating and a complete one-eighty than it had been when he'd requested I get her on the line. "But we need the offer by five p.m. today, or the seller is going to accept the offer that's already come in."

Lance won't be happy if he loses this purchase. I don't think men like Lance Byers know how to lose, and I can't imagine what his night was like after he dropped me off.

You're such an idiot, I tell myself for the hundred and twenty-first time. The moment I'd gotten out of his car, I'd wanted to get right back in. I wanted to tell him I'd made a huge mistake, and of course—absolutely of course—it was fine that he didn't want our dating to be fake. I don't want to fake it either. *Take me to dinner right now.*

I press my eyes closed in the silence, and then Lance says, "You're lucky I got us until this afternoon," and his voice is far too close for him to be at his desk.

I whip open my eyes, and sure enough, he's standing in the doorway. His eyebrows are an angry V, and he somehow raises them in the same position. His question is clear: *What are you doing, lurking here against the wall?*

I wish I knew.

My heart pounds so dang hard I'm sure it's going to crack a rib.

"Five o'clock," he says, and then he lowers his hand holding the phone. "Miss Dunaway?"

I take a steeling breath and throw myself off the cliff. "I need to talk to you," I say. "In private."

Lance's angry-V disappears, his eyebrows still sky-high. He steps back and gestures toward his office. "This better be quick."

CHAPTER FOURTEEN

LANCE

I'M ALREADY BACK TO MY DESK BY THE TIME JESS takes a seat. She promptly gets back up, and I stay on my feet too. With the desk between us, I feel like I might be able to hold my composure for however long this conversation is going to be.

When she doesn't say anything, I go, "Well?" I have plenty to do today, and I can't believe Kyle Corison is going to sell that property out from under me. My blood boils at the thought, and Jess's bright blue sweater with a star right in the middle of it isn't enough to distract me.

"I made a mistake," she says, twisting her fingers around one another.

I reach up and pinch my fingers along my forehead. I didn't sleep last night but spent hours tossing and turning in some level of dozing, thinking about Jess.

Then, the line at Legacy Brew was twenty cars deep,

and I'd skipped it, knowing there'd be coffee here. Then Kyle had called, and I still haven't been properly caffeinated.

"With what?" I ask, trying to think through what houses we've been working on. I shuffle a couple of files on my desk just to have something to do with my hands. "If you can't book Laura for the pictures for the Gilmore estate, just get—"

"With you," Jess blurts out. "I was so stupid last night. I don't want to fake-date either."

My eyes fly to hers, noting how much anxiety she carries in her shoulders, her face, and even her stance.

"I like holding your hand," she says, licking her lips— completely distracting me yet again. "I loved riding with you in that convertible, and talking to you over lunch—and I don't mean about business things. Just...Lance things."

I have no idea what to say. An insane amount of hope builds in my chest, but I will not let it out. Not yet. Not until I'm sure Jess knows what she's saying—and means it.

I blink, and Jess relaxes slightly. "Maybe it was a one-time offer," she says. "I know you're doing this female-fast thing, and I don't want to break that for you. Maybe we could just, I don't know, give it a try, and if it doesn't work out, it doesn't work out."

I start nodding about halfway through. "If you want." My voice grinds through my throat as if I've been stung by a jellyfish.

"Is there some office policy or something?" she asks.

"Like, maybe then, if I know you can't fire me just because it doesn't work out..."

Ah, so she wants assurance she's not going to lose her job. *That's smart*, I tell myself, just like I did all of last night. I've never thought Jessie Dunaway was stupid, that's for sure.

"I own the agency," I say slowly. "Well, Peter and I do. There's no official policy against two co-workers dating, and we've never had a problem with it." I sit down, my feet and knees thanking me instantly.

"You own this place?" Jess asks, dumbfounded.

"Yes," I say.

She falls into her seat. "I didn't know that. I've been here for two weeks. Why didn't you say so?"

I shrug, because I didn't feel the need to tell her. "My step-dad co-founded Finley and Frank with one of his best friends. Simon Frank. Peter is his son. I'm Aaron Finley's son. We co-own it." I click my mouse like this is no big deal. To me, it isn't.

"No wonder you have a convertible," she says.

I look over to her, a smile forming in my soul and working its way toward my mouth. The silence in the office isn't quite so charged anymore, and I like that. Jess, of course, brings a shot of electricity to my blood every time I look at her, so there's definitely still some current. It's just not as angry or frustrated.

"I can guarantee you that the only reason I would fire

you is if you mess up on a job-related item," I say. "Is that good enough?"

Her face lights up. "A personal guarantee from the great Lance Byers?"

"Stop it," I say, letting the smile touch my mouth. I don't want her to know how tightly she's got me wrapped around her finger already.

"I'd say that's enough," she says.

"Great," I say, not sure what to do next. There's all this real estate work, but now that we've decided to maybe not be fake-dating, shouldn't I ask her out or something? "So... what are your plans for tonight?"

"No plans," she says sweetly.

"Dinner, then?" I ask, and I make sure I'm looking right into her eyes when I add, "And we won't be talking about business."

A flush fills her cheeks, and dang if that doesn't make me ten times hotter than I already am. She nods, gets to her feet, and says, "Stand up. We need to fix your tie."

I grin from ear to ear as I do what she says. She moves over to the bank of cabinets beside the entrance to my office and opens the one closest to the door. "Let's see..." She checks over her shoulder a couple of times as I unknot the tie around my neck. "This one."

She plucks down a dark red, orange, and purple tie that's covered with polka dots of varying sizes.

"Really?" I hand her the offending tie, which I thought

matched the baby blue shirt I'm wearing. It's navy blue, so it's in the same color family.

"Contrasting is always better," she says as I loop the tie around my neck. "You'll see."

I finish up with the tie and smooth it down my chest and abdomen, my eyes following it. "I do like it."

"It's fabulous," she says. "Now, if you'll excuse me, I have to go return a call for my client."

I chuckle as she walks away, wondering if she knows she's adding an extra swing to those sexy hips. If she doesn't, she's simply amazing. "You like saying that, don't you?"

"You know what?" She turns back at the door, her smile oh-so-beautiful. "I really do."

———

A COUPLE OF HOURS LATER, I'm neck-deep in going over an offer that came in on one of my properties—which has pushed my regular work to the side—when I hear a couple of voices I don't recognize.

That's not all that abnormal, because we have clients in and out of the agency all the time. Besides Peter and me, there are six other agents working at Finley & Frank, all of them buying and selling real estate and commercial properties in the Charleston and surrounding areas.

But these voices sound angry.

"Let's go in here," Jess says, and she appears in my

doorway. She's clearly out of her element and her league, and she throws me a look that screams *help me, Lance!*

I get to my feet, the proposed offer forgotten, and round the desk just as Sabrina Shadows bustles by Jess. Right on her heels is Jason Finch.

"...walk away like that," Jason says, clearly upset. "And don't think that just because you've hired one of the best real estate agents in the city means that you can get away with undercutting me." He glares at Sabrina, who keeps her back to him, and looks at me. "Hey, Lance."

"Hey," I say as Sabrina whips around.

"You know him?"

"Of course I know him," Jason fires back at her.

She cocks one hip so hard I'm sure she's going to fall. I even lunge toward her just in case. She gives me the dirtiest look a woman has ever given me and switches her glare back to Jason. "I suppose you're going to hire him to sell the house."

Jason lifts his chin. "Yes."

"What is going on here?" I ask, holding up both hands. I even step between Jason and Sabrina, because one of them is going to start throwing punches at the other. My bet is on Sabrina, because that woman is not afraid of anything or anyone.

"Miss Shadows found a property she liked," Jess says, those hands winding and twining. I need to tell her to knock that off. She should be the Power Suit in the room, not the Nervous Nellie.

I take a step toward her and put my hands over hers. "And?"

She stills and looks up at me. "And Jason—uh, Mister Finch—owns it. Sabrina wanted to put in an offer below asking price, and I called Jason, who's selling his own property. You know, a FSBO? Anyway." She swallows and does her deep-breathing thing. "Things sort of snowballed from there."

"And by snowballed, she means *Miss Shadows*," Jason sneers. "Put in an offer at half the listed price. It's insulting."

"Jess," I say, trying not to be condescending.

"That's not true," Jess says, removing her hands from beneath mine. They clench into fists as she steps next to me. "There was no offer made. I wouldn't do that, because I know the value of your property, Mister Finch, and I was advising my client—"

"It's not my job to pad your bank account," Sabrina says over Jess.

I want to tell her to duck and cover, but I'm too proud of her. Of course she did her homework on the property Sabrina liked. And of course she didn't try to low-ball the seller.

"It's not my job to sell to you for half the value just because you want it," Jason snaps back.

"You're so used to everyone bending to your will, because you're so good-looking," Sabrina hurls at him. "Or you think you are."

"No one bends to my will," Jason says. "I work hard for what I have."

"So do I."

"Do you?" he challenges, even taking a step forward. "Did you bring me the Callahan case files from storage last week when I asked for them?"

"I'm not your paralegal," Sabrina growls.

"No." Jason wears a dark, dark look. "You're my *junior partner*. That means you work on cases *with* me, and I shouldn't have had to waste my afternoon at the depository to get that case."

"I shouldn't have had to either."

"You put in a request, and they send it!" he yells. "Neither of us should've had to, but you didn't do what I asked you to do."

"Okay," I say, stepping in, because this fight really has nothing to do with me or Jess. "You two need to deal with your work issues somewhere else." I look between them, giving them each a fierce enough glare that they both back down. "Miss Shadows, Jess cannot put in an offer that isn't fair for the seller. If you'd rather not work with someone of her caliber, that's fine, but I don't think you'll find any agents here at Finley and Frank that will do that for you."

Message: *Take your business somewhere else.*

"I'm happy to show you the properties I found," Jess says, her voice as sweet as sugar pops. "Including a tour of Mister Finch's century-old house. But there are market values we want to observe." She cuts a quick look at Jason, who now wears a smug look. I want to slap him and tell him he's not doing himself any favors.

"Jason," I grumble out of the corner of my mouth.

He looks at me and takes his arrogance down a notch, praise the heavens. "I don't think I'm needed here," he says.

"That you are not," Sabrina says. "And if you follow me again, I'm calling the cops."

"You do what you have to do," Jason says breezily as he exits the office.

Jess and I are left with Miss Trouble, and I look at her, trying to anticipate Sabrina's next move.

"Don't look at me like that," she snaps. "It's men like you who make women sit out in cubicles." She looks me up and down. "With your fancy ties and jackets, you act like you own the world." She stomps past me and then Jess, who doesn't linger in my office.

She goes after Sabrina with, "Miss Shadows, he is one of the top five real estate agents in the state. He isn't *taking* anything from me or anyone else."

I smile to myself, because Jess has some fire inside her too. You just have to know how to light it. I move to the edge of the doorway and listen, much the same way Jess did to me this morning.

Eavesdropping...who knew I'd be reduced to this inside my own agency?

"He's teaching me everything he knows," Jess says as her office chair squeaks. "Besides, he can't match his ties to his shirts to save his life, so he's definitely not perfect." She inhales, and I hope that quells her nerves for her.

"Please, sit down, and let's look at these. I found some great places." She sounds in control and professional, and I'm so, so proud of her.

"You're only saying that because you're dating him," Sabrina says.

"No," Jess says firmly. "Lance and I are seeing one another, but that has nothing to do with the professional respect I have for him. Now, this one has the big windows you said you wanted."

Professional respect.

I ease away from the door and let Jess handle Sabrina, no eavesdropping needed. She's obviously better at it than I am—than anyone else—and as I go back to my own offer, I pray that Jess will be able to put together this deal...and that I won't mess up too badly tonight at dinner.

CHAPTER FIFTEEN

JESSIE

My phone bleeps out several *BLOOPETY-BLINK-BLIPS*, and I realize I was probably in a dead-zone. I'm not sure, but I suspect the texts are from Lance. I glance at the clock and realize he can't be here yet. My adrenaline has spiked already, and I do see his name on my phone.

All of the texts are from him, and I smile to myself. A warm feeling envelops me, and I lean against the wall and tap to open the messages. My goodness, he's sent me five pictures, each numbered, mind you, that show an outfit lying on the bed.

They each have a pair of slacks, a light-colored shirt—everything from pale canary to baby-girl-pink—and a tie in them.

Do any of these match? he'd asked.

I giggle to myself, finding him utterly adorable. The

man is thirty-seven and asking me what he should wear on our first date. Can he get any cuter?

None of these, I tap out quickly. I send the message, and then I take a breath. If I know him even a little, I know he'll call.

Sure enough, my phone rings, and Lance's polished, professional agent picture comes up on my screen. "Okay," I say instead of hello. "We're going to dinner where?"

"Oh, uh, I thought we'd try this place called Panini Palace."

I burst out laughing. "You're kidding."

"No," he says, his voice somewhat wounded. "Why? I'll admit, it's a bit of a cheesy name, but it's getting really good reviews on all the foodie blogs around Charleston."

"And you think you need to wear slacks and a tie?"

"I—" He cuts off, and I can't stop smiling.

"Honey," I say, really drawling out the word. "It's the end of October, so maybe not shorts. But put on some jeans and a polo. Shoes you don't have to shine. And come pick me up."

Silence comes through the line, and I check my device to see if the call is still connected. It is. "Lance?"

"I don't actually own a pair of jeans."

I laugh again, because AFD—A-Freaking-Dorable.

"Khakis?" I suggest.

"I have those," he says.

"Great," I say. "Those. Loafers—not dress shoes. And Lance, search your closet for something that isn't pastel."

"Isn't...pastel..." He says the words like he's not sure what they mean.

"And then surprise me," I say.

"What are you going to wear?"

I glance down at myself. "I'm not sure. I was just on my way to get ready from the pool."

"I'll be there in half an hour."

"I'll be ready," I promise, and the call ends. I can't decide if he sounded nervous as he'd said his last statement or not. I tell myself not to obsess about anything, and I pull the oversized blouse covered with splashy flowers over my head. I've paired the red, orange, and blue shirt with a pair of black skinny jeans, and as I shimmy into those, I feel so great about myself.

I can't do much to tame my curls, but I spray in my de-tangler and run my fingers through my hair. It actually looks pretty good, and I swipe on a pale purple lip gloss and a few dashes of mascara.

I leave my bedroom, pausing just outside the door. I think about what Lance said about not having privacy, and I reach back around to lock the doorknob. I have the key on my ring, and a sense of power fills me as I walk down the wide hallway.

"Jessie," Uncle Jack says as I move past the dining room.

I pause and hold my breath before I turn toward the doorway. "Yes?"

He holds his soup spoon above a gold-rimmed bowl,

but at least he's the only one seated at the table tonight. "Going out?"

"Yes, sir," I say.

"With whom?"

"My new boyfriend," I say, hoping he'll text those exact words to Mama the moment I turn my back. Or right now. "He's almost here, so I have to jet." I wave to him and smile widely. "Have a good night, Uncle Jack."

I don't need to antagonize him. I am grateful that he's let me live here for the past few months. He provided a sense of freedom and safety for me I hadn't had in Beaufort, and that will always mean a lot to me.

Leaving the mansion goes down like a breath of fresh air, and I practically skip past the marble pillars and down the steps. I'm wearing a pair of strappy sandals that leave my heels flapping, and I should know better than to skip.

My shoes trip me, and I stumble down the last couple of steps to the graveled drive. It looks like someone's raked it recently, and now I've caused a couple of foot-sized potholes.

I manage not to fall, which is a miracle, and only a couple of seconds later, Mammoth's growl fills the air. His headlights light the night, and I step back up onto the bottom step of the sweeping staircase that leads up to the cement front porch with all those columns.

I can't wipe the smile from my face, and I wait right where I am as Lance puts Mammoth in park and gets down. He jogs around the front of the truck, and he's wearing a big grin too. It goes well with his light gray cotton pants and the deep, midnight black polo that hugs his shoulders and chest.

Such a lucky piece of cloth. I wonder if it knew it would get to touch Lance's body when it was sewn into a shirt. Probably not.

"Howdy, ma'am," he says, and then he wraps me into a hug. This is so different from his demeanor and greeting at the agency, but I don't complain. Not even a little bit.

"Hi." I run my hands up his back, getting the silky quality of the polo. "This shirt sure looks nice."

"Does it?" He steps back and brushes something down his abs. "I found it buried in the back of my closet."

"You don't like dark colors," I say as a statement of fact.

"Not particularly."

"You should wear them, though," I say. "You're fair, Lance. Blond men do well in navies, blacks, eggplant, or ooh, you know what you'd look amazing in?"

"Do tell," he says, plenty of teasing in his voice.

"You're not going to like it," I say, waiting for him to open my door. He does and steps out of the way so I can put my foot on the runner and boost myself into Mammoth's interior.

"Tell me anyway," he says, looking and sounding more relaxed than I thought he'd be. He did say I was easy to talk to, and I hope we can pick up our alphabet adjective game tonight.

"Brick red," I say, noting the fixed seatbelt inside Mammoth.

He chuckles and shakes his head. "Never gonna happen."

I boost myself into the truck without falling backward into my boss, thankfully, and when I'm seated, I ask, "What about mustard? Or burnt orange?"

"Those are doable," he says. He leans in and adds, "You look amazing tonight, Jess. I'm glad we're doing this." Before I can answer, he steps back and closes the door.

I watch him walk through the headlights and back to the driver's side, and I can admit to myself that I'm glad we're doing this too. Really glad.

Giddy-glad, and I hope that my enthusiasm for this new relationship doesn't kill it before it can get legs and start to grow.

"So," he says. "It's your turn. We're on L."

"L," I repeat, my brain matter firing adjectives at me. *Lucky. Lazy. Large.*

I could kill the relationship—and lose my job—with this letter.

"Nothing?" he teases, his phone brightening the cab of the truck. He glances at it, and then quickly grabs the device. "This is Rich." A pause. "He's got an apartment we can go see tomorrow."

"You're kidding," I say, my breath catching in my throat. "One bedroom? In my price range?"

Lance's grin is illuminated by the blue light on the

phone, and he is so sexy my muscles quiver. "Yep," he says, his fingers flying over the screen. "I'm going to tell him I'll have my assistant check my schedule, and we'll let him know when we can go tomorrow."

I giggle—and then get busy checking his schedule on my own phone. As he drives us toward the city, we decide we can go look at the apartment tomorrow after lunch. I take his phone and send the message to Rich, as if I'm Lance, and with that all settled, a glow starts in my chest.

Things are finally starting to look up. I just might have a chance at the life I want, instead of the one that's been dictated to me for three decades.

"You're not getting out of L," Lance says.

"I don't have anything," I say. "What would you say about me for L?"

"We can come back to it," he says. "I have M for you, and I'm going to go with *mesmerizing*."

I laugh, because everything is better with a man when I don't have to pretend. This is going to be a great date, and I have an apartment to see tomorrow too.

"Limitless," I blurt out. I swing my attention toward him. "You're limitless."

He nods, not saying anything right away. "Yeah," he says slowly. "I like that. Thanks, Jess." He speaks with such a genuine quality to his voice, and I sink further into the seat—and into him as he continues toward the city.

———

I EASE Lucille to a stop in front of a little white house that sits back from the road. Neither Lance nor I say anything. I'm taking in the blackness of the roof, and the fact that the flowerbeds have been cleared for the winter. The grass is neat and trimmed, and the driveway is flat and runs along the side of the house.

"It's a basement apartment," Lance says.

"Yes." My voice is barely loud enough to leave my throat. I have a very good feeling about this place, just like I had a great feeling last night after Lance had dropped me off after our date.

We'd had the best night—good food, fun conversation, and lots of laughter. He'd held my hand, ordered six desserts so we could try them all, and walked me all the way to the front doors of the mansion. There had been no kiss—at least not on the lips—and I'd slipped into the house feeling like toasted marshmallows from head to toe.

We'd worked like a well-oiled machine at the agency that morning, and now, I was looking at the house where I was going to live. I just knew it.

"Okay." I take a big breath and open the door.

"You left your keys," Lance says, and I duck back into the sedan to pull them from the ignition. So I'm nervous. BFD. The last time I'd looked at an apartment with Lance, my hair had gotten ripped out by a jackalope. I certainly don't want to repeat that.

He meets me at the front of the car and takes my hand in his. "Rich said this place was nice," he says. "It's not on the listings yet, so you don't need to make a decision in the next five minutes."

"I know how to weigh options," I say.

"Hm."

I let this go, because he lets me tease him about being ADHD. So I tend to see something or hear something and make a decision quickly. That's not a crime, thank you very much.

A door sits halfway back on the side of the house, right in the driveway, and it's painted a bright yellow. *Ew*, I think, but I can live with a yellow door if it's the golden ticket to my own place. The yellow brick road to Oz. Something.

"They said it would be unlocked," I say, and the knob turns like a greased watermelon going down a slip-n-slide.

I expect a pungent scent to punch me in the face, but I get...lilacs. My soul swells, and I look right and up a few steps to a closed door. Another set of steps on my left goes down, and I move first to go that way. Eight stairs later, I reach the basement floor.

The hallway branches left and right, and I look both ways while Lance crowds in close behind me. "Sorry," I say, realizing I've stopped right in the way. "Bedroom is this way." I look to the left, and that's actually the bathroom. It has the standard stuff, and right next to it, in the corner of the apartment is the laundry room.

"Washer and dryer," I say. "That's nice. Did you know it had this?"

"No," Lance says, and I watch him scan his eyes over the window in the bathroom and up to the ceiling. I need to be more like that. More discerning. More observant. See more details.

"That's it over here," I say, and I go down the skinny hallway. Maybe I could get a couch in here if I had two strong men to tip it on its side. The room opens up then, and the dining room, living room, and kitchen take up the rest of what I can see.

"A couch will fit in here," Lance says. "Maybe not a love seat, but definitely a recliner too."

"Mm." The dining room table has four chairs compared to the jackalope's two, and I don't see any mounted Elky's. So it's a win all around. The kitchen holds outdated appliances, but I figure a stove with coiled burners still cooks.

My stomach swoops as I realize I'm going to have to cook my own meals, and I suddenly wonder if I'm ready for this.

Thankfully, that only lasts a moment, because I am so ready to live on my own. Do my own laundry. Pay my own bills, buy my own groceries, and cook my own meals.

The windows actually let in a lot of light, something I wasn't expecting for an apartment halfway under the ground. They don't have curtains, and most of them are only a few feet long anyway.

"I don't get it," I finally say, turning toward Lance, who's standing in front of the microwave, frowning.

He turns fully toward me. "What?"

"There's no bedroom." I also don't have furniture, nor the funds to buy much, but I can make do if they'll leave the dining room table and chairs. "Is it a studio?" If so, I don't know where the bed is hiding.

"No," Lance says slowly. "Rich said it's a one-bed, one-bath." He enters the living room too, and he points to the door in the corner. "Gotta be back there."

I didn't even see that door, but now I move toward it, Lance hot on my heels. The door opens into the bedroom, which is far larger than I anticipated. "Wow."

"This is great, Jess," Lance says.

"Kind of a long trip to the bathroom in the middle of the night," I say. "But at least anyone breaking in won't be able to find the bedroom." I grin at him, and he shakes his head.

"You should talk to Callie. She'll come over and serial-killer-proof this place for you."

"Yeah?"

"Yeah." Lance's hand slips along my waist, causing me to suck in a breath. The man causes sparks and sizzles to zip through my whole body. "Do you like this place?"

"Yes," I whisper. "Can I afford it?"

"Rich said nine-fifty."

I can afford it, and my nerves begin shouting at me to *take it. Take it. Take it!*

"I want it," I say, turning into him in excitement. "I can't believe this, Lance. My own apartment." Joy and wonder parade through me, and I gaze into his eyes, wondering what he sees when he looks at me.

"What do you think?" I ask, searching his face now.

"I think…" He reaches up and runs his fingertips down the side of my face. "I think you're pretty." He leans down and touches his lips to my cheek. "Passionate." His mouth slides down to my jaw, and I lean into his touch.

This man lights me up in all the best ways, and my heartbeat hammers at me while my mind tells me to enjoy this moment. Just enjoy the clean linen scent of him, and the warmth of his mouth against my throat, and the way his husky voice says, "Powerful," just before he pulls away.

I've fisted my hands in the collar of his dress shirt—which is a marvelous mauve today, and which I paired with a very Auburn blue-and-orange striped tie—and I don't settle back onto my feet. My eyes are only half open, and when Lance exhales, his breath cascades over my cheek.

"Jess."

"That was a lot of P-words," I say, my own voice filled with plenty of emotion. "I meant what do you think of the apartment?"

"I'll tell you after," he whispers.

"After what?" I sway, or maybe that's the earth moving because of how near Lance stands to me.

"After I kiss you." He gives me a second, then two, to deny him, and when I don't, he touches his mouth to mine.

Explosions go off in every cell in my body, and I'm certainly going to combust before my next breath.

Praise the stars above that I don't, because Lance and I breathe in together, and then he kisses me again, his mouth the most delicious thing I've ever tasted. The earth is definitely swinging wildly now, and nothing I do will stop it.

So I just keep experiencing the very best kiss of my entire life.

CHAPTER SIXTEEN

LANCE

I can't stop kissing Jessie. I don't *WANT* to stop kissing her, despite the way my muscles have tensed from toe to scalp. I want to relax into the motion, really enjoy the stroke of her mouth against mine, and the feel of her hair through my fingers.

But everything is on high alert, and it's not until we breathe in together, our lips only millimeters apart, and then simultaneously close the distance between us again that I relax. Instantly, I feel the silkiness of her hair between my fingers, and I slide my hands down her face and along her neck. Over her shoulders and to her back, where I keep her pressed right against me.

She tastes like strawberries, something spicy, and hope. I tell myself to get in control of my hormones and stop all this kissing, but it takes me another couple of seconds to do it.

My chest inflates as I pull in a long breath, and I'm aware enough to notice the way Jess has to breathe in and out rapidly a couple of times. I open my eyes and look at her. Her eyes are still closed, and I haven't backed up a single step. I don't give her an inch, and at some point, I press her against the wall right next to the door leading into her bedroom.

She opens her eyes and looks at me. I don't laugh, or smile, or duck my head in embarrassment. I'm not embarrassed that I kissed her. I wanted to do it, and I want to do a lot more of it.

"Okay?" I ask, because I need her to be okay with what just happened. Kissing her has changed a whole lot in my life, but it can't be weird between us at work.

"Yeah," she says, a smile revealing her expensively straight white teeth. "I'm okay."

The tension in my muscles eases a bit more, and I allow myself to duck my head and touch my mouth against her delicious throat again. "Okay." I breathe in deep again, getting her floral perfume with a hint of oranges in it, and back up a step, then two. "So you want it."

"Yes," she says again. "I want it." She edges along the wall and into the doorway of the bedroom. Facing it, she adds, "You cheated, you know."

I have no idea what she's talking about. That kiss was Life Changing, with a capital L and C, and I'm going to need some time to wrap my head around what that means. "On what?"

"We were on the letter N," she says, turning toward me and cocking one sexy hip into the doorway. "Which is my letter for you. Then you were supposed to have O for me. P is my letter." She steps toward me, her expression only made of flirt. "You cheated."

I grin at her, easily taking her into my arms again. "Yeah? Are you going to punish me for going out of order? Or stealing your letter?"

"Mm." She runs her hands up the front of my shirt, which lights all of my skin cells from sole to forehead on fire. "Both, I think." She tips up and touches her lips to mine again. This kiss is sweet and special. *Sacred*, I think, once again wondering what that means, and then Jess is out of my arms again.

"This is Alec," she says, holding up her phone. I hadn't heard it ring or chime. "Can I?"

"Of course," I say, grinding my voice through my throat. "I'll text Rich that we want this apartment."

Jess doesn't answer the phone. Instead, her hand holding it drops to her side. "My friendship with Alec isn't going to be a problem for you, is it?" Her blue eyes are so innocent, so wide.

"No," I tell her honestly. "I know Alec. Seriously, you should've answered." Surely the call has ended now, and Jess lifts her phone to find the screen dark. "Call him back," I say, swiping to get to Rich's name. "I'm going to call Rich."

As she chats with her best friend, and I tell Rich we

want this apartment, I relive the kiss in the back of my mind. Again and again, because it was that spectacular. As soon as I get off the phone with Rich, I get a text from Ruth.

My heart jolts as if someone has hooked it to a live wire, because there's no way I can talk to my sister and not tell her about this LC kiss with Jess. I glance over to the blonde woman who's turned my world upside down in only a couple of weeks, and I smile as she tips her head back and laughs.

Ruth can wait. I approach Jess, feeling a buzz in my veins I haven't in so long. Even when I was with Hadley, I didn't feel this...alive.

Jess ends the call and meets my eyes when I'm only a couple of paces away. "What's so funny?" I ask.

"He's got a new puppy," she says, shaking her head as she pockets her phone. "So Mister Byers. Do we have time to go by his apartment and see a little German shepherd puppy?" She looks at me with puppy dog eyes, and I would never say no to her when she looks at me like that.

"Sure," I say, my voice lodged somewhere in my throat. "Let's go."

———

"NOTORIOUS," Jess says as I push the button to call the elevator in Alec's building.

"Notorious?" I repeat, glancing at her. I held her hand

from the parking lot to here, and I take it in mine again. I wasn't expecting to have anything but ashes in my chest where my heart is, but somehow, Jess has made something out of the chaos there.

I never thought I'd hear my heart beat as loud as it does right now, as she turns and looks at me, her smile as wide as the Mississippi. "What's wrong with notorious?"

I try to tell my pulse to settle the heck down, but it doesn't comply. Confusion runs through me at how this woman has restrung me with a simple kiss. Then I remind myself that she is not simple, and neither was that kiss.

"I'm not a fugitive," I say, shaking my head as the elevator dings its arrival.

"Notorious means famous," she says, leading me into the car.

"For something bad," I add. "Come on. Something else."

"I might need to come back to it." She presses the button for Alec's floor, which is great, because I don't know where he lives. "What about you? O?"

"Open-minded," I say without thinking too hard about it.

"I'll accept that answer."

I just smile at her and ask, "What do you want to do about P? Since I 'stole' it from you."

Her grin is made of sunshine and flirtatiousness. "You did."

"Mm, yeah," I say, turning toward her fully. "I don't

regret it." I kiss her again, still stunned I've found my way out of the darkness that's been living in my soul since Hadley left. I don't carry on nearly as long as I did in the basement apartment, mostly because the elevator is fast, and our kiss slow.

The chime dings again, and the doors start to slide open. A mother stands there with her two boys who look to be about ten or eleven. I'm super-glad Jess and I stopped kissing before they could see us, and they step back so we can get off.

Jess talks to them like she knows them, but I just enjoy the taste of her lip gloss in my mouth and the feel of her skin against mine until she starts to walk down the hall toward Alec's apartment.

When we arrive, Jess cocks her head and pauses. "Do you hear that?"

"I'd have to be deaf not to hear that," I say, recognizing all the yips and cries as dogs. As in multiple dogs. Puppies. Lots of them. Above it all, a bird screeches like she's allergic to canines, and Jess heaves a sigh as she opens the door.

"Alec?" she calls, and he says, "Don't let them out!" in an urgent voice.

Jess and I duck inside, dodging no less than six German shepherd puppies, who converge on us like we're fresh meat. Because we are. Jess giggles, and key lime mango pie, the sound ignites another part of me I thought had died when Hadley left Charleston.

I find myself smiling and crouching down the same way Jess does. She released my hand when we walked in, and she's all the way down on the floor, four of the pups licking her face and vying for attention.

I watch her for a moment, because she embodies joy in that moment, and I want to feel like that too. My smile softens everything in my body, and I barely notice the chaos around me. Jess erases it all, and I'm once again left wondering what that means and if I need to do anything about it.

Then Jess says, "Alec, why are there so many?"

I glance away from her to find the other man's gaze glued to me. He saw me watching her, and I quickly duck my head to the single shepherd who deemed me better than Jess. I drop to my knees too, and the little dog climbs right up into my lap.

"Ohh, you're in trouble," Jess singsongs. "That one's yours."

"No," I say, though I'm stroking the puppy like I'll take him home to meet Cha-Cha. Jessie giggles and fends off one of the German shepherds just to have two more lunge for her. She starts cooing at them, and Alec hasn't looked away from me.

I meet his eyes, and his eyebrows go up. I shake my head once, a silent way to say, *Nothing's changed. Don't make a big deal out of this.*

Internally, my relationship with Jess is already a big, huge, humongo deal, and I need time and space to think about it before I start talking about it. Especially with Alec. I like the guy, but he's not my best friend and he is Jess's. The real problem is, Dawson won't be much help either.

I think of Ruth, and I figure I better be calling her sooner rather than later.

"Why are there so many?" Jess asks again, and Alec finally switches his gaze to hers.

"The guy said I could pick any one of them I wanted. Tara's on her way to help, and I figured you should weigh in too."

She grins at him, then the pups, then me. "Well, obviously not that one." She's glowing she's so happy, and I've completely forgotten what that feels like. I want to feel that way again, and Jess thaws part of me that had frozen maybe when my first fiancé had called off the wedding.

"I'm not taking a puppy home," I say, but the little dog in my lap looks up at me as if to ask me *why not?* He nips at my hand as I stroke his head, and I immediately curl my fingers into a fist.

"Boy or girl?" Jess asks, picking up one puppy and getting back to her feet. The others don't like that, and a couple of them start to cry.

Peaches goes ballistic inside her cage, and she hands the dog to Alec as he says, "I'm thinking girl. The two I like best are females."

"Peaches," Jessie sings to the bird. "Calm down and I'll let you out."

"At your own risk," Alec says, eyeing the bird. "She's acting like she'll have to let the dog sleep in her cage."

"She's just jealous," Jess says, opening the door and putting her hand inside for the green and white parrot to jump onto. "Aren't you, sweetheart?"

"Bacon," the bird yells. I mean, I knew she could talk, but I didn't realize how vocal she could be. "Motorbike, I love you!" She hops up onto Jess's head, and for some reason, that sight tickles everything inside me that makes me laugh.

Jess doesn't mind at all, and as I start to chuckle at the sight in front of me, she just strikes a pose. Then another one. I laugh and laugh, and some of that happiness Jess exudes finally, finally enters my heart.

———

FINE, I say a couple of weeks later. *I'm sending one picture, and that's it, Ruthie.*

I can practically hear my older sister growl through the text, and I smile though it's far too late for me to even be awake. Jess and I have a couple of meetings in the morning, and I've been texting her for most of the evening about her solo meeting with Sabrina Shadows tomorrow afternoon.

It better be a good one, Lance, Ruth texts. *Full faces for both of you.*

It's a good thing Jess takes pictures of everything and

she's a pro at selfies, otherwise I wouldn't have a picture of us. The past couple of weeks have been close to magical, and while there's no company policy against dating a co-worker, Jess and I have managed to keep everything professional at the agency.

I've kissed her on the front sidewalk and around the corner of the building. At her car in the lot, and against the doors of Mammoth. But never in my office.

I think about that and if I want to kiss Jess in my office or not while I find the best selfie Jess has sent me and attach it to a text to Ruth. I've told her about Jess—almost everything about her—and without my sister, I'm not sure what kind of knots I'd still be in.

Ruth is a voice of reason, and since she doesn't live here and there's zero chance of running into her around Charleston, she's been an impartial source for me. I've been able to tell her about kissing Jess, working with Jess, and getting to know Jess. I've kept my healing and feelings about having a girlfriend again to myself, though Ruth does know how to pry well enough to have gotten a few things out of me.

My phone rings, and I swipe on the call from Ruth. "That was a good picture," I say, absent-mindedly stroking Cha-Cha. I did manage to resist getting one of the German shepherds, but Alec had gotten two. According to Jessie, Peaches had calmed down, and his trio of pets has started to figure out how to get along.

"Lance," Ruth says, and she's not barking or warning. She also doesn't say anything else.

"What?" I ask her. "It's late, Ruth."

"She's gorgeous," Ruth says, and her voice breaks. Like, legit breaks.

"Yes," I say, because I did say Jess was pretty. Gorgeous works just fine too.

"You look so happy with her," Ruth says.

"Ruth," I warn her. "Don't."

"I'm just saying, I've seen plenty of pictures of you and Hadley, and in none of them were your eyes shining like they are in this one."

"I'm hanging up."

"Lance," Ruth says again, and I pause. I say nothing, and several seconds of silence pass through the line, both of us sitting there together.

"I know, okay?" I say.

"I'm just saying."

"I really do have to work early in the morning," I say, my voice almost a whisper. "I'll talk to you later."

"Love you, Lance," Ruth says.

"Love you too, Ruth." I end the call then and let the phone fall to my chest. I heard everything Ruth said in that silence.

You're happy with her, Lance.

You're falling in love with her, Lance.

What are you going to do about all of the above, Lance?

I reach over and plug in my phone, neither confirming or denying anything Ruth didn't say. As I fall asleep, I imagine kissing Jess in my office the next day. I've never kissed a woman in my office, and it's always been a safe spot for me after every one of my past relationships has ended.

Maybe, this relationship with Jess won't end.

Maybe I don't need my office to escape to anymore.

Maybe.

CHAPTER SEVENTEEN

SABRINA

I HAVE ALL OF THE DOCUMENTS PRINTED AND LINED up in the conference room when my assistant comes on-speaker with, "Miss Shadows, Jessica Dunaway is here to see you."

"Yes." I lean forward to speak into the phone, but I don't know why. It's a habit, I guess, and one I'm supremely glad no one has seen me do. "Send her to conference room four, please, Cheryl." I stand and reach for my cardigan. My mother told me it adds fifteen years to my age, but I don't care. At least I pretended like I didn't when she'd said it. Now, I wear the sweater into the office, shed it and let it keep the back of my chair warm, and then put it back on when necessary.

"Conference room four?" Cheryl repeats.

"Yes," I say, already clicking my way toward my office door. I made junior partner several months ago, and that perk came with an office with four walls and one window. One door, and a secretary who sits down the hall and keeps unwanted people away from me.

Since I don't really like people in general, I wish I could zip Cheryl into a suitcase and take her home with me too. That sounds way worse than I thought it would...

"Ma'am," Cheryl says, and that alone stops me in my tracks. I'm thirty-four, which is nowhere near "ma'am" status. "Mister Finch just had me send clients into conference room four for him..." She trails off at the end, which is about when my vision starts to go red along the edges.

"Didn't you tell him I reserved it on the calendar?" I ask, though I realize a moment later that the question is a waste of my time. Cheryl's not going to fix this problem.

My hands shake as I open my office door and stride out into the hall. At least I try to stride. The skirts I've been wearing have gotten a little more narrow and usually don't go below my knees, so the length of my stride might not be as long or as powerful as I'd like it to be.

Since I'm also only a hair over five-foot-three, I'm neither commanding nor intimidating, while the tall, tan, dark, delicious Jason Finch is.

He's not delicious, I tell myself as I march down the hall toward the quad of conference rooms in the back of our offices here on the seventeenth floor.

He is with clients, but I open the door anyway and poke my head in. He stops speaking as he sees it's me, a look of great distaste entering those midnight eyes. "Can I help you, Miss Shadows?" he asks without bothering to get to his feet.

"Yes," I say as sweetly as I can, which means it still sounds like I want to poison him. "Can I talk to you for a moment out here?" My eyes sweep the table, and all of my documents are gone. That man.

My stomach quakes as I back into the hall, and I pace from one side of it to the other three times before he graces me with his presence. I stop and hold my ground as he closes the door behind him.

"What?" he barks.

"I reserved this conference room for today at two," I say, gesturing toward the blinded windows. "I had my documents laid out in there."

Jason blinks, and I see the truth slide right through that expression. "You did?"

"You saw them, you snake," I hiss at him, very much the one who's acting like a snake. "Where are they?"

"I had Brenda come in and prep the room for the Wintcrings," Jason says smoothly, which is how he says everything. The man is a player if I've ever seen one. He's slippery, and he'll say anything to get the spotlight either on him or off of him, whatever suits him the most.

"That is not true," I say, calling him on the lie. I park my hands on my hips and lean forward. "Brenda took a half-day today to go to her almost-daughter-in-law's bridal shower."

I once again watch Jason blink, but this time it's more

like a *bl-blink, bal-blink-blink.* Maybe he's not used to being caught so blatantly in his lies.

"Sabrina," Jessie Dunaway says smoothly as she comes down the hall. "Jason. How good to see you."

I swing my attention to her at the same time Jason does, and she's wearing what I wish I could. But Jess is a few inches taller than me, so the long maxi dress with soaring butterflies on it doesn't make her look like she's a beach ball.

Her eyes meet mine, and I try to smile. I fail, and Jessie sees it. She steps over to Jason and presses a kiss to his cheek. "What have you done to her, you scoundrel?" She gives a light laugh as she moves to my side, but I know she's not kidding.

"I didn't do anything," Jason says with his signature chin-raise. I swear, one day, I'm going to make that head lower in acquiescence to me. "Conference room four is occupied." He turns to go back inside, but I lunge for him.

"Jason," I say, grabbing onto his arm. He's opened the door, and he's halfway turned, so he's not steady on his feet. I'm certainly not steady in any regard, least of all physically. We both topple into the room, me right behind him. He stumbles a couple of times to try to catch himself, but in the end, he fails.

He calls out and grabs onto the nearest chair. *He'll save us,* I think, but unfortunately, all of our chairs in the conference rooms roll, and the chair is no good to us as an anchor.

We're going down, I think just as we do exactly that.

The chair goes spinning toward the far wall, where it clunks noisily while several people start to exclaim. I can't make out all the voices, though I'm sure Jessie's is in there somewhere. All I can focus on is breathing, which I'm doing in a rapid fashion.

Jason is too—I know, because both of my hands are planted against his chest. I actually slide them down, feeling the ridges in his abs, before I figure out what I'm actually doing.

My eyes fly to his, and our gazes lock. In that moment, everything falls away—the other voices, the sound of chairs moving, everything—and I only see Jason Finch.

The man is incredibly good-looking, whether I want to admit it or not. In one breath of time, I see something in his eyes I don't think he wants me to see. He's...soft, which is so unlike every other persona he's allowed me to witness.

I've seen Lawyer-Jason, and he's fierce and talented. I've seen Playboy-Jason, and he's eyeroll-worthy and actually a little cringy. I've seen Arrogant-Jason, and he's the guy I want to punch most of the time. I wish I could see Soft-Jason more, or even Mentor-Jason, but either he doesn't exist or Jason won't let him out of the closet, because he still refuses to help me with any of our shared cases.

"Sabrina," Jessie says, her voice finally loud enough and close enough to break me from the trance. Her hands touch my elbows and forearms and help me to my feet.

"I'm so sorry," I say, adopting my professional voice. I smooth down my cardigan when I really want to rip it off and tell Cheryl to put it through the shredder. Cheryl's standing by the door, wringing her hands, as I turn that way.

"We can meet in my office," I say, putting my own chin in the air as others move to help Pretty-Boy-With Good-Abs-Jason to his feet. I'm several feet down the hall when Jason calls my name.

My face already burns with humiliation. What more can he take from me? So I turn around and glare my *Yes, Mister Finch?* in his direction.

A storm mars his handsome face, and it takes him a few seconds to say, "Your...'documents' are on my desk."

———

I SIGH as I put my feet up on the same coffee table where Macie has hers. She looks over at me, her mug already at her lips. "Rough day?"

I nod, because I don't want to talk. Macie said I could have all the free coffee I wanted—and that I didn't have to talk.

"You didn't find a new place?"

I shake my head and stir my cappuccino. Maybe she'll get the hint and just let me exist inside my own mind. Macie and I have been friends for years. She's the reason I'm not homeless right now, and I often stop by Legacy

Brew on the way back from the law office just to see how her day is going.

She's off for the evening, but we like to sit on this orange couch and nurse a hot drink for a bit before retreating into our private lives. Her mom and my mom are best friends, so we've known each other for a while. She knows how prickly I can be, and that I can't hide how I'm feeling very well, and I expect another question in oh, less than seven seconds.

Sure enough, only six later, Macie says, "I'm sure it wasn't that bad."

I take a sip of my coffee and lean forward to set the cup next to my feet. "Jessie stopped by, didn't she?"

"She may have been here after work, that's all." Macie takes a ginormous bite of her lemon pound cake, her way of saying, *Yes, and she told me all about the two-body-pile-up in conference room four.*

I close my eyes and lean my head back against the cushy couch. "She says there's at least two places that will work for you," Macie says. I listen between the lines, which only makes my mood darker.

"I want amazing," I say. "Not something that merely *works*." I open my eyes and meet Macie's. "You're okay if I stay with you a little longer, right?"

"Of course." Macie waves away my concern. "I just don't see why you want an old house."

"I want charm," I say, something I've told her in the past. "I want a project."

"Honey," Macie says, giving me an up-down look. "You're a project all your own."

"Hey," I say, though when I look down, I discover I *am* wearing the cardigan. At least it's black and slims me slightly. I sigh again, my thoughts flying right back to Jason.

I'd collected my printouts of the houses Jessie had sent me from his office, and Jess and I had gone over things in mine. I'd gone to look at a couple of places with her—the two best ones. Truth be told, either of them probably would work. One had some great calico brick and an in-ground pool. The other had gargoyles guarding the front gate, and while that definitely isn't something I want, I can only imagine my joy at knocking them down.

Really pounding my anger and frustration into the stones and watching them crumble, imagining Jason's face on each of the gargoyle's.

I reach for my cappuccino without a tremor in my hand, which is something I haven't achieved for a few hours now. I just need this hot coffee and then a hot bath, and everything will be fine.

"When are you going to just tell him he better ask you to dinner?"

I choke on the sip I've just taken, and hot liquid splashes over the rim of the cup and onto the back of my hand. I yelp, and all that does is draw attention to me in my should-be-burned-ugly cardigan.

Macie hands me a couple of napkins, her left eyebrow

cocked higher than her right. She says nothing while I glare at her and then mop up the mess.

"I'm not interested in Jason Finch," I say through clenched teeth.

"Yeah, and I don't pine over Andrew Cash." Macie sighs as I toss the wad of wet and ruined napkins on the table.

I look over to her, and a beat of silence passes between us. "You actually have a shot with him," I say. "Jason looks at me like I'm something he scraped off the bottom of his thousand-dollar shoes."

"Oh, please," Macie says, waving her hand. "That's because he feels cornered by you. He knows you're better than him, and he's nervous."

"Yeah, I doubt that." I pick up my coffee again and lift both of my eyebrows at her. "Am I safe to sip this time?"

"Safe to sip," she says with a grin.

I do, and then say, "Why don't you ask Andy to take you out? Or better yet...to stop by for coffee one evening after you get off? He could be sitting right here instead of me." I grin at Macie, the perfect date happening in my imagination.

Macie smiles too and shakes her head. We both giggle, and the last of my tension from my day at the law office fades into relaxation.

Then a woman says, "Hey, Mace," and I glance up to see Callie Houser plopping down on the other side of Macie. She looks at her husband. "Our usual, honey."

Dawson goes to get whatever their usual is, taking Alec Ward—one of his best friends—with him. Behind him walks Lance Byers, but Jessie and Tara detour toward us already on the couches. I smile at them, though we're not all besties yet. I have such a hard time making friends with women, because most of them want me to change who I am. At the very least, they don't appreciate a good messy bun or my knowledge of the law.

I choke on my cappuccino again when I see Jason enter the coffee shop after holding the door for another couple. *So chivalrous*, I think, and then I tell my heartbeat to stop betraying me by banging so dang hard against my ribcage.

He meets my eyes, and I wish I could sever our connection. I feel the eyes of the other women already in the seating area, and I know they're thinking Things That Aren't True.

Or maybe they are...

"Hey," he says, his eyes flitting away from mine first. "Looks like the guys got in line."

"Yeah," Callie chirps. "But you can just sit right there on the end next to Sabrina. I'll text Dawson to get what you want."

I switch my glare to Callie, but she's made of iron, because she simply smiles back, her fingers moving a mile a millisecond across her screen.

CHAPTER EIGHTEEN

JASON

I feel like a real schmuck, which honestly isn't a new feeling for me. It's been happening more and more lately, and I'm not sure what to do about it. With Jessie Dunaway, I did nothing. I played things off as ha-ha-friendly, and she still speaks to me.

She won't go out with me, but that's okay. I don't think she's really my type anyway.

No, I'm not super into blondes, despite what my last several dates have looked like. I swallow as I look at Sabrina Shadows.

I really like a woman with dark hair and fire in her dark eyes—which is exactly what a man gets with Miss Shadows. Not only that, but she's intelligent and sharp, and I have the very distinct feeling I'm going to get gutted by this woman before long.

I don't squeeze onto the oversized couch beside her,

though in the past, I might have. I definitely would have, because a past version of myself liked to get women's numbers and go out with three or four women in a week. It was fun. It was thrilling. I never had to be too serious or settle down for too long.

Only a few months have passed since I started feeling myself change, but it's long enough to know I can't rebuild a bridge I might burn, especially with Sabrina Shadows.

I sigh as I sink into an armchair perpendicular to where she sits. "Did you see anything good this afternoon?" I ask, not truly looking at her.

She turns her head toward me, her eyes wide. She folds her arms as those eyes narrows. "A couple of things," she says evasively.

Part of me wants to quip at her. Ask her if she's going to put in half-price offers on good real estate, the way she almost did to me. I bite my tongue—a real feat for me—and give her a smile instead. She looks utterly confused, as if she doesn't know how to take the gesture.

From me, maybe she doesn't.

That's not a maybe, Jace, I tell myself. Since Sabrina's become my junior partner, my life in the office has gotten harder, not easier. She's my first junior partner, but I've seen plenty of others before me get their juniors. I have a mentor who's given me advice for how to mentor Sabrina along. She makes everything difficult though, because she wants to be in my position when she hasn't earned it yet.

I need to have her into my office for a meeting, but the truth is, I've been too much of a chicken to do it.

I'm going to name my next hen Jason, Tara told me twenty minutes ago when I told her what had happened between me and Bri at the office today. Alec had remained silent, thankfully, but Tara's never held back with me.

She even made chickeny bok-bok-bok sounds at me after I'd admitted that I haven't scheduled my initial junior partner meeting with Bri yet. It's a good thing I didn't tell her about cleaning up Bri's real estate papers and putting them on my desk, as if I didn't know she wanted to use the conference room.

I still don't know why I did it. Maybe so there would be a reason Bri would have to talk to me? Come into my office and look me in the eye? Bring in that curvy body and the scent of her perfume, and be less than six feet from me?

"Are you going to stare at me for much longer?" she asks now, leaning forward to set her empty coffee cup on the table. She looks at me, and I meet those dark eyes with mine.

"No," I say, forcing myself to look somewhere else. I hadn't even realized I'd been staring at her. The woman dominates my thoughts, which is just another annoying thing about her. "Listen," I add. "We need to schedule a meeting."

She settles back into the orange couch again. Those arms cinch right over her chest. "We do?"

"Yes." I clear my throat. "I should've done it a month ago. We need to talk about our...working relationship with you as my junior partner."

Further darkness enters her expression. I expect her to spit like a camel and stalk out, the same way she did this afternoon. I'd barely gotten back to my feet before I'd realized Bri was long gone.

Instead, something shutters over the emotion in her eyes, and she says, "Okay." She pulls her phone out from under her leg, which only draws my attention there. The woman has great legs, and I quickly yank my eyes back to hers.

She's scrolling on her phone, only glancing up without truly looking at me once. "When?"

"Whenever is convenient for you," I say. "My schedule is synced with yours." That happens when a junior is assigned to a regular partner, so I know her schedule too.

"Next week is free for both of us on Thursday," she says, her voice set on the type of professional I hate. "Before ten."

"Nine then," I say, the headache behind my eyes intensifying. Dawson better be hurrying with that coffee. I look over to him, and he's taking his card back from the cashier.

"Nine," she says, tapping on her phone. "Your office?"

"Yes, please."

Bri's gaze is heavy now, and I look fully at her. "Please?"

"I've said please before," I say.

"Not to me," she says.

"No bickering tonight," Macie says. "I can't handle it after today."

"Me either," Callie says.

"Yeah," Tara says dryly. "Since you didn't go in until two o'clock this afternoon, I can see how tired you must be." She grins at Callie, who smiles back.

"Helping my best friend with her wedding gown was *very* taxing," Callie says, and the two of them laugh. I love Tara with my whole heart. She's never given up on me, ever, for any reason. She always invites me over to her house or next door to Mr. Reynolds' when she's got a new recipe she wants us to try. She stops by and gives me dinner just because.

"Did you get the dress done?" I ask, once again glancing at Bri. She's like a North Pole to my South, and I can't help myself.

"Almost," Tara says. "Oh, and be warned, Jason. My mother is coming in this weekend to do a few wedding things. She's calling your mom tonight to see if she wants to come." She glances up as Alec appears at her side, her coffee in his hand. She beams at him as she takes it, and he perches on the armrest of the couch beside her.

Dawson hands me my coffee and goes to sit beside Callie, which shifts Bri and Macie down, closer to me.

"Great," I say dryly, then take a sip of my coffee. The last thing I need is to deal with Cynthia Finch, but I keep that to myself. The five-letter word made of desert sand said enough. At least to anyone listening.

Tara gives me a sympathetic look—she was listening.

Bri's look is curious—she was listening too. My pulse jumps into the back of my throat, and it's everything I can do not to ask her to dinner for that night. She'd say no anyway, and I'd be embarrassed in front of the only seven people who I can call friends.

Well, I do have a few friends at the office, but not anyone I really want to hang out with like this.

"I've got to get going," Bri says before Lance arrives with his and Jessie's coffee, and though Macie, Callie, and Tara all protest, she stands, gives everyone a smile and a few air-cheek-kisses, and then walks out.

The wake she leaves behind is laced with discomfort, though I'm sure I'm the only one who can feel it. Lance and Jessie arrive, and I move over to the couch next to Macie so they can share the armchair.

"So," Macie says oh-so-casually. The lawyer ears I have hear everything in those two letters, and I feel the insatiable need to bolt. Now.

"So no," I say, but Macie says, "When are you going to ask her out?" anyway.

No one says anything, and they all stare at me.

"I'm not," I say, lifting my mug to my lips in a calm, controlled manner. "She's just my partner."

"Bok, bok, bok," Tara says under her breath, though definitely loud enough for everyone to hear.

"I'm not," I insist, glancing around at the lot of them. In that moment, I see three couples who work together. They blur, and I'm not sure how I didn't put all of that together until this moment. "I'm not really dating right now. Decided to take a break."

Lance starts to laugh, but I don't see what's so dang funny. I glare at him and bark, "What?"

"That's what I told myself too," he says, still chuckling. Then he lifts Jessie's hand to his lips and kisses it. They look at one another, and it's so sweet, I almost throw up.

"Yeah, I'm pretty sure I said 'she's just my secretary' about five thousand times," Dawson says, grinning at me. He tries to hide behind his coffee mug but fails.

"But she was," I insist, glancing at Callie. "For a long time. A really long time."

"Until she wasn't," Dawson says, beaming at his wife. They make me sick too.

I get to my feet, saying, "I have to go."

"Don't go, Jace," Tara says, jumping up too.

"Good to see you all," I drawl out. "Thanks for inviting me."

"Jason," Macie says. "I'm sorry."

"Nothing to be sorry about." I set down my coffee and head for the door, Tara right behind me.

"Jason," she says.

"Tara," I say back, finally reaching the door. I practically punch the bar that will release the latch and let me into the fresh air.

"Will you stop for two seconds?" she asks.

I do, my chest heaving for some reason I can't name. I also can't look at her. She stands right in front of me, almost as tall as me, but I can't meet her gaze. "You've changed," she says quietly. "I didn't see it until now."

"I'm fine," I say.

"I know you are," she says. "Of course you are." She puts one hand on the side of my face and guides me to look at her. I do, seeing so much of myself in her eyes. It makes sense. Our dads are brothers, and we both have the Finch eyes and the slope of the Finch nose. "Dinner at my place tomorrow night," she says.

"You're catering that cowboy gala tomorrow night," I tell her, feeling wicked inside. I hate feeling like this. When I do is when I say the wrong thing and go out with too many women.

"Breakfast on Saturday," she says.

"Gonna have to be brunch," I say. "I know how late you sleep. And your mom is coming into town."

"Nine a.m.," she says. "Not a minute later." Fierceness enters her eyes. "It's okay to be someone different than you were before."

"I know," I say, though I don't. I don't know who I am anymore, or what I want. I thought I did. I thought I had my whole life figured out, but I don't. Not even close.

She nods and drops her hand. "Text me when you get home, so I know you're safe."

"Okay." My heart pinches at the love my cousin has for me. Tara's been such a Godsend in my life, and I'm too chicken to tell her. I open my mouth to say more, but she's already heading back inside.

It's just as well. I can communicate with clients, but that's head-thinking. Heart-thinking and emotional-talk... I am the worst at both of those.

So I head for my car, which is parked around the block. I think about Sabrina on the way home, which is nothing new. Now that we have a meeting on our schedule, perhaps she'll mentally go away and leave me alone. Maybe I'll be able to go back to the man I was before, which would be a relief to me. At least I knew who I was and what I wanted.

Now? Now, I'm not so sure, but being one-half of a couple who looks at one another with starshine in their eyes sounds really nice...

Really, really nice.

CHAPTER NINETEEN

JESSIE

"Just that last bag," I say, indicating the colossal-sized laundry basket of clothes. Moving for me is mostly about fabrics and hangers and less about boxes and furniture. Hey, Lance, Dawson, and Jason should be thankful they don't have to try to fit a settee through the narrow doorways and down the microscopic steps in my new basement apartment.

I feel like I've been waiting my whole life for this day, this very moment, and I pause in the doorway of the bedroom at my uncle's mansion after Jason takes the collapsible laundry basket into the hall. Over the past two days, this room has looked like a bomb has gone off. Now, it looks like an upscale guest room Uncle Jack can offer to his richest acquaintance.

Or another wayward niece, I suppose.

I've scrubbed the windowsills and oiled the tracks on

the closet doors. I washed all the blankets and sheets and remade the bed. Lance vacuumed not twenty minutes ago, while I wiped the mirror and continued to direct Dawson and Jason to take out the things I'd packed.

A sadness I was not expecting creeps up on me, striking me hotly behind the heart. I pull in a breath as tears touch my eyes.

"You're all done?"

I turn toward Uncle Jack, one betraying tear sliding down my face. I swipe at it and fly into his arms. "Yes," I say.

He holds me tight, and while I ran from Beaufort too, I still got to hug Mama and Daddy this way too. They still love me.

Uncle Jack steps back and sniffs, about all the emotion I've ever seen from him. He's wearing his usual attire for the day—slacks and a button-up shirt, no tie yet. Even Lance had on his gym shorts this Saturday morning, along with a T-shirt that clung to his biceps in a way that told me he works out with weights.

"We'll miss you," Uncle Jack says, glancing toward the open bedroom door. "You come on back if you need anything." He looks at me again. "Anything, Jessie, okay?"

I nod, not sure how to get my voice to work properly. I hate crying. It makes my face all puffy and my eyes red, and I already have a pretty amazing albino look going on with my pale skin and light hair. I don't need the red eyes too.

"I know what life is like with your mama," Uncle Jack says with a sigh. "She's proud of you, whether she'll ever say it or not." He smiles at me and tucks his hands in his pockets. "I'm proud of you too."

"Thank you, Uncle Jack." I mean it too, and I nod. "For everything."

"It's amazing what a little confidence will do for a person."

It is, but I can't say that. I came here with nothing, and while I'm leaving with about the same stuff I brought, I do have so much more.

"Jess?"

I turn toward Lance as he comes toward me. He slings his arm around my waist easily, and I lean into his strength. I look up at him as he looks at Uncle Jack. "So great to finally meet you," he says again, extending his hand for Uncle Jack to shake.

"You take care of her," Uncle Jack says.

"He's not moving in with me," I say, switching my attention to my uncle. "I can take care of myself."

Lance chuckles. "You heard her. I'm not getting in the way of that." He gazes down at me with adoration in his eyes. I'm not sure how or when he started doing that, and surprise bolts through me. "You're all ready?"

"Yes," I say.

"Said your good-byes?"

"Yes." I eye the bedroom door. I've only ever had a bedroom in someone else's house. I don't even know what apartment living will be like. I know I made a few phone calls to set up utilities. The apartment comes with cable from the couple upstairs. It's mostly furnished, so I don't need a lot, other than what I have.

I take a Big Bird Breath—BBB—and face Uncle Jack. "I'm ready."

"Let's go then," Lance says. "Dawson is already complaining about how long this is taking."

"It's been thirty minutes," I say, turning with him. "Dawson...I'm going to drive Lucy as slow as possible on the way over."

Lance laughs again and says, "That'll show him."

I don't really want to upset Dawson. I know he's had some big clients at work lately, and he's likely headed downtown after this. Outside, he waits next to Mammoth, typing furiously on his phone.

"Dawson," I say sweetly. "You can go if you need to."

He looks up, his eyes glazed. "What?"

"He's not going," Lance says, glaring at me and then his best friend. "Callie's handling everything, and he can give us another hour."

Dawson meets Lance's eye, and something bromantic or bro-related passes between them. He shoves his phone in his shorts pocket. He's wearing gym shorts too, and it's like he and Lance went shopping for their workout attire together. "Yeah, no problem," he says, and it actually sounds like he means it.

"Great," I say. "I've got the keys, and y'all can follow me."

Jason nods and gets in the backseat while Lance goes around to the driver's seat. I wait for Dawson to move toward the front passenger seat, and then I head for Lucy. I get behind the wheel and start her up.

"All right, Luce," I say, just like I did in the driveway at the mansion in Beaufort. "Another new adventure. We've got a new place to live, and you're going to love it so much." I clench my fingers around the steering wheel and look out the windshield.

Then I put Lucy in drive, and we head down the dirt lane with all the live oaks standing sentinel, the mansion in our rearview mirror—and the future wide open in front of us.

———

A COUPLE OF DAYS LATER, I lean in the doorway of Lance's office. He's got three ties laid out on the front of his desk, but he's typing furiously on his keyboard. "Just a sec," he says, and he's the most focused I've seen him in a while.

Only a few seconds later, he turns, his expression changing instantly. How he does that, I'll never know. "My tie, if you would. I have a golf date with Mister Nickelson in thirty-five minutes." He stands and comes around the desk as I enter his office.

I scrutinize the ties he's selected. "What do you think?" I ask, refusing to look at him. I told him on Monday that he should start to at least try to pick out his own tie. I can tell him why or why not, and he can learn.

Isn't that what you're always telling me? I'd teased with his office door closed. Lance won't kiss me in his office. He never has, not even once. When I tried to tip up onto my toes and press my mouth to his, he backed away.

I'd been stung, sure. But he said he wanted to keep things professional around the office. He didn't want others to be uncomfortable around us, or worry that they might walk into a room anywhere at the agency— including his office—and see something they didn't want to.

Once he'd laid out his argument, I could see the wisdom in it. We try to keep our meetings open-door, and I even asked Olive if she was uncomfortable with any of the exchanges she's heard between me and Lance.

She said she absolutely wasn't, and if there's anyone who sees and hears and knows everything in any office, it's the front desk receptionist.

Now, he sighs like I've asked him to eat his vegetables before he can be excused from the dinner table.

"I sent the escrow statement to Debbie Hymas," I say, still refusing to look at him.

That stops him. "You did? You filled it out?"

"Yes, sir," I drawl, finally looking up and into those brilliant blue eyes. I want to dive into them and never get out of that pool. I can feel myself falling in love with Lance Byers, and I wish there was something to do about it. Since I've never been in love, I don't know how long the falling lasts, or if there's anything anyone can do to stop it.

"If I can learn what an escrow statement even is, you can at least try to pick a tie from three. You have a one-third shot of getting it right." I grin at him and indicate the ties.

"So there's only one good choice here?" he asks, stepping beside me.

"In my opinion."

"Yours is the one I want," he mutters as he reaches out and picks the yellow tie with black and white stripes. He's wearing a baby blue dress shirt, buttoned all the way to the collar, with a pair of black slacks. I've managed to get him off the pastels for polos, but not for his office attire.

It's fine, because he looks good in soft colors, dark pants, and bright ties.

"Bravo," I say. "Now, why is that the one?"

"Contrasting colors?" he guesses as he starts to loop the tie around his neck.

"Mm." I brush his hands away and reach up to do the tie myself. "You want a thick knot on this too, Mister Byers. It's a skinnier tie, and they look better with bigger knots, especially for a man your size."

"Is that a fat joke?" He grins down at me, one hand coming to rest on my hip. He barely touches me in the office, and I didn't realize how much I crave his warmth until I instinctively lean into his palm.

I smile and keep my chin down. "Dinner tonight? My place?"

"You just like saying my place," he teases. "Did they get the toilet fixed?"

"This morning before I left," I say, looking up at him. Time freezes, and I think he'll finally lean down and kiss me right here in his office.

His eyes blaze with the desire to do so, though his mouth has told me he won't.

His intercom beeps, startling both of us. "Mister Byers," Olive says crisply. "Your father is on his way in."

"Thank you," Lance says at the same time he backs up. I do the same, not realizing how freakishly close I'd been standing to the chairs situated in front of his desk. My wedged heel catches on one of them, and my leg goes limp. My body has the worst ways of betraying me sometimes.

I fall to one knee with an "Oof," at the same time a man's voice booms through the agency. The whole world, really.

"There he is," Aaron Finley bellows to the world, his laughter just as loud as it fills the room a moment after he finishes speaking. He swallows Lance in an embrace, and I'm left to myself to get back to my feet.

I manage it by holding onto the desk with one hand and the chair with the other, wondering why I'd worn this ridiculous pencil skirt. Callie had told me I'd look good in one, what with the legs I have and all of my cute shoes.

I never should've invited her over to help me unpack.

I wipe my hand through my hair, feeling the sweat along my brow, as I face Lance and his dad. Technically, his step-dad, but as they part, they sure do look alike.

"Dad," Lance says, very obviously nervous. "This is Jess, my..." He clears his throat, panic evident in his eyes. It practically burns me, but I don't know what to say either.

"Jessica Dunaway," Lance tries again. "She works here."

"I'm his assistant," I say, thrusting out my hand. "Here at Finley and Frank, which is an amazing agency, sir." I give him my brightest Southern Socialite Smile—the triple S. Mama taught it to me when I was six years old. She says nothing beats the Triple S.

The way Aaron Finley returns my smile and pumps my hand tells me Mama was right.

"He's also my mentor and teacher," I say, shooting a professional smile at Lance. "He's been helping me learn the real estate business too. And he's my boyfriend once the clock strikes five, and usually all weekend, unless we have an open house."

I pull back my hand and watch Aaron's face as surprise and then glee tramples across it. "Well, now," he says, and though he's been living in Florida for a few years now, he sure sounds Southern. "I like her." He grins at

Lance. "Assistant, student, and girlfriend. We better be callin' your momma the moment we get in the car."

Lance smiles and shakes his head. "I suppose so." He reaches for his jacket, which he draped over the back of the chair that tripped me. "We'll be back before lunch," he says. "If the Bowmans get here before I do, you can—"

"I'll have their docs ready," I say. "I'll pull in Leann if I need to." I smile sweetly at Lance and clasp my hands in front of me so I don't fidget with them. Lance taught me that, and I have to say I'm a very good student.

A moment freezes where Lance and I get lost in each other, and then he jolts and turns back to his dad. "All right," he says. "Let's go see how badly Byron wants to destroy us today."

Aaron laughs like a cowboy and says, "I don't have to lose to him anymore, son. That's just your job," as they leave the office. Honestly, the lack of sound Aaron Finley leaves in his wake echoes in my ears, and I stand in Lance's office for a few seconds while everything rings the tiniest bit.

Then I head for my desk, because I have work to do too. My phone lights up as I sit, and I pull my rolling chair forward and grab the phone when I see the 212 number.

"New York," I whisper to myself, and then I swipe on the call. My mouth tastes like metal and is as dry as cotton on a heat-wave-summer day. Yet somehow I manage to say, "This is Jessie Dunaway," as if I get calls from New York City every minute of every day.

The fashion capital of the US screams through my mind.

"Yes, hello, Miss Dunaway," a woman says, her accent definitely from up north. "I'm Kira Chatwood, and one of my assistants put your portfolio on my desk this morning. I'm quite interested in speaking with you about it. Do you have a few minutes?"

I blink at my computer screen, which has two hundred and fifteen unread messages. I have docs to print, and forms to fill out. I have listings to look at, and if I don't speak with Sabrina today, I will regret it for the rest of my life.

I press my eyes closed, shut all of it out, and with my heartbeat tap dancing through my whole body, I say, "Yes, I do. How nice to hear from you Kira."

CHAPTER TWENTY

LANCE

"Ma, can you stop?" I smile to myself in Mammoth's rearview mirror, and then switch my grin over to Cha-Cha, who's riding shotgun. "I'm not answering any more questions about Jess."

"Just one more," my mother says, and since I can't say no to her, I say nothing. "Are you going to ask her to marry you?"

My foot jams on the gas pedal of its own accord. "No," barks out of my mouth.

"Lance, sugar," my mom coos at me. I've seen women do this before—most recently, Jess, when she was trying to calm down Peaches. I'm not a parrot, or a cat, or a dog, and I don't need to be stroked

"Mom," I say firmly. "I'm going to tell you the same thing I told you last weekend, when Daddy made me call you. It's new still. Of course I like her, or I wouldn't be dating her. But we're dating. That's all."

I dated Hadley for over two years before I asked her to marry me. I can't help feeling like there are huge, vast, cavernous differences between Hadley and Jess, but I keep that to myself. I have all kinds of secrets I don't let out of my bedroom, as I have a hard time falling asleep at night, and my thoughts have a way of running off on tangents.

"Okay," Momma says, managing to turn the simple word into three syllables. "I love you, baby."

I pull up to the white-brick house and crane my neck to see if Jess is coming down the drive. "Love you too, Momma." The call ends, and Cha-Cha turns to look at me expectantly. "Do you need to get out?" I ask her, which sets her little tail stub to wagging. "Fine."

I heave a sigh as I get out of the truck and go around to let Cha-Cha out. She jumps down despite her tiny legs, her nose already to the ground. I hope she has to take care of number one, because I packed all the bags, and I don't want to dig through granola bars and pretzels to find them.

I glance around in the awkward silence that always accompanies a dog and their ritual to find the precise spot to relieve themselves. I don't see any neighbors, nor the owners of the house...or Lucille Ball.

As I pull out my phone to call Jess, Cha-Cha finally finds the right spot, and thankfully, I don't need a bag. "Hey," I say when Jess answers. "I think someone forgot our morning date." I grin, because *finally*. The woman doesn't forget anything, and she's always on time—early even. She never passes an opportunity to tease me about having to buy clothes to get dressed to go see that first apartment, and I've been trying to catch her off her game for over a month now.

"Not true," she singsongs. "I'm coming around the corner now. I just had to run Tara's dress over to her, and I stopped to get breakfast on the way back."

I frown. "I thought we were dropping by that French bakery." I may or may not have practiced pronouncing a couple of their menu items.

"I see you," Jess says. "I'm hanging up."

Lightning strikes through me as her beat-up white sedan pulls up to the curb behind Mammoth. Cha-Cha seems to know exactly who'll be behind the wheel of that car, and she barks and bounds over to Lucy.

"Hey, Chachy," Jess sings to the dog as she comes around the hood. She takes a moment to pat my dog, then she straightens and nearly blinds me with her smile.

"What is going on?" I ask, though my own mouth starts to curl up. "You have mischief written all over your face." I take her into my arms, enjoying the nearness and the scent of her skin, but looking past her to Lucy.

"Nothing," Jess says. "Just that you're dating a woman who's now made her first real estate sale."

I yank back, my eyes searching hers. "Did Jemma Jones sign?"

"She signed, she sealed, I delivered the paperwork by

six p.m." She starts to laugh, and I join her. I can't tell her —or my momma—that I'm falling in love with her. I don't understand how my heart can even be ready for such a thing. Nothing between me and Jess makes all that much sense, and yet, I'm the happiest I've been in years. Even when I was with Hadley, I wasn't happy.

I was…hopeful. I was comfortable. I was willing to do whatever she wanted me to do.

"Jess," I say as my chuckles fade. "That's so amazing. Congratulations." I lean down and kiss her, but her mouth doesn't straighten for long.

"No kissing this morning," she says, taking my hand and leading me toward the car. "Let's get the pastries and hit the road. We've got sights to see today."

I shake my head, but she doesn't see me. She opens the front door of her car and hands me a big, brown box, with a very French flourish on the top.

"You stopped at the French bakery."

"Oui," she says, giggling afterward. "Do you have a leash for Chachy? Or should I go get the one I have here?"

Just the fact that she has a leash here isn't all that lost on me. Fine, it's not lost at all. Cheese and crackers, this woman has me knotted and unknotted in the best ways possible.

"I have one," I say, turning to take the pastries to Mammoth. "I hope you have your hiking shoes." I turn back to her to find Cha-Cha glued to her side and a plastic grocery sack in her hand.

"I do." She holds up the bag, her face once again made of enough light to rival the sun, moon, and stars. Combined.

She is Beautiful with a capital B, and I can't see myself with anyone else. The thought terrifies me, and I stuff it back inside the box where it belongs. "All right," I say. "Come get in, then. It's an hour to our first stop."

About seventy minutes later—Jess had to stop to use the bathroom—we pull up to the sign marking the trail-head for the Appalachian Waterfall. Jess changes out of her sandals and into her hiking boots while I leash Cha-Cha.

We've eaten fancy French pastries, sipped juice, and talked about everything at work. I don't want the rest of the day to have any acronyms—at least real estate ones—or client names or anything related to Finley & Frank in it.

When Jess gets down and shoulders her backpack, I say, "I don't want to talk about work again today."

"Deal," she says, grinning at me.

I smile back at her and face the trail. I have a pack with water, snacks, and food for Cha-Cha, as well as appropriate bags to pick up her waste should I have to. "It's a short one," I say. "Only half a mile."

"I might die," Jess says. "The most exercise I get is when I sprint into your office."

I tuck her into my side and kiss her forehead. "You'll be fine."

"You go first anyway," she says.

I do, because while I'm not a huge hiker, I do run a lot, and I can help guide her if the path is wet or rocky or whatever.

"Lance," she says behind me, and I glance over my shoulder. "I wanted to talk to you about something."

"Sure."

"I...well, I need a few days off."

I pause and step to the side of the trail. It's really only big enough for one person to walk comfortably in either direction, but it's November now and there weren't hardly any cars in the lot. "A few days off? Why? When?"

She smiles at me, but I see the nerves right there in her blue eyes. "Do you not allow your assistants to take time off? I've been at the agency for almost two months now."

"We have a vacation policy," I say automatically, still confused. "Are you going to go visit your folks?" She told me she might, though she didn't ask me to come with her. She met my dad, but I haven't planned a trip to Florida for her to meet my mom.

We're barely six weeks into a relationship. I don't need to rush.

"No," she says slowly, moving past me on the trail and continuing up. "I sent a portfolio of my sketches to a designer in New York, and she wants to meet with me."

The words are English, but I have no idea what they mean. "A portfolio?"

"Yes."

"How many designs did you send?"

"Why does that matter?"

"How many is she interested in?"

Jess stops and turns back to me. "Again, why does that matter?" She shoots fire at me with just her eyes, but I can't look away.

"I thought you wanted to be a real estate agent," I say. I've been teaching her morning, noon, and night for two months. She'd be a great asset to Finley & Frank.

But I know that's not the real reason her simple request for time off has turned into five hundred needles stabbing at the backs of my eyes. I don't want her to leave Charleston.

Leave *me*.

Everyone in my life has left me behind in Charleston, and I can't... If Jess goes to New York, I have the very real feeling, she won't be coming back.

Jess wears a crestfallen look, but the walls around my heart have suddenly grown about twenty-nine feet.

"This is no big deal," she says. "It's just a trip to see what she says."

"NBD," I say. "Sure." I try to step past her, but she holds up one hand.

"What's going on?"

"How many designs is she interested in?"

Jess raises her chin. "Just one." She crosses her arms across her chest, and that's always a bad sign, at least for Jess. We work so well together, both at the agency and out of it. She told me I have an R-REF, which is so similar to her mama's RBF. After I'd laughed and laughed, I'd asked what my acronym meant.

Resting Real Estate Face, she'd said. *And trust me, Lance, no client wants to see you glaring at them.*

I don't glare, I'd told her. It might have been a bark, but Jess has been at F&F for two months, and I've worked there for almost two decades. She has no idea what every day with me has been like.

No, maybe not, she'd said. *But every client wants to feel like they're your most important client, whether they are or not. And your R-REF doesn't convey that to them.*

I'm sure I have an R-REF right now. "How many in the portfolio?"

"It's meant to be a collection," Jess says. "That's how fashion works. You don't send less than ten."

"So less than ten percent."

"Why are you being such a jerk about this?" She spins in her hiking boot, which she somehow makes look natural and sexy at the same time. "I've been racking my brain for X and Z adjectives, and I was totally going to finish today." She strides away on the path, leaving me to feel like I've made a huge mistake.

Which, of course, I have. But watching her walk away from me...it's torture. I wish it wasn't. I wish my heart was all those ashes I'd once assumed it was. I wish it was filled with cement and so hard, no woman will ever penetrate it again.

"Jess," I say, pushing myself to catch her. My calves

scream at me that they run on flat ground, and hey, can I take the jogging uphill down a notch? Like, all the way to nothing.

"Jess," I say, panting once I get right behind her. "Come on. I'm sorry."

She spins again, and I nearly ram into her. "For what, Lance Byers?"

"Not being excited for you," I say even as a pinch of hurt runs from my ears to my ankles. "You didn't even tell me you were sending off a portfolio to New York."

Her expression softens, probably because of the wounded quality of my voice. She heaves a sigh, following it with a huge breath. "I know."

"Why not?"

"Because, then after six months or a year or whatever, when I didn't hear back, no one would ask me about it."

I look down at the ground and then take her hand in mine. I like the way our fingers look twined together. "How's Tara's dress?"

"It's going to be done on time," Jess whispers.

"Are you going to New York before or after the wedding?"

Alec didn't want a long engagement, and Tara set a date that barely gave her enough time to get a gown. Jess designed it and has been doing a lot of the embellishments as the pieces have been tailored. The whole dress came back from the seamstress a couple of days ago, and I lost my girlfriend in the evenings to beads, baubles, and other blitzy things.

Tara and Alec are getting married in only two more weeks, the weekend before the week of Thanksgiving, and maybe Jess will go after that.

"I was hoping to take an evening flight next Wednesday," Jess says. "It's fine if I can't. I told Kira I needed to talk to my boss." She gives me a look with such a dangerous glint that I feel a slice go right through my throat.

"You can go," I say, trying to think through next week. "I'm sure I can handle whatever Thursday and Friday hold."

"I rescheduled Sabrina," Jess says with a smile. "Other than that, you'll be fine." She focuses on our hands near our waists too, and I use my free hand to lift her face back to mine.

"I'm sorry," I say sincerely. "I just..." I exhale, because I don't know how to explain. I don't want to explain. It's too soon, and I can't be saying any of the things that run through my mind at night. I can't.

"Can I see the portfolio?" I ask gently, which brings her gaze back to mine. "You never show me anything."

"You make that sound so scandalous," she teases, inching closer to me. She stands on higher ground, which means she's about the same height as me right now.

"Well, we can talk about that too," I say, a slow grin tracing its way across my face. "But really, Jess. I'm interested in your fashion design. I'm not going to make fun of it."

"I know," she says lightly, almost in a tone that suggests she doesn't believe me. "It's not that I think you'll make fun of it."

We start up the path, her hand trailing behind her so she can keep it in mine. I sure do like that, and I smile to myself. "What is it then?" I ask, because I can keep the conversation on this track.

"I don't want suggestions," she says. "I know some of them aren't quite right, but I want to be the one to figure out what the design needs."

My immediate reaction is to deny that I'd suggest anything to her. But I practically bite my tongue I snap my mouth closed so fast. I do tend to be a fixer. If someone comes to me with a problem, we brainstorm solutions. Jess doesn't want that.

Which is Fine with a capital F. "I won't make any suggestions," I say.

"I know you, Mister Byers," Jess says, her voice back on Flirt. "You will."

"I won't," I insist. "If I do, you can...I don't know, cut off my tongue."

She bursts out laughing, and that brings a smile to my face.

"I'm gonna need that in writing," Jess says, turning back to me again as the path flattens for a few steps. "Is there a contract at the agency about cutting out tongues?"

"Oh, sure," I say breezily. "The COT clause. Haven't I told you about that one yet?"

———

I LET Dawson drive past me and lay up the basketball without opposition. The ball bounces back to the floor as he turns to face me. He wipes the sweat from his brow. "This is boring," he says. "You're not even trying."

"Yeah, well, I already ran five miles this morning." I give him a sour look—at least it feels sour all the way down to the soles of my sneakers. "I only came because you wanted to." I palm the ball and get it to bounce high enough to catch.

"What's eating at you?" He takes the ball from me, and we start toward the bleachers where we've stowed our stuff.

I collapse onto the bench seat and stare out at the shiny blonde-wood floor. "Nothing."

"Sure," Dawson says with the quality of the Sahara. "Because when I played like this, there was nothing wrong with me either." He starts packing up his stuff. "Let's go get breakfast at Alec's."

"Is he working today?"

"Not at Saucebilities," Dawson says. "But the girls are off doing the dress, and he texted me to say he was working on a breakfast sandwich if I wanted to offer advice."

I don't let my jealousy take root. Alec probably texted me the same thing, but I don't check my phone as often as Dawson does, especially on the weekend. "Fine."

"Are you angry or hurt?" Dawson asks.

I think about it for a moment. "Both. I need an AA meeting."

Dawson jerks his attention back to me. "AA? It's that bad?"

I realize what I've said, and I quickly shake my head. I forget not everyone and their platypus makes an acronym out of something. "I'm angry, and I'm...anguished," I say. "AA."

"Did you drink alone last night?" he asks. "Because I needed a drink *bad*."

I grin at him and shake my head again. "No. Jess showed me her sketches. She's going to New York on Wednesday." So much more is said in those few words, and understanding dawns on Dawson's face.

"I don't want to talk it to death," I say, pulling my phone from the pocket of my duffle. I swipe and type and look up. "It's thirteen minutes to Alec's apartment. That's how long you get."

"I hate these terms, for the official record," Dawson says, but he's grinning as he says it. "One day, I'm gonna tell Momma Byers that she cursed me when she implemented speaking time limits for you."

I just grin at him and act like I'm starting a timer. I pick up my bag as Dawson does, and then he says, "Okay, so here's what I think." He glances at me as if he needs permission to keep talking.

I say nothing. I don't even look at him. He's going to continue no matter what I say. I gave him thirteen minutes.

"I've known you forever," Dawson says. "Through the Diane Disaster, and all through Hurricane Hadley. A— I've never seen you this happy."

"You're going to letter it all?"

"That's right," he snaps at me. "So buckle in, Byers. B —" He cuts off as if there is no B. We exit the building, and I head for Mammoth, as I picked up Dawson that morning when he wouldn't let me get out of playing basketball at the rec center.

"Okay, look," Dawson says, obviously abandoning the lettering. "Jess is so different than anyone you've ever been out with. You're this buttoned-up, never-wears-anything-but-slacks real estate agent. You're dang good at what you do, and you expect excellence from everyone you come in contact with."

"I don't know if this is a compliment or not," I say. It doesn't sound like one.

"Jess is about the opposite of that. She's the opposite of Hadley, of Diane, of anyone you've ever shown interest in." He gets in the passenger seat, and as he's buckling, he adds, "Think about your second date with Hadley. What did she make you do?"

"I don't know, man," I say. "I'm not going into the

memory bank for her." I glare at him, and he raises one hand in acquiescence.

"You wanted to take her to the beach. Casual. I think there was a fair or something there that weekend. She said absolutely not. You two went to The Roof, and I'm pretty sure you wore a five-piece suit and then attended the symphony."

He's not wrong, so I say nothing.

"Now, let's consider Jess."

I pull out onto the street without looking both ways. Maybe if I get us to Alec's faster, Dawson won't be able to finish his point. I think I know what it is already anyway.

"She's so easy, bro."

"She is not easy," I throw back at him.

"You know what I mean."

"I'm sure I don't."

"Don't kill us," Dawson says, reaching for the handle above the door as someone honks at us. "Maybe you do need an AA meeting." He shakes his head and relaxes. "She's so easy for you to be with. She's convertible easy. You text her about going for a ride in the convertible, and what did she do? She came flying outside in a prom dress, happy as a clam to go. What would Hadley have done?"

I don't need him to answer the question for me. I know exactly what Hadley would've done, because I tried to take her for a ride in the convertible plenty of times. She never wanted to mess up her hair, and the one time I got her in the passenger seat, she wrapped her head all up

Jackie-Kennedy-style, complete with the huge sunglasses, and said, "I hope no one I know sees me."

Hadley and I weren't even compatible, and how I thought we could make a marriage work baffles me to this day. What did I miss when I was with her? Did I just not want to be alone?

"I'm just saying," Dawson says. "Jess is good for you. She's alive, Lance, and she wants to taste life. You need that in your life. You need someone trying to get you to loosen up and unbutton that shirt. That's all I'm saying."

"Okay," I say, because if I agree, maybe he'll stop talking. I know what he's saying, and I don't need a lecture. Thankfully, Dawson and I know when to quit with the other, and he doesn't say anything for the last six minutes to Alec's.

The scent of something salty and something cheesy meets my nose several doors down from Alec's, and Dawson goes into his apartment the same way Jess does—he knocks and then just turns the knob.

Alec's two puppies don't move from their spots on some imaginary line just outside the kitchen, but Peaches sure is happy to see us.

"Tara, I love you!" she screeches, and for some reason, that makes me so dang happy. I laugh and hold out my arm so the parrot will come to me. She does, and I use one finger to stroke her head.

"I love you," Peaches says again, her voice quieter now.

"I love you too," I whisper back to her as Alec says

something to Dawson several paces away in the kitchen. Peaches imitates the doorbell, her sentiment for me forgotten. But I needed to be reminded that I'm lovable, and whether that comes from a Quaker parrot, my momma, or my best friend, I guess it doesn't matter.

"Get in here," Alec says, coming toward me. He grins and takes Peaches, setting the bird on his shoulder. "Dawson says I can't put cranberry preserves on a turkey bacon breakfast sandwich, and I need you to back me up." He looks at me with energy blazing from his dark eyes, and I grin.

"You got it, man," I say, following him into the kitchen. I take the half-sandwich still sitting on the plate, wondering what felon invented turkey bacon. Seriously, the stuff should be banned and sales of it should be criminal. I take a bite anyway, and somehow, Alec has made the stuff mostly palatable.

I don't hate the cranberry preserves on the sandwich, but they're not my favorite either. I chew and smack my lips. "Tastes like Thanksgiving morning," I say.

"See?" Alec's eyebrows go up in Dawson's direction, and then he grins heartily at me.

"Conspiracy," Dawson mutters, though he finishes his half of the sandwich without another complaint.

"Whatever," I say. "No conspiracy."

"Jess is gonna be back before the wedding, right?" Alec asks. "She was vague on the details of her trip this weekend." He won't look at me as he speaks, and that right there is a conspiracy.

"Overdone steak and potatoes," I say, straightening and staring at Dawson. "How fast can you talk, man?"

"I said nothing." Dawson actually looks like he believes himself.

Alec can't hide his smile though. "Seriously, Lance. She won't stop texting me about New York City."

"I'm sure that's true," I say, trying to keep the bark and bite beneath my tongue.

"The only thing she's ever talked this much about before is...you." He grins and finishes his sandwich. After he swallows, he adds, "She did say she's going to miss Peaches the most, but you're a close second."

"Shut up," I say, laughing with him. "I'm always going to lose to that bird, aren't I?"

"Don't worry, man," Alec says. "She steals every heart she comes in contact with."

"I love you!" Peaches yells, but I can't help wondering if Alec meant her...or Jess. I know one thing—I've got to figure out how to be with Jess, with all the ways she loves life and wants to taste it and smell it, or I'm going to lose her.

My heart flops in my chest, because I know one more thing: I don't want to lose Jessica Dunaway.

CHAPTER TWENTY-ONE

JESSIE

My apartment feels like someone trying to stuff more meat into a casing than it can hold. Callie, Tara, and Macie have come to see the dress, and I don't have it ready yet. "Five more minutes," I'd told Tara when she'd arrived with the other women oh, about twenty minutes ago now.

She laughs from the kitchen, but the stress settling on my shoulders presses me further into the chair in front of my sewing machine.

This is her wedding dress. I have to get it exactly right. Not only that, but the wedding is in thirteen days, and I'm going to be gone for four of them. I want the dress done before I board the plane. Tara wants the dress done fifteen minutes ago, when I said it would be.

I glance over to them, my vision blurring for a few seconds. I've been staring at white fabric, glitzy gems, and driven-snow-colored lace for what feels like ages. All that color voidance can obviously mess with a person.

"How's it coming?" Callie asks. If she wasn't so nice, I might think she's hinting I shouldn't even be looking up right now.

"Good," I say, returning my attention to the yards and yards of fabric. I can admit that I've spent a lot of time thinking about what my wedding dress will look like. In my head, I see ruffles and a train a mile long. I see eggshell fabric, with a white lace covering. I've imagined so many things, and I presented Tara with three designs I'd worked on in the past.

Tears fill my eyes, because this is the first sketch that's actually come to life. "I just need to get two more panels in place." The dress had come back from the professional seamstress—of which I am not—ready to be bedazzled and bejeweled. I've been working on that non-stop for a few days now, only taking a break yesterday to go with Lance on a Carolina excursion that had actually taken us down into Georgia too.

"Oh, honey," Callie says, running her hand along my shoulders. "Why are you crying?" She pulls out the only other seat at the dining room table and sits.

I sniff, which somehow draws the attention of the other two women in the kitchen. I've dubbed this area the breakfast nook, though there's nothing breakfasty or nooky about it. I don't even eat breakfast now that the muffin bar at the mansion isn't an option.

I shake my head. "I just want to get the dress right." I glance up. "Sorry, Tara."

"It's fine," she drawls, and I wish I was as refined as her. She owns her own business. She's renowned around the city now. I've always felt small and insignificant in comparison to her, and I hate that feeling. After she worked through some things with Alec, she's been nothing but kind to me, and I just want this dress to be perfect for her. It almost feels symbolic of our friendship, and I *need* it to be precisely right.

I feed a newly jeweled piece of fabric under the pressure foot of my machine, but don't put that foot down. I can't, or something's gonna break. I've made the stitches ultra-small, which means I can't run my machine faster than a snail moves.

The weight of Callie's gaze stays heavy on my forehead as I work, and a couple of minutes later, that panel is in. I pull the dress out and stand up. "Tara."

She's right there, her dark eyes searching my face. "It's bad."

Fear strikes me behind the heart, lashing at me horribly. "What?"

Tara looks at Callie, uber-serious. "She hasn't even heard us."

"Honey." Macie takes the dress from me, which is quite the feat given how much fabric there is. I simply watch it flow from my hands as I stand there, not quite sure what's happening. "Tell us what's going on."

"Nothing's going on," I say, refusing to look at Callie. I know Lance is with Dawson this morning, but I don't know how much Dawson knows and how much he's told Callie. They're married, and just because my mama and daddy hardly talk doesn't mean that's how every marriage is.

"You haven't touched the pecan rolls," Callie says.

"Okay, this isn't about breakfast," Tara says. "Although, I did spend a lot of time on those this morning, and they are divine." She offers me a smile, which I swear breaks me.

My lip quivers, and the next thing I know, Tara's gathering me into her arms. "Told y'all," she says. "It's bad."

"It's going to be done soon," I say, my voice too high.

"This isn't about the dress," Macie says. "She really didn't hear us."

I cling to Tara for another moment and then step back. I need Peaches here to lighten the moment by screaming about motorbikes and casseroles and whatever else Alec has taught her. She could chime like my doorbell, except I haven't got one.

"I don't know what you mean."

"Of course you don't, because you weren't listening."

"I was sewing," I say, turning away from the lot of them to get the dress. Macie blocks me, and I look into her eyes, truly surprised. She's been nothing short of amazing, and I didn't know she had any bones in her body that could cause conflict. She knows how to handle huge crowds at Legacy Brew, and I've never seen her without a smile for me or for anyone else who walks in.

Sure, she gets tired. She is human, after all. Today, she wears something vibrant in her hazel-eyed expression, and I can't release her gaze.

"Is it Lance?" she asks. "Something with your mama?" She swallows and glances over to the other girls. "Help me out here, ladies."

"Jess," Tara says at the same time Callie says, "This is more than the dress, Jess."

I scan all three of them, not really looking them in the eyes. If I can't tell them, who can I tell? *This is NBD*, I tell myself. "I'm going to New York City on Wednesday night." The words nearly choke me, and I take a deep, deep breath after I've said them.

"Why?" Callie asks, really making the one-syllable word into two. *Why-uh?*

My hands run around and around each other, and I feel the ghost of Lance's over them, calming me in his office from weeks ago. I smooth down my blouse, which is a fantastic pale pink number I found at a second-hand store last night. I'd bought Lance a striped polo in black, fawn, and navy, but I haven't given it to him yet.

"Listen," I say. "I don't want anyone to get all worked up. It's nothing—and it really can be nothing in less time than it takes to breathe." My heart pounds, trapped by all those ribs.

Tara folds her arms, her eyes telling me I better keep talking, and keep talking fast.

"I sent in a portfolio to a design agency," I say. "They were having a contest, and their executive director called last week. She likes one of my designs, and I'm going to talk to her."

The calm before the storm only last half a second, and then both Macie and Callie erupt into congratulations and why didn't you tell us's. Tara takes another moment, her smile plenty big, before she says, "That's so great, Jess."

"Yes." I adopt my agency persona. "Now, let me finish the dress so you can try it on, so I can have a real, live emblem of one of my designs." I meet her eyes, all of my confidence gone. "You'll model it for me, right? Let me take your picture?"

"Of course," Tara says, her gaze moving to the dress. "Absolutely I will."

I nod and reach for the dress again. Macie blocks me again, and I don't know what to do. In situations like this, I clam up and split. But this is my apartment, and these women would just track me down and make me talk.

"There's more," she says, narrowing her eyes at me.

"No," I insist, because I'm not going to tell my friends that Lance's reaction to this same news wasn't the same as theirs. I'm not. He came around, and he just needed more time to process. His background is just different. "I have one more panel, and then I'm going to eat all the pecan buns in that tray." I give them all a warning-eye. "So if y'all want more, you better eat fast."

"I'll get the butter out," Tara says.

"I'll brew another pot of coffee." Callie follows her into the microscopic kitchen, the action taking three steps.

Macie watches me, those eyes all-seeing despite the way she's set them into squints. "Jess."

"Please, Macie," I say, almost under my breath.

She straightens her shoulders and shakes her hair over them. She's got gorgeous curly hair she hardly ever wears down. "Fine," she whisper-says. "But you can't hide much from Callie for long. Tara either; she just works more."

"I'm not hiding anything," I say, but we both know that's not true. She lets me gather the dress, and I get back to work as the scent of coffee fills my nose.

Quirky runs through my mind. Lance had given me that Q-word. I'd called him a *running champ*. He said I was *stylish*.

Our adjective game has gone on, but I still don't have a X-word or a Z-word for him. I got the two hardest letters of the alphabet.

Talented, understood, valued, wonderful.

When he'd told me I was *understood*, I very nearly started crying. I wonder if he feels the same way now or if he realizes how very un-understood he made me feel when he turned into BBL on our hike yesterday.

I really don't like the barky, bossy Lance—BBL—but I also don't know how to tell him that. With all the thinking, the panel gets done, and I say, "All right, Tara. Come put this on."

———

"YOU'VE GOT EVERYTHING?" Lance asks from behind the steering wheel.

"Yes." I clutch my purse, my carry-on in Mammoth's bed.

"You need your driver's license to board." He glances over at me.

I give him my best withering look, and he actually turns to dust. "All right," he mumbles. "You've got everything."

That's right, I do. Just because I've barely left South Carolina doesn't mean I don't know how. I have my ID. I have money. I have a toothbrush. Whatever else I forgot, I can buy in the city. I'll be fine.

I've been telling myself these things for days and days, and I don't need my boyfriend to insinuate that I'm not suited for the Big Apple. My stomach feels like a swarm of angry bees has attacked, and I don't know how to settle them down. Maybe I'll just be this perpetually sick for the next four days.

Things with Lance have been...okay at the agency. His strict rules and definitive lines in the sand actually came in very handy this week. I know how to deal with being his assistant, and he knows how to keep things professional between us.

I did notice that his professional real estate advice hardly came this week at all, but I didn't say anything. I remind myself one more time that we all have things we're working through. Just like Lance has to say *you've got everything*—that *you have* in his question so proper—I have to figure out what I really want my life to be.

I've never really wanted to leave Carolina. I love the South, and I love being Southern. My sketches have always been...an escape. Something only for me to look at, to dream about, and to keep me company. I don't know if I'm ready for them to be more.

I simply didn't want to marry someone I didn't love. I didn't want to wear hoop skirts and ball gowns all day, every day. I don't care about the weather or walking through gardens. Okay, that last bit is sometimes nice, depending on the heat.

My word, I hate all of my thoughts. They feel like they belong to someone else, like I'm doing something inside someone else's body. Something that's not me.

You sent in the portfolio, I tell myself. *Just go see.*

Go see, go see, go see.

I need to go see. I've always needed to know for myself, something Daddy told me before I left. *Go see, sugar-doll. You won't be satisfied until you go see.*

I'm going. I'm seeing. Then I'll know.

The drive to the airport doesn't take very long. Or

maybe I blinked, passed out from my nerves, and then we arrived. No matter what, we're here, and Lance is getting down from Mammoth to retrieve my bag.

I nearly fall as I stumble from the truck, and a curb-side attendant lunges toward me. "You okay, ma'am?"

I brush back my hair as he removes his hand from me. "Fine, thank you."

Lance looks at him and then me before setting my suit-case on the sidewalk. "Jess?"

"I'm fine," I repeat, wishing I don't feel like someone has cut me into fifteen pieces and the sewed me back together wrong. "Mammoth just tried to kill me. It's not the first time." I put a smile on my face, because I know Lance won't.

He frowns at his truck and meets my eyes. "Cha-Cha wasn't happy she didn't get to come say good-bye."

"It's not good-bye," I say, stepping closer to him, a silent indication I want him to take me into his arms. I want him to hold me and tell me everything will be okay. That if New York City chews me up and spits me out, I can show up on his doorstep and find refuge.

He slides his arms around me, and I can breathe again. I take a deep breath of the scent of his shirt—cotton and dryer sheets and probably a little Cha-Cha in there too. "It's four days," I say. "I'll call you when I'm settled at the hotel. You'll come get me on Sunday?"

He grunts, which is Emotional-Lance-Speak for *yes, of course. I love you and don't worry, Jess. Everything is going to be fine. That designer is such an idiot if she doesn't like every single design you've ever sketched.*

It's amazing what a grunt can really mean. Or how disillusioned I am. One or the other.

"Sir," the attendant says, and Lance steps back.

"Be safe, Jess," he says, already turning to walk away.

"Wait," I say, and he faces me again. I can't go without kissing him. I can't. He's not going to kiss me, so I step back into his arms and tip up to touch my lips to his. It's a simple, beautiful, chaste kiss, and it means so much more than what it looks like on the outside.

"Thank you, Lance," I whisper. "I'll see you soon."

He nods, no smile in sight, and then I'm ready to grip the handle on my suitcase and walk into the airport. And I do exactly that, wondering what lies in front of me...and what I'm truly leaving behind.

CHAPTER TWENTY-TWO

LANCE

I LOOK TOWARD THE DOOR AGAIN, WONDERING WHERE in the world Dawson and Callie are. I can't believe I agreed to come to dinner with them and the Tara-Alec combo. I like them. Of course I like them. It's not like I want to spend Friday night alone while my girlfriend is out of town.

Callie has some sort of pigeon homing device or something, and she zeroed in on me the moment Jess boarded the plane. Someone knocked on my door two minutes after I'd gotten home from the airport, and there stood a pizza delivery guy.

Dawson and Callie didn't say anything, but it was the fried green tomato type, with plenty of bacon and cheese. Pretty much only Dawson knows I like that, and that I'm a closet-eater of it. Then Callie herself texted me before six a.m. this morning, inviting me to dinner with them tonight.

I glance across the table to Macie Wilheim, my "date" for tonight. She utters a sound of disgust and looks up from her phone. "I'm not answering him," she says, flipping the phone over and leaving it face-down on the tabletop. "I swear, he thinks he rules the world."

She huffs and folds her arms. I see the indecision in her face, despite what she's said. "Coy?" I ask anyway, though I know exactly who she's talking about.

She gives me a dirty look, her hazel eyes more brown than green, almost the color of old dirt. Her hair is the curly-curly type, and it goes almost to her waist. She's a pretty woman—when she's not stark raving mad. "Who else?"

"What does he want now?"

"He wants me to go to Veterans Brew and see how they mix their blends." She scoffs, as if market research is such a terrible burden.

"Dawson and Cal handle their marketing," I say, once again glancing toward the door. On the outside, I'm cool and collected. I made it through two days alone at F&F, and it was by sheer will, let me tell you. "They might have some insights."

"They do?" Macie asks.

I merely nod, because I'm starting to get Peeved with a capital P. Dawson and Callie are late, and if Alec and Tara are supposed to be here, they are too. If they don't walk through the door in the next five minutes, I'm leaving. I can order pizza again, or drive through somewhere on my way home to Cha-Cha.

Unfortunately, Dawson walks in before I can take my next breath, and my stomach falls to my loafers. It rebounds quickly, especially when I see the storm on his face. I don't have to ask what the problem is—both he and Callie are both still dressed in their office clothes. Dressed-down-for-Friday for Dawson is his usual clothes, minus a tie. I could take a leaf from his book, in all honesty, and I'm glad I changed out my pale yellow—lemon meringue, Jess had called it—dress shirt for this polo. It gives the illusion that I've been home when I haven't. Plus, I haven't been able to wear a tie for two days anyway, because Jess isn't here to make sure it matches.

I rise from the booth so I can sit on the end and give Dawson a look and Callie a hug. "Thanks for the pizza," I say as I pull away.

She smiles at me and slides against the wall. "Sorry we're late," she says. "We needed to go over a couple of things and get the project off to the printer before we could leave."

"And we couldn't get Jeremiah out of the blasted office," Dawson says. "Cal here had to fake an injury to get him to go."

I grin at him as he slides into the booth too, but he barely cracks a smile. "What kind of injury?"

"Bad back," Callie says in mock sincerity. "I needed so

many pills, and I just had to get off my feet." She smiles across the table to Macie. "Uh oh. What's wrong with you?"

"Coy," we say together, and I give her a smile too.

"Sorry," Tara says, rushing over to the table. Since I stopped watching the door, I didn't see her. She stands at the end of the table while Alec joins her. "But guess what?" She bounces on the balls of her feet, a big, yellow-brown envelope clutched in her hand.

Callie squeals and tries to crawl over Dawson to get out of the booth. "I'm sitting here, baby."

"Get out, get out," Callie says. "That's from a publisher. Tara Lynn Finch, is that from a publisher?"

I jump to my feet, because Dawson's getting out of the booth whether I do or not. Tara thrusts the envelope into the air, her face shining out as much radiance as a spotlight. "It's from a publisher!" she yells. She giggles, and Macie and Callie converge on her, the three of them jumping up and down in a girl-circle as they squeal and offer congratulations.

Alec wisely stands out of the way, and Dawson and I join him. "Book deal," he says, obvious pride in his voice. "She's been writing a cookbook for a while. Your mother really came through, Dawson."

"She usually does," he says, and he steps into the fray to hug Tara the moment it seems safe to do so.

I follow suit, telling her, "This is amazing, Tara.

Congrats," before we all settle back into our seats. Macie sits against the wall, leaving me to face Alec. I don't mind. He's a great guy, and he won't badger me to death about Jess. In fact, he and Dawson have made a semi-effective wall against the women, and I'm so, so grateful for that.

"How's Jess?" Dawson asks, betraying me completely.

All the gushing conversation and passing of papers from the envelope stops, everyone focusing on me.

"Fine," I say, glaring at him. "She called last night, saying the city is great. Her meeting went well. She had another one today, but I haven't heard from her yet." I reach for my water glass, realizing it's empty, as I drank it all while waiting for everyone to arrive.

"I'm not answering questions about her," I add. "That's it. She's fine. I'm fine. We're fine." I lean forward a little bit. "I don't need pizza or meals. Believe it or not, I've lived on my own for a while now."

Callie's shoulders go right up. "I'm going to send pizza if I want to."

I nod, trying to take down the BBL—what Jess calls me when I'm being bossy-barky-Lance at work. I'm not sure if I have my R-REF on or not, but I try to smooth it away. "And I appreciate it. But I'm okay."

"We know you're okay," Dawson says quietly, but I think he worries about me. I get it; for a while there, I worried about him too. He's *so happy* now, and I want that more than anything in my life.

"Okay," I say, blowing out my breath. "So, Mace. Tell us what Coy's doing now. Maybe Dawson and Callie can help." That gets the attention off me, which is where I need it right now. The conversation switches from that, to the book contract, to the wedding, and I'm happy to go with the flow.

I check my phone a few times, just to make sure it still has power. It does, but there are no messages from Jess. I know the city never sleeps, and I hope she's okay and having a good time. She had a party tonight, hosted by the designer who called and liked her work.

She'll call later, I tell myself. *It's not even late yet.*

Dinner ends, I drive home, and I scrub Cha-Cha from front paws to back. I shower, even though I'm going straight to bed, and the clock chimes midnight.

Jess still hasn't messaged or called. Since texting is a two-way street, I tap out a quick message to her. *Going to bed. Give me a call tomorrow if you have a minute. I want to hear how today went.*

Then I do go to bed, telling myself she's fine. I don't have to hear from her before I sleep. My thoughts circle and tangle, the way they usually do, and then I fall asleep, the way I usually do. All I can do is hope that everything really is okay for Jess, and that she really will call tomorrow.

———

I RUN SATURDAY MORNING, the girl's track team hot on my heels. I let them pass me once, but I'm not letting that happen today. I half-expect Jess to call in the middle of my run again, but she doesn't.

I have no idea what I do during the day. Probably stare piningly at my phone or something, willing it to ring. It doesn't. I send Jess another couple of texts, trying to stay upbeat and hopeful. I want her to know I miss her and I'm anxious to hear her news, whatever it is. *Good or bad*, I tell her. *It'll be okay.*

I want her to know she can come back to Charleston proud of herself, no matter what. That I'll be here, and the agency is here, and she can keep trying with the fashion design. She doesn't answer, and she doesn't call.

About five, I order some food, and twenty minutes later, I open the map app to see where the driver is. He's close—but so is Dawson. He shared his location pin with me years ago, because we both like to run, and when he's not on the treadmill, he's out on the trails. I like knowing I can be found should something happen to me, and now, seeing Dawson only five minutes from my house throws me into action.

I hurry into the bedroom, pulling my shirt over my head while yelling at Cha-Cha to get ready for a run. I didn't take her this morning, so she should be fine to go tonight. I've changed and leashed Cha-Cha, and I'm even down my front steps and a few strides down the sidewalk when Dawson pulls into my driveway.

Callie is with him, and I pause. Have they come to deliver bad news?

Of course they have, I tell myself. The concern in Callie's eyes, even through the windshield, is a dead giveaway.

Dawson gets out of the car while I tighten my hold on Cha-Cha's leash. "Going running?" he asks.

"Yep."

"Didn't you run this morning?"

"Yep." I don't have to explain anything to him.

He sighs and looks toward the house and back to me. "Listen, Lance," he says, keeping his head low as he approaches me. I hate that. I'm not a squirrel he's going to scare away. If I wanted to leave Charleston, I'd have done it when Hadley did, taking three months' worth of my money in the form of a diamond ring with her.

"She's going to come back," he says.

I narrow my eyes at him. "What are you talking about?"

"Haven't you talked to Jess?"

I cock my head at him and finally let Cha-Cha go to Callie, who crouches down and gives her love, the same way Jess does. What is with women and corgis?

"If I'd talked to Jess, do you think I'd be going for a second run?" I ask Dawson.

Alarm pulls all the way across his face, and he looks over to Callie. She too wears a bit of horror in her expression, and my curiosity gets the best of me.

"What's going on?"

"Nothing," Callie yells above whatever Dawson says. His mouth moved, but I couldn't hear him. "She'll call soon, I'm sure."

I may not have been able to get to the altar with a woman yet, even after two failed engagements. But I'm not an idiot either. "You talked to her," I say, and I'm not asking. Why in the world would Jess call Callie when she could use her obviously sparse and precious time to call me?

A knife jabs through my ribs and right into the fleshiest part of my heart.

I turn away from the truth, because it hurts too much. "Come on, Cha-Cha," I say, and I pick up my stride.

"Lance," Dawson calls after me, but I keep on going. If my dog comes, great. If she doesn't, perhaps Callie and Dawson will be kind enough to put her back in the house for me.

But I'm not going back. I'm not talking to them about Jess—who they've talked to and gotten news from—when I haven't spoken to her yet.

I'm not. I'm not. I'm not.

My feet beat out a rhythm with the words, and soon enough they're screaming through my head too.

————

THE FOLLOWING MORNING, I don't text Jess. I can't stand the thought of sending her six texts without getting an answer. Somehow five was okay, but half a dozen is my limit. I think of how she called me *limitless*, and wow, how wrong she was about that.

It's funny how wrong we can be sometimes. I've been over and over my feelings for her, and I can't figure out if they're right or wrong. Was I imagining the happiness? Had I pretended to start falling in love with her? How does the human heart and soul even know what love is?

I dial her, because either I'm speaking to her today or I'm never talking to her again. That's where I am right now, and praise the heavens and stars and sky above, she answers.

"Hey, Lance."

As I pace from one side of my kitchen to the other, I can't tell how she's feeling. I can't decipher her voice and qualify it into apprehension, happiness, fear, anything.

"Hey," I say, not sure how I sound either. "I haven't heard from you, and I was actually starting to get worried..." I let my words hang there, because I have the very real feeling it's not me who has to talk. I gaze out the window above the sink, wishing life was as simple as wind in tree limbs.

"I know." Jess takes a big breath I can hear over the line—not good. She does these big breath things—a BBT! —when she's nervous and trying to calm herself down—

and then exhales. "I'm so sorry, Lance, but I need another day off. Maybe two..."

My mind spins, and I turn away from my backyard. "What?" I'm not entirely sure what's on our calendar for tomorrow and Tuesday. A few swipes or clicks and I'd know. Right now, I can barely see past the chairs at the bar to Cha-Cha lying on the floor by the front door.

"Sabrina Shadows is coming in tomorrow morning," Jess says in a rush. "I can text her and say you'll meet with her."

"Sabrina Shadows?" My mind can't form coherent thoughts yet.

"It's just that Kira wanted to show my stuff to another designer. This guy name Tim? But he's in Paris. Or he was. I guess he's flying home today, and she wants me to meet him, and well, he might not be ready for guests tomorrow what with the jet lag and all."

She keeps talking, but it's all just a jumble of sounds in her pretty voice. I find myself nodding as if she can see me —she can't—and when she finally stops explaining, I say, "Sure, take the time you need."

A pause comes through the line. "Really?"

"What am I supposed to say?" I challenge her, anger touching my voice and chest. "Come home now or I'll fire you?" I shake my head. She must think me the worst boss on the planet. "Honestly, Jess, I thought we were past that." I can't help the biting tone flowing from me now. "Are you going to make it to the wedding?"

Tara and Alec are getting married on Saturday. She designed the dress. "Yes," she says.

"I hate that you didn't call me on Friday," I say, thinking I might as well lay everything out for her. I walk through the kitchen to the living room, and Cha-Cha lifts her head. "Or Saturday. And I have a very strong suspicion you weren't going to call today. That instead of calling me, your boyfriend and boss, you called Callie Houser and told *her* everything."

Jess doesn't deny it immediately, and I've seen her stand up for herself. I remember her snapping at Sabrina Shadows about the type of real estate agent I was, and her defense of me. There's none of that now.

I sink into the couch. "Tell me I'm wrong," I say quietly, pressing my eyes closed. Cha-Cha jumps up next to me, and I reach over to take comfort from her by stroking her.

"I just called Callie to get some advice," Jess says, zero fire in sight. Not even a hint of smoke.

Anguish pours through me, the kind made of all capital letters. Everything feels so hard, and so dark, and I can't figure out what to say. With one more thought, sunshine pours through the chaos, and I open my eyes.

"Jess," I say as calmly as I can, glad I'm sitting now. "Or rather, Miss Dunaway, please do let me know when you'll be back at work. I'll expect you Wednesday unless I get a call directly from you."

"Miss Dunaway?" Her voice is definitely made of shock now.

"Yes," I say. "I think it's best if we...go back to being professionals." I press my mouth shut, everything in my life crashing and burning. "You're a good assistant, Jess. I'd hate to lose you at Finley and Frank."

"Are you breaking up with me?"

I don't think. I can't. I shut off the feelings, the emotions, the rushing of blood through my body. "Yes."

"Lance."

"I'm sorry," I say again as Cha-Cha jumps down from the couch, her nails clicking across the hard floor toward the back door. "But you couldn't even call me and tell me how your meeting on Friday went, or about the party. I texted you and texted you, and you call Callie? I think you broke up with me, Jess. On Saturday."

"That is not true." She speaks with the fire now, but I honestly think it's a little too late.

"Good luck with your meeting tomorrow," I say, getting to my feet and following Cha-Cha. "And do remember you have to give two weeks' notice to quit the agency." That last part's not entirely true, but I can't keep talking to her. "I have to go. Cha-Cha needs to go out."

I give her a moment—several, in fact—to protest, but she doesn't. She doesn't apologize. I do hear a sniff, and then she says, "I'll talk to you soon, Mister Byers," and the call ends.

I stand in my kitchen, my phone going silent and dark,

and Cha-Cha waiting at the back door. I step over to it and open it for her, a bellow gathering in my stomach, then my chest, and then my throat.

At least I haven't asked her to marry me yet, I think, and then I yell my frustration and hurt into the South Carolina sky.

CHAPTER TWENTY-THREE

JESSIE

I SHOULD BE WEARING A CROWN FOR HOW PRINCESS-like I feel. There's low music playing, and people milling about. I'm holding a flute of champagne exactly the way my mama taught me. No white gloves like I used to wear at my Socialite parties, but close enough.

I haven't stopped smiling since I arrived, and I think anyone in fashion would be doing the same as me.

See, I'm wearing a Victoria Lyons dress, and for anyone who knows, that's *something*. It hugs my curves and really boosts up my chest, and plenty of people have stopped by to compliment me on the burgundy fabric with the black roses velveted in. The dress might be a tad dark for me, but I'm wearing it like a champion, as one must when in the company of the rich, famous, and fashionable.

"You look lovely," a man says, coming to a stop in front

of me. His eyes scan from my cleavage to my Choos, and all I can do is giggle and smile.

"Thank you," I say. "It's Lyons."

"Of course it is." He looks at me like I've lost my mind, because anyone who's anyone at this party is wearing something designed by someone else at this party. Not me, though, and the bitterness from the alcohol slides right down my throat.

"You wear this extremely well," he says, circling me. He's wearing a pair of slacks that looks like he's outgrown them—the current style. His shoes are black and shiny, and his glasses are big and bulky and black. They're perfectly round too, and he looks at me through the lenses. "Do you model?"

"No, sir," I say in my Southern twang. Kira said it makes me sound different, and in this industry, different is usually good. Sometimes it can kill a career though, so I don't put in the sway in my voice I might if I was still in Carolina.

"You should," he says, reaching into his inside jacket pocket. "I'm Stephon Grishwald, photographer. Email me, and I'll call you when I've got plus-size jobs."

I take the card, completely stunned. I look at the letters on the card, and sure enough, he's got a website and an email address. I'm not sure I know what those things are at the moment, and by the time I look up, Stephon is gone.

"Thank you," I call out to no one in particular, a

certain giddiness romping through me. I have nowhere to tuck the card, and I turn in a circle, completely lost.

Good or bad, runs through my mind. *It'll be okay.*

Lance's text from Friday night. Suddenly, I don't want to be at this party. I don't care if I can make connections here in New York City, because I don't live and design here. I live and work at a real estate office in Charleston, South Carolina.

The distinct thought of *What am I doing here?* barrels through my thoughts, and I honestly have no idea.

Lance had sent me four or five more texts, each sweet and reassuring. I could tell he was getting more and more worried about me, and then he came right out and said it when we finally did talk.

I should've called him. I know it, and I tip my head back and down the rest of my drink. The champagne burns my throat, and I set my empty flute on a table and walk away, the skirts of the Victoria Lyons dress swishing all the while.

New York isn't nearly as warm as Carolina, and Kira has given me a fur stole to wear with the dress when we're outside. I've left my phone with that, and this card needs to go there too. I'm not going to email Stephon though.

Am I?

Honestly, I don't know much of anything anymore. I sniffle as I enter the coat closet, not really watching where I'm going. I hear some rustling I definitely don't want to hear, and I say, "Excuse me. I'm coming in here."

A man parts the coats in the back of the room, his guilt written all over his face. He says nothing but it's clear he wants me to leave. I'm about to burst into tears, so I don't dare go back out to the party. As it is, I'm going to have to text Kira—or something. She hasn't actually given me her number.

She arranges everything, and I just wait like a lemming on the sidewalk for the car to show up. Tonight's was an hour late, and I didn't dare go back inside the hotel for fear of missing it. It's a miracle I still have my toes, as there's a cold spell in the city right now.

"I'm about to cry," I tell him. "Do you want to deal with that, or can I be alone?"

Something sort of like sympathy crosses his face, and he drags a woman out of the coats as he starts to walk. My sniffling only increases with every step he takes, and the woman trailing behind him in her ultra-high heels—we used to call those UGHs back home. Ultra-glorious heels. I honestly don't know what I was thinking back then— gives me a look that says she understands.

She'll probably spend some part of tonight crying too, if the good-looking, well-dressed, seemingly put together man in front of her is any indication.

I hold back my tears for as long as I can. Long enough to find my fur and remove my phone from the zipper pocket along the right shoulder. I tuck the card in there, but everything is blurry now.

I can't believe I'm still here, a full twenty-four hours

after Lance broke up with me. I sat on the couch in the hotel for a good fifteen minutes before his words had sunk all the way into my brain. I'd called him back, but he hadn't answered.

After I swipe on my phone, I go to his texts. I like being tortured, apparently. He sent me five, starting Friday night and running through Sunday morning. Early, like just after midnight.

I hope today was amazing. I can't wait to hear about it. Good or bad. It'll all be okay.

I miss you, Jess. How's New York? How was the design meeting with Kira? Call me when you get a minute.

Hey, I know we don't do real estate on weekends, but Jason Finch says he wants to hire you and not me to sell his house. Doable? I miss you. Let me know.

I close my eyes, squishing out the tears. They run down my face in a warm-then-cold drip, but I can't read any more texts. I miss Lance too. I do. Of course I do. Today's the first Monday in a while I haven't arrived at Finley & Frank, waited in his office for him to show up, picked his tie, and then outlined our week.

Our week. Not his week.

How in the world am I going to work at that agency and not be his girlfriend? No wonder he kept so many lines and so many compartments around our relationship. Him not kissing me in his office? Genius on his part, because now he can work there without having to imagine it.

"He doesn't care anyway," I whisper, though I know that can't be true. I *hope* it can't be true.

I tip my head back and blink rapidly, using my fingers to get the tears attached to my eyelashes. Hopefully my makeup isn't too badly ruined, but I'm not sure why I care. I've just taken the deepest breath of my life, but I haven't decided if I'm going back to the party or calling a cab and going to the hotel, when Kira says, "There you are, darling."

The "darling" gives her away. I cringe as I turn to face her, masking the movement of my shoulders as I reach to pick up my skirts. "Kira, hello," I say as if I've just arrived for the festivities.

"Come meet Tim Vincent," she says, gesturing for me to go with her. She wears a painted on smile of red lipstick, but she's a shark. She hasn't said a single word about my designs without me needling her, and at this point, I think I might be dealing with a Cruella de Ville. You know, someone who steals other people's designs and passes them off as her own.

She has my portfolio, and I'm determined to get it back before I board the plane Tuesday afternoon. So I paste a smile on my own lips—mine are painted raspberry—and loop my arm through hers.

"Have you had a chance to decide on the jumper or the skirt?" I ask her. She has told me she's narrowed it to those two, and she wants to know what textiles I'd use with them. I told her I wanted to know which one she would construct before we went any further. That took me all day Friday, and then I attended another ghastly party until well after midnight.

"Oh, we don't talk business at parties, dear." She trills out a laugh, and an older gentleman turns from the piece of art he's studying. He's got gray along his temples, and he's wearing a proper suit in dusty charcoal. A bowtie adorns his neck, and it's very nearly the same color as my dress.

"I love your tie," I say, grinning at him. If Kira thought I wouldn't be able to handle her high society fashion parties, she was dead wrong. I've been attending these things since I was four years old. "You belong with me, Mister Vincent. We match." I switch my arm from Kira's to his, his smile encouraging me all the way.

I leave Kira in the dust as I aim us back to the party. "Tell me, where did you get that tie? I'd love to get one for my boyfriend." The word sticks in my throat, choking me no matter how much I eat, drink, or talk.

And I know. I have to do something about Lance, or I'm going to lose, well, everything.

———

THE FOLLOWING MORNING, my phone rings from somewhere beside me, waking me. I have no idea what time it is, but someone snuck into my room in the middle of the night and replaced my saliva with cat hair.

My mouth is stuck together it's so dry, and I slap at the nightstand to find my phone. I see Sabrina's name on the screen and sit straight up in bed. "Hello," I say, reminding myself this is a business call. "This is Jessie Dunaway."

"Praise the Lord you answered," Sabrina spits. Oh, she's mad, and my heart begins to pound like a cowboy setting a fence.

"Yes," I say, glancing at the clock. It's past ten already, and another round of panic parades through me. My flight is at three, and I have to be out of this hotel room in one hour. "What can I do for you?"

I throw back the blanket, only half-listening. I can't stay in this city for another day, though I'd originally planned to go home tomorrow. I'd called the airline this morning and changed my flight, and the hotel said I could leave early too.

Lance isn't expecting me until Thursday, and I don't know what I'll do tomorrow. "Look for a job," I mutter, and Sabrina goes, "What?"

"I'm sorry," I say, straightening and focusing on the conversation at hand. "My attention was divided, but now it's all yours. What did you say?"

"I said, I got your autoresponder that you were out of the office and to contact Lance, but he's not answering his phone either."

First, I answered my phone, but I don't say that. "He should be in the office," I say, frowning. When I walk in a room, I just drop my clothes wherever they happen to fall, and I have stuff everywhere. "What do you need?"

"I went and asked at that farmhouse, like you suggested."

My heart takes flight, and my lipstick-stained lips curve up. "You did? Sabrina, that's great."

"The owners are interested in hearing more about what their property is worth," she says without acknowledging what I've said. "I told them someone from Finley and Frank would call them yesterday, and Lance did not."

"I'll call him and find out what's going on." I get to my feet and pick up the hotel pen and pad of paper. I'd wondered what anyone would use this for, and now I know. "Tell me the name and number of the owners. I'll call them today if I can't get in touch with Lance."

"Thank you," Sabrina says, and she lists the name and number of who I need to talk to in order to appease her.

The call ends, and I reach down to pull on my big girl panties and make a phone call I don't want to make.

I take a breath and then another one, and I don't think there's enough deep breaths in the world to prepare me to call Lance.

My finger shakes as I swipe and tap, his name staring me in the face. I can't tap the button. I can't. Maybe I can just text him.

"Grow up," I tell myself. We work together, and I'm not quitting. If Lance can't stand to be around me, he's going to have to find an issue with my performance at the agency and fire me.

I tap the button and lift my trembling phone to my ear. "Be strong," I recite to myself as the line rings. And rings. And rings. I want to tell him the only reason I called Callie was to get her advice on what to say to Lance, how to ask him for more time off in a professional way.

Lance doesn't answer, and his voice comes over the recording, making my heart clench. "Hey," I chirp into my phone. I pace toward the window, where I stood for at least ten minutes the first time I arrived in the hotel room. "I just got off the phone with Sabrina, and she said she tried to get in touch with you. Are you not in the office today? She wanted you to call the owners of the farmhouse."

I turn back to the nightstand where I jotted down the name. My brain can't hold anything at the moment, and I know exactly why. I'm as nervous now as I was when I first showed up at Finley & Frank for my interview with Lance. I've still never told him I was right about the time, and the thought gives me the shot of confidence I need in this moment.

"The Owens?" I say into the message. "I have their number." I rattle it off and then freeze. Finally, I say, "Okay, thanks," and hang up. I drop my phone onto the messy bed as if it's caught fire, and I take another deep breath. Then another.

"You did it," I tell myself. I'm not sure if Lance will

call me back, but my guess is he won't. He's not a chicken or afraid of a challenge, but he'll either text or he won't respond at all.

I start packing, because I have to get out of this hotel. I have to get back to Charleston, and not so I can appease Sabrina.

I have to get back so I can look Lance in the face and apologize. I have to get back to Carolina so I can explain everything to him. If he can just try to see things from my point of view, I know he'll forgive me.

I have to get back, because I have to get Lance Byers back into my life.

CHAPTER TWENTY-FOUR

SABRINA

I FIT MY KEY INTO THE LOCK AND TWIST, JUGGLING MY huge purse with the ginormous paper bag of books I bought at the store just now. I'd already been home from the law office when I'd remembered I needed a new novel.

I'd meant to stop on the way home from the downtown office, but when my meeting with Jason Finch had gotten postponed *again*, I'd left the seventeenth floor in a bit of a fit. Honestly, most walking I do is a bit stridey. A little like a march.

All I know is it keeps people away, and that's where I want them. Away.

I enter my apartment—which I'd found only a week or so ago, the stench of beets or boots coming from the place next door. This place isn't much better than crashing in Macie's spare bedroom, but Jess is out of town until tomorrow, and while she called me back yesterday afternoon to let me know she has a meeting with the Owens out at the Century Farm, nothing moves fast enough for me.

I drop the books and my purse onto the couch, the burden finally relieved from my arms. I exhale as I shrug out of my denim jacket and hang it on the coat rack beside the door. I close that and lock the deadbolt. I don't feel safe if I don't, though I live in a quiet neighborhood tucked off any main thoroughfares in Charleston.

For what I have, it's a nice enough place. One bedroom. One bath. A living room with a dining nook and a kitchen. Big windows take up the back of the apartment, and my sister even sent some sunny curtains from California where she lives.

I look that way, kick off my shoes, and stop by the couch to pick up one of my romance novels before continuing into the kitchen. My stomach growls at me for something to eat, as it's nearly seven and I haven't had dinner yet. Chelsea will text me to find out if I've eaten, as if she can do anything about it from almost three thousand miles away.

She likes to cook, which is a good thing as she lives up in the mountains in Northern California and there's no such thing as Carry or CarryEats. Her husband is a chef, and if I ask if Doritos count as dinner, I get both of them texting me.

"Oh," I say, the word leaking from my mouth as I see the pot on the stove. I'm a terrible cook—I can burn water, literally—and I toss the romance paperback on the counter and reach for the pot.

The flame isn't on underneath it, but I distinctly remember lighting the burner. I'd filled this pot halfway with water, but as I tip it toward me, there's not a single drop left.

There are also no eggs, and I absolutely, one-hundred percent, for-certain put six eggs in this pot before I remembered I needed a new nightly read and then dashed off to the bookstore.

I look left. I look right.

No eggs. No eggs. Where are the eggs?

With horror cascading through my whole body, my eyes get drawn to the sunny curtains. There's no longer simply smiling cartoon suns on the fabric. Bits of egg—hard-boiled beyond belief egg—cling to the curtains.

And the windowsill. And the wall. All the way to the ceiling, where it looks like hard-boiled shrapnel has been missiled into the plaster.

"Ohhh." Another sigh leaks from my mouth, my heartbeat clogging my throat and nose. How on God's green earth am I going to get this cleaned up? I can't. This apartment needs to be burned to the ground, and even then, the fire marshal will likely find bits of egg white, egg yolk, and eggshell in the ashes.

I stand there in the poultrified crime scene, wondering how to even start cleaning it up. Eventually, I reach out and brush my fingers against the sunny-eggy-something. It doesn't budge, and I recoil from the texture of it.

"Those are going in the garbage," I say, making an executive decision. I do that all day at work, and my house is no different. "Chelsea simply doesn't need to know."

I nearly rip the curtain rod off the wall in my attempt to get the curtains down, and as I look down at the ruined fabric in the trashcan, I have a moment of clarity.

I need to move. I need to move so badly, and when I do, I'll simply lose my cleaning deposit. I should've torn down the curtain rod, because there's no way I'm getting a cent of my money back. The landlord is going to have to bring in a power-washer, strip the paint, replaster, and then repaint. When the contractor put in *eggshell*-white paint, I don't think this was what he intended.

I lift the pot from the defunct burner—both of which are still warm to the touch—and set it in the sink. Then I pick up my romance novel and march out of the kitchen. Out of sight, out of mind, right?

Maybe with exploded eggs and ugly denim jackets. I shed my clothes and step into silky pajamas. With a sigh, I climb between the crisp, clean, cool sheets of the bed I make meticulously every morning. I open the paperback, determined not to think about work, my clients, the farmhouse, or Jason Finch.

It's that last item on the list that trips me up every time. It's not really his fault that our meeting has been postponed a few times now. Well, some of it is. It's mine too though, so I haven't given him a piece of my mind. Yet.

"You're not giving him a piece of anything," I mutter to myself, focusing on the first line in chapter one *again*. Definitely not my heart, mind, or soul. The whole reason I moved to Charleston a few years ago was to regain all that I'd given away to a man so very much like Mister Finch, and I won't be making that mistake again. Oh, no, I will not.

My eyes move down the lines of text, but I'm not comprehending them. When my phone chimes, I practically lunge for it, insanely hoping it will be Jason.

It's not. Of course it's not. While he has my number, he wouldn't be texting me after work mid-week unless it was an emergency. Since we're not working any emergent cases right now—or any cases together at all—*of course* it's not going to be him.

It's Chelsea. *Did you eat?*

My stomach roars, and my sister probably heard that in her cabin in the woods. She literally lives in a mountain Hallmark town, and she probably has a three-course meal on the table right now.

Does a handful of M&M's count? I send to her, already knowing it does not. *I was going to make egg salad*, I start to type out to her as her answer-in-the-negative comes in. *But it didn't work out.*

Chelsea calls, as I knew she would. One, she hates egg

salad, so I'll hear about that. Two, she senses a good story, and boy oh boy, do I have one for her.

I flip on the call. "Hey."

"Didn't work out? Define *didn't work out.*"

THE ALARM on my phone goes off though I'm staring right at it. I set it for another minute, stand, and start shuffling folders around on my desk. I can see the seconds counting down, but I pretend like I can't.

I'm now two minutes late for my meeting with Jason, which is finally happening today. My stomach has been sick for hours, and I just want to skip out of the office early on this Thursday afternoon. It would be more like a half-day, but at this point, I'm willing to take the vacation day.

I wonder if it's too late to postpone, then I mutter to myself that of course it is. I don't need a folder. I don't need an excuse to stop by his office. There's no stopping by anyway, as his office sits in a hallway that one only goes down if they're supposed to be there. It's not like I can just "happen by" and he wouldn't wonder why.

I pick up the notebook and array of pens I've had ready for the past hour. My alarm goes off again, and this time I swipe it silent and face my door. "You've got this," I tell myself, but really I want to run to the women's room and throw up. There's nothing in my stomach, because I haven't been able to eat since last night.

Even then, I only ate because Jess stopped by with coffee and pastries, and we went over everything she's learned about Century Farm. Bottom line—it's out of my price range. I don't really want a whole farm to take care of anyway. I just want the charming, white farmhouse.

I want old. I want quaint. I want something I can work on in the evenings. No one—not even my sister—knows I read romance novels by lamplight, and I want to keep it that way. So I need another hobby, and I've always liked fixing things up.

I tug on my cardigan as I leave the office, pulling it up and over the smaller of my breasts. I hate being lopsided, and I'm sure everyone who ever looks at me is thinking how off-kilter I am. If I'm being honest, that's why I wear jackets and cardigans and other things that cover me up. It's easier to hide the bulk on the right side and try to boost the lack of bulk on the left.

I arrive at Jason's office exactly four minutes late. The door is open, but I stop in the doorway and knock. He looks over from his computer, waves me in, and says, "I have to run, Paul. I'll call you back, okay?"

He doesn't wait for confirmation before hanging up. That, or Paul is the fastest talker on the planet. I can't even think *okay* before Jason pulls the headset from his ears and tosses it on his desk. He stands, exhales heavily, and puts both hands on his back. He pushes forward, stretching his lower back, and my hormones betray me violently.

So Jason Finch is good-looking. My younger half-sister

would say something more like *drop-dead gorgeous* or *hotter than a tin roof on a Texas summer day.*

And he is. Any woman who denies that doesn't have functional eyes. Jason himself has dark eyes, and they know how to soak a woman right up. His hair is just as delicious and midnighty, but I keep those thoughts to myself.

He wears the latest fashions for men, and I'm not sure if I like that or don't. The skinny ties, the bright dress shirts, the pants that don't even reach the ankle. All of it is trying too hard in my opinion, and Jason... Well, he doesn't need to try that hard. Let's leave it at that.

"Come in," he says, and I realize I'm lurking in the doorway, staring at him.

"Your button is undone," I say stupidly, my eyes still focused somewhere in his abdominal region.

He looks down and finds the button, deftly doing it right up. Shame, as I thought I saw a peek of tan skin under all that bright blue.

I take a step toward his desk, my notebook clutched to my mismatched girls, hoping he hasn't noticed yet. All we do is bicker, so he probably hasn't. A junior partner can dream.

"I'm glad we're finally sitting down together," he says, and if I had to classify his voice, I'd call it pleasant.

I instantly narrow my eyes. Is he playing some game I don't know about yet? Does Farmer, Buhler, and Cason have some sort of hazing ritual for their junior partners?

No snakes pop out and sprinklers don't spring to life on the ceiling, so I pull out the chair, step around it, and sit.

"You can relax, Sabrina," he says, giving me a smile. I wonder how many women he's charmed with that blindingly white thing. My guess is a lot. I used to be wowed by men like him. I dated one for a year, was engaged to him for another two, and then found out that he was already married with a wife and two kids in Great Falls.

Needless to say, I left Montana before the sun rose the next day, and I nomad'ed my way around for a bit, finally landing in Charleston, at this firm.

"Okay," he says with a sigh, as I have not released a single muscle in my body. I tell myself to melt into the chair, just let go and relax, but I don't know *how*.

Jason plunks a binder on the desk between us. It's at least a two-incher, and for anyone who's been to law school, we can gauge the size of a binder in less time than it takes to blink.

"Here at FB-and-C, we have a mentoring program for junior partners," he says. "I have a senior partner as my mentor, and we all learn vertically." He has a nice speaking voice, and I almost lose my attention to the roll and swell of it. He nudges the binder a little closer to me, a clear indication I should open it.

I reach out and pull it in front of me, perching right on the front edge of the chair. I look at my array of pens and click into action a red one.

"Going for the red ink, huh?" he asks, and when I look at him, a teasing glint sits in those eyes. Oh, those eyes.

"Yes," I say simply, because my brain has gone bird on me. Small and not much there. All I can think is *peck, peck, pec-without-a-K.* My eyes drop to his chest, and he's certainly not non-symmetrical. He can probably go to the beach and do very well. Very well indeed.

"There's nothing to mark up in there," Jason says, still smiling at me. "I'd definitely go blue or black. Oh, you even brought—is that a brown pen?" He reaches for it, and I almost smack his hand away. I love my pens, and no one but me touches them.

"It is a brown pen," he says, clicking it open and closed a couple of times. He's got a plant on his desk that's seen better days, as well as a picture frame with him and Tara in one photo and him and a couple of older people in another. His parents, I'm assuming.

I hold out my hand, and he delivers my pen back to me.

"You're an interesting woman," he says, and that alone makes everything in my body light up.

"What does that mean?" I ask, and to my own surprise, it's not a snap. It's just a question.

He leans forward, his happy-go-lucky-lawyer persona —the Playboy Lawyer, I've dubbed this particular person- ally—completely gone. Just like that. A blink, and the man is someone else.

He might be a combination of the Soft Jason and the

Mentor Jason I've been dreaming about. I'm not entirely sure, because most of our interactions have been filled with snipes or silence.

"It means I think you're interesting," he says, no smile in sight. "Listen, Tara is getting married tomorrow, and I need a date. Might you be interested in going with me? She's a chef, and so is her husband. Best catering company in the city, in fact. The food will at least be good."

He shrugs like he doesn't care if I come with him or not, and I honestly can't imagine why he would. My brain goes into Big Bird mode, screaming at me in a raspy, muppety voice that *he just asked you out! He asked you out!*

"Is it a date?" I ask, sounding like Big Bird and clearing my throat to get out the feathers.

"If you'd like," he says coolly.

"No," I say just as slowly. Just because I'm not Southern born and bred doesn't mean I don't know how to do the accent. "You tell me what it is. A date to your cousin's wedding? Or a casual thing between two co-workers because you don't want to go to a wedding alone?"

I'm thirty-four, not stupid. I've seen romcoms and TV shows, and hey, I've read plenty of romance novels where the couple gets together simply to go to a wedding so they don't have to be alone. Then they fall in love. A tiny part of me wants to live out my own romance novel, and the other bigger, louder part reminds me of what happened in Montana.

Jason smiles at me now, some of all of his personalities shining through. He's smart—really smart. He likes that I can see through him, and that I don't put up with any garbage from him. He's arrogant, but right now, it's in an adorable way. Almost like him challenging me to shoot him down and make him go to his cousin's wedding alone.

"You know what?" he asks. "I'm not sure. Right now, I'm about torn right in half."

Something inside me is tearing right in half too. I raise my chin and prepare to answer him, praying my voice box won't betray me.

When I open my mouth...I don't say no.

CHAPTER TWENTY-FIVE

LANCE

"Momma," I say, my most disapproving voice set on high. "I told you I don't need a breakfast bar in the morning." I can't even take in all the food on the table. The fruit platter alone is big enough to choke a man to death. Probably several men.

"You go do your run," she says, bustling over to the groaning dining room table with a plate of bacon that practically drips grease. "This isn't for you anyway."

"The breakfast gals," Dad says, squeezing past me and sneaking a piece of bacon as Mom turns to smile at me.

I stay right where I am and let her embrace me, her smile wider than the ocean. She may live in Florida now, but my Southern momma did try to fatten me up this week. She's succeeded too, as I arrived on Monday with an empty belly to match my barren heart.

It was time for me to come visit her anyway. It doesn't

matter that she got the whole story about Jess out of me in less than an hour, and that I ate two plates of pot roast while I talked. Having everything out actually makes things easier for me to start to heal.

Strangely, however, I don't feel any better than I did when I first rang the doorbell four days ago.

"Cha-Cha and I are just going for a short run," I say as Momma steps back. I glance down at Cha-Cha, who grins up at me with her adorable corgi face. "My plane leaves at one-fifteen."

"Yep," Momma says, turning her back on me. "Aaron," she barks. "You stay away from that bacon." She marches toward him, and Daddy scoots into the living room, chuckling. I smile at them too, at the easy way they love each other and exist together. They have what I want. Something easy and casual. Something comfortable to come home to every night, and someone to share my every thought—dangerous, emotional, overjoyed —with.

I'm not sure I know what that feels like, though I thought I've been in love before. I twist the doorknob and exit the twinhome where my parents live in a fifty-five-plus community. The morning is sleepy and mostly silent, with a lawn mower buzzing somewhere one block over.

As I'm stretching out my calves, a huge Lincoln towncar the color of ruby red apples pulls up to the curb. A woman with a silver bob emerges from the passenger seat, and then the back door opens. More ladies my mother's age spill from the car, one after the other, almost like a clown car.

I hitch a smile in place, knowing I'm going to have to say hello to all of them.

"My, my," the passenger says, scanning me from head to toe. I do have my running shorts on, as well as a tank top. I mean, I haven't even started yet. "That is a good-looking...dog."

I laugh right out loud and say, "Good morning, ma'am. My momma is inside."

"Oh, a Southern boy," she says. "Even better." She gives me a wink I'm not quite sure what to do with and goes right by me. She doesn't knock or ring the bell, but simply enters the house.

All of the "breakfast gals" parade past me, each with a smile on their face. "Good morning," I drawl several times, grinning for all I'm worth. It's nice to feel like I'm worth anything at all, and I push against my feelings of self-loathing.

"Charity," the last woman says. "There's a Southern gentleman out here. Who is he?"

"Let's go, Chachy," I say to the dog. It's definitely time to get out of here.

A few hours later, I've showered, packed my bag, and stand in the kitchen again. The fruit platter is half-gone, which is a miracle in my opinion. Those ladies made short work of the bagels and bacon, and I had to eat a bowl of oatmeal with strawberries and blueberries after my run.

"Okay, Momma," I say. "I have to go. My ride will be here in a couple of minutes."

"Are you sure you have to go?" she asks as she gets up from the couch. She wears a pout as she shuffles toward me.

"Yes," I say, taking her into my arms. I don't care how old a man gets, there's nothing better than hugging his momma. I close my eyes and hold her tight, wishing she could stitch up all the loose things in my life. "Tara's getting married tomorrow, and I will never be forgiven if I miss it."

"Maybe Jess will be there," Momma says, stepping back. She wears such bright hope in her face, and I wish I could erase it for her.

"Momma," I say. I don't have much else to add. "I broke up with her."

"Yes, but you didn't want to. Just talk to her, baby. She's not going to abandon you, I just know it."

I nod, because if I agree, then we can leave with smiles and hugs, not an open argument. Jess has called a couple of times, but I didn't answer. She left messages that nearly filleted my muscles right from my bones, and I texted her back with a few crisp words about what she should do.

Both messages held pauses, and in those, I heard so many things. I've laid awake at night every day since Sunday, wondering what I can or should do about her. As far as I know, she returned to Charleston on Thursday, as she'd planned to do. Yes, her plans had changed over time, but she'd communicated them to me professionally. I have no cause to fire her. Yet I cannot stand the thought of walking into Finley & Frank on Monday morning and seeing her in my office.

I simply can't do it. I couldn't even go to work this week and see her desk, with its picture frames and neat to-do trays and that lamp she'd bought on our weekend excursion only a couple of days before she'd gone to the city. The base was a high-fashion woman going to the Kentucky Derby, with the shade as her ridiculously huge hat.

Jess had confessed that she's always wanted to go to the Derby and wear a big hat and a skirt that flared out only on one side. I'd asked her if she'd designed the skirt already, and she'd said yes, she had a sketch of it somewhere.

My phone chimes, reminding me I'm still standing in my parents' kitchen. "My ride is here," I say, and Momma moves out of the way so I can hug my dad.

"Travel safe, son," he says. "And listen to your momma." He hasn't given me a lot of lectures this week. He just let me go golfing with him—neither of us having to lose to the other. He talked to me about the agency and family life. He put on movies at night so I could zone out.

"I love you," I say to him, and he nods as he steps back.

"Love you too, Lance."

With that, I pick up Cha-Cha's leash in one hand and grip the handle on her carrier and the one on my suitcase, and we head for the door. Aaron opens it for me, and I leave the sanctuary I've found this week.

On the plane back to South Carolina, I wonder if I should drop Chachy at home and then drive south. Beaufort is only an hour from Charleston, and I could just drop by the Dunaways. Perhaps I could learn something more about Jess. Perhaps I could talk to her daddy and tell him I'm in love with his daughter, but I made a mistake. Ask him how to fix it.

My eyes drift closed as my thoughts do their train-thing and run across the country and back.

I've ignored Dawson and Callie all week, and they'll probably be at the airport with pitchforks and protest signs. Or pizza. Probably pizza. I smile to myself, something my momma said popping into my mind.

I don't see why you have to propose, she'd says. *You can say I love you without asking will you marry me?*

I'd told Momma I wasn't in love with Jess. I'd denied it vehemently, in fact. I didn't need to say anything more to her. I just needed...time. Just like with Hadley, I need *time* to figure out where I went wrong, and if it's worth even trying ever again. No matter what I do with a woman, it always ends up the same. Me alone, with my heart broken, and I'm really, really tired of that.

The plane lands, as planes do, and Cha-Cha and I wait our turn to get off. I've carried everything on with me, so I head for the doggie potty and then the regular one before making my way past security and toward the airport exit.

I drove myself to the airport and parked in the expensive lot, but I don't care. I couldn't ask Dawson to help me run away, and I didn't even tell him I wasn't in Charleston until he texted on Tuesday night, asking it I wanted to meet him for a game of basketball.

"Lance!" someone yells, and I know exactly who it is. Callie.

I turn toward her, my heart doing this stupid swelling thing at the sight of her, Dawson, Tara, and Alec all standing behind the barrier that keeps those waiting for their loved ones out of the flow of traffic.

They're here. They're here for me, even with everything I lack in my life. I want to cry, but I smile instead, pushing back the embarrassing tears.

"Oh, you let me have Cha-Cha," Tara says, as if I've been abusing her by making her fly to visit my parents. She got duck treats every few minutes on the plane, for crying out loud. She takes the leash from me just before Dawson grips me in a huge hug.

"You're never to leave the city without telling me again," he says thickly.

He's my very best friend in the world, and I should've known I can go to him. The problem is, the last time a woman cracked my heart in half, Dawson had broken up with Callie. He'd run to my rescue instead of hers, and I just can't be responsible for that again.

He steps back, his dark eyes actually harboring anger. "Do you hear me?"

"Yes, sir," I drawl at him, nodding seriously. His wife engulfs me too, telling me she almost flew down there just to make sure I was safe, and she would have if Dawson hadn't shown her my pin and told her I was with my momma.

When she looks me in the eye, I see her concern. I don't need another mother, but at the same time, it sure is nice to know she wants to take care of me. I clap Alec in a hug, and then Tara, and I get my suitcase moving. "You guys ready for the wedding tomorrow?"

"Absolutely," Alec says, throwing Tara a smile. She melts like marshmallows in the microwave and nods.

"Nope," Callie says firmly. "We're not talking about the wedding."

I look at her, surprised. "Oh-kay?"

She's got a power walk going, her heels clicking along the tile as she strides toward the rectangle of light that's the exit. "No," she says firmly again. "And you're not taking your car. You're riding with us."

"It's ten dollars a day to park here," I say. "I'm not leaving Mammoth for another—" I cut off when I name my truck. I freeze right to the spot, unable to keep walking.

Everyone else slows too, taking an extra step or two before realizing I've halted.

My mind races, and I blink, everything around me fading and muting. Callie grins, and Dawson steps toward me. White noise fills my ears, and while I'm extremely grateful my friends have come to greet me, I wish Jess were here.

I clear my throat and say, "I wish Jess were here."

"Exactly," Callie says.

I look at her and then Tara, who also wears a kind smile. "I need help," I say, sounding like I've swallowed sand. "How do I get her back? Do I just show up and what? Apologize?"

Callie loops her arm through mine. "Okay, I'm going to tell you something, Lance Byers, and you will not be upset. Deal?"

I glance at Dawson as Callie gently tows me toward the exit. He grins and shrugs one shoulder, his eyebrows going up in sync with his arm.

"I'll try," I say.

"Tara and I, we talk to Jess," Callie says. "I don't know a lot of details, but she has mentioned an alphabet adjective game you two have been playing...yes? You know what I'm talking about?"

"Yes, ma'am," I say, my throat as narrow as a straw.

"She's going to be at the wedding tomorrow," Tara says, drawing my attention to her. "I'm sure there will be a few minutes where the mic is...open." She glances at Alec, who nods.

"So you want me to..." I leave the sentence there, wishing these women would fill it in with a complete plan. Bullet points would be ideal.

"Dress up nice," Callie says. "Show up to the wedding. Have a speech prepared that uses your little game. She'll take you back."

"You've forgiven her, right?" Alec asks.

I nod, because I have. She didn't really do anything wrong, unless I want to label chasing your dreams as wrong. I don't. Not for Jess. She has big wings that have been tied to her back for decades. I'm not going to be the one to clip them or re-bind them. I can't believe I did in the first place.

Ideas pop through my head, and I let Callie lead me to the bus stop. "If you're not at our house in thirty minutes, I'm coming over," she says. "We have a lot more planning to do, Mister."

"Yes, ma'am," I say again, and I give them all one more big hug before they leave with Cha-Cha and her kennel and I wait for the bus that will take me back to Mammoth.

A public apology isn't really my style, but it might be time to unbutton that top button and let loose a little. I've never wanted to do that, but for Jess...

I'll do anything for Jess.

CHAPTER TWENTY-SIX

TARA

I turn as someone ducks into the room, thinking it might be Alec. He's been trying to get in and sneak a peek at my dress all day. Or at least he's been teasing me about it.

It's not my fiancé—about to become my husband—but it is a man. "Lance," I say, hurrying toward him though I barely wear any clothes. Jess and Callie are a little late with the dress, that's all. Callie's never late to anything, but Jess texted to say there "might have been a mishap," but that she was taking care of it.

I'd texted back in all caps—*TELL ME WHAT YOU MEAN BY MISHAP*—and she hasn't responded. I'm about four seconds away from losing my cool, but I take a deep breath and flick a look over to my mother. She doesn't even tear her attention from her phone, so she must really be texting up a storm with her sister-in-law.

Jason's mother is out front right now, making sure all of the flowers and tablecloths get set up in the right place. I know how to keep Aunt Cynthia busy, and that's to give her something that she feels in control of. I haven't told her that I met with the decorators four separate times, and they know what they're doing without her help.

I told Janet, the lead wedding planner, to text me if my aunt becomes a problem.

"What are you doing here?" I hiss at Lance. "Jess could walk in at any moment."

"Dawson has Callie on maps," he says. "They're seven minutes away." He glances around the room as if just now realizing that he's standing in the brides' room. He focuses on my face again, his nerves higher than mine. "Tara."

"No," I tell him in my best kitchen-boss voice, which admittedly, isn't impressive. "Lance, you've got this. Now, this is my wedding, and I'm letting you intrude on it." I link my arm through his and lead him toward the door. "You shouldn't be in here. You have roses to arrange and a banner to check on."

His real estate game face slides into position. "You're right. Of course you're right." He opens the door and takes a step into the hall at the same time Dawson yells his name.

"The app hadn't updated," he says, jogging down the hall in his dark suit and tie. "They just pulled in. Let's go. Out this door." He hustles Lance out the door at the wrong end of the hall, and I hold my breath, waiting for the emergency exit alarm to sound.

It doesn't, and I retreat back to the full-length mirror, stinging ants in my stomach. I'm not nervous about marrying Alec. I'm in love with him, and I already know he's here. He's moved about half of what he owns into my house already, and Tommy and Goose seem to like him more than me, the canine traitors.

I worry about being enough for him. Not him, exactly. His mother. She has not come into the brides' room, though I personally invited her via text, email, and a direct phone call. She's...iffy on giving me her plans, and I have to force myself not to care. Merging two lives is hard, and while Alec doesn't seem super-close to his family, I know he's been working on his relationships with them.

The door opens again, and I spin as a giant white dress enters before the woman holding it. "It's fine," Callie says from somewhere in all the lace and fabric. "Nothing to worry about, Tara."

"Mishap?" I say, practically running in my slip and undergarments toward her. We'd gone bra shopping together, and I do have the best support on the market for a wedding dress. Jess and I have tried the dress on at least a dozen times, and it's perfect. But that was all before the word *mishap* got sent.

"We were loading the dress," Jess says, coming into the room and closing the door. Her hair is extra-curly today, and she is so...perfect for Lance. I smile at her, and she lets

Callie handle the dress while my mom gets to her feet. "And my upstairs-neighbor's cat comes streaking out of the backyard, right?"

Jess steps into me and gives me a light hug. "Cats have claws, you know."

I look at the dress, which doesn't seem to be clawed to shreds. "This is why I have dogs."

"Dogs have claws too," Callie says, turning to face us. "And Claude Monet is declawed. Don't blame this on the whole species."

I grin at her, and she smiles back, tilting her head. "You're getting married today."

I open my arms to her, and she flies into them. We hold each other tightly, because this is a big day for me. My first marriage was oh-so-bad, and I really want to make the second go-round work. I can. I will. Alec loves me.

"Anyway," Jess says, plunking down her purse. "There was a little mishap. I needed my sewing machine, and I got it all sorted."

I step back from Callie, and we both look at the dress. "I'm getting cold in this slip," I say. "Mom."

She abandons her phone, and together with Callie and Jess, they help me into my wedding gown. I've worn it before. I've seen myself in it from toes to the top of my head. Somehow, today, it's different.

The four of us stand there and look at my image in the mirror, and I'm in love with the dress. "It's perfect," I whisper.

"So are you," Callie says. "Now, come on. Put on your shoes, and let's go."

I do what she says, my heart thumping out a couple of extra beats, because I know what's coming for Jess. I glance at her a couple of times, and she seems relatively normal. She's distracted and busy right now, though, and I wonder what it's been like for her at night this past week.

Probably terrible, and once she has my feet in the right shoes and the box put away, she meets my eyes. "What?" she asks.

"Nothing."

"You've been staring at me," she says, planting her hands on her thighs and straightening. She's a bridesmaid —which really helped the plan with Lance—and she wears the lavender dress like a pro. So does Callie, of course, because she can make any dress, skirt, or blouse look like a million bucks.

"How are you?" I ask. "I feel like I haven't seen you... in a while."

"I was literally at your house until nine o'clock last night," she says, cocking her hip. She looks at Callie, who wears a forced, I'm-so-innocent smile. "This is about Lance."

"Hey, she can say his name," Callie says, looking at me.

"I'm not talking about Lance," Jess says, picking up her purse and then putting it back down. "I don't need this."

"No," I say, grinning at her. "What did you eat for breakfast this morning?"

Jess's eyes fly right back to mine. Several seconds go by before she says, "I don't want to say."

"Probably cereal with orange juice," Callie says. "That's what happened to this friend of mine when her boyfriend broke up with her."

"I can't even remember the days after me and Alec broke up," I say. "They're like this black hole."

"Stop it," Jess says, but her voice holds no power. "He's going to be here, and I already don't know what to say to him." She shakes her head and looks away. "I'm fine. We'll be fine."

"Maybe you should just not say anything," Callie says. "You can just find him and kiss him."

Jess's laughter explodes out of her. "Right," she says with plenty of sarcasm. She brushes at her eyes. "If I want to ruin Tara's wedding, which I don't."

"Tara, five minutes," someone says from the doorway, and I wave to acknowledge I've heard Janet. "Bridesmaids are lining up," she adds.

Since I only have three, and two-thirds of them are standing in front of me, we have time.

Jess sniffles once, her makeup still perfect. "I'm walking with Jason, yes?" she asks.

I don't have the heart to lie to her, so I don't say anything. She doesn't wait for an answer anyway. I'd texted Jason about walking down the aisle with Jess the moment I'd heard she and Lance had split up.

Then, once Lance got home, I'd texted again that the plan had changed. He'd told me not to worry about him, that he'd found a date to the wedding. He won't tell me who it is, and I haven't had time to go spy.

"Okay," Callie says with a big sigh. "Let's get these chickens married."

She leads the way out of the brides' room, my mom hot on her heels. I exit last, and my daddy is waiting right there for me. I smile at him and link my arm through his.

"You're beautiful," he says, and we wait in the hallway while the others go get in line. Since I've catered for so many people around the city, I was able to book the indoor gardens at the library, which is a wonderful, if intimate, space. I don't mind, because Alec didn't want a big wedding.

My family isn't huge, but I do have employees and important clients I wanted to invite. In all, there should be about sixty or seventy people in the grand hall, and we'll feed everyone a dinner Alec and I put together ourselves.

The line in front of me starts to move, and there's no fighting or screeching, so Jason must have Jess on his arm. Lance will be further up in the line—the first, actually—with Dawson between Jason and Jess. Jared, one of my chefs, is also walking in the wedding party, as well as both of Alec's brothers. They all have wives, and I'm fine with the ladies walking down the aisle ahead of me too.

Janet waves to me from the cusp of the hallway, and I move forward with my father. The crowd starts to come into view, and my heart races around my inside my chest. I deliberately move slow, and I tell myself not to look toward the altar the moment I make it past the corner of the wall.

I fail, and my eyes land on Alec instantly. Everything in the world is now oh-so-right, and I can't help the huge smile that touches my face. He's grinning too, and he actually lifts one hand in a shoulder-height wave. He is just the absolute cutest, and I can't believe he chose me.

I don't wave back, because one hand holds my enormous bouquet, and the other is tucked in my dad's elbow. I can't take my eyes from him, though, as we arrive at the head of the aisle.

Alec clasps his hands in front of him, his smile beaming the way toward him. I hope he'll be able to put up with my squawking chickens, and our late nights together, and me running next door to Mr. Reynolds all the time.

And Callie and Dawson, and Jess, and Jason, and everyone else in my life who is so important to me.

Dad takes me down the aisle, shakes Alec's hand, and passes me to him. Alec wears stars in his eyes, and he leans in close, takes a deep breath of me, and says, "I love you, Tara."

I don't need anyone else or anything else, and we turn toward the altar. As I do, I see Sabrina Shadows sitting on the front row, an empty seat next to her. I jolt, my eyes flying to Jason's. He gives nothing away—which totally gives him away.

Even as my mind races down a path, screaming, *I thought he didn't like her!* I shelve the information to deal with later.

I'm getting married right now, after all.

"Welcome to the wedding of Tara and Alec," the pastor says as the guests start to seat themselves.

"Wait," a man calls out, and I glance to my left, where the sound of Lance's voice came from. Alec's hand in mine tightens, and we grin at each other.

This is going to be perfect.

CHAPTER TWENTY-SEVEN

LANCE

I STEP OUT OF THE LINE, MY HEART BEATING LIKE A great big, huge bass drum. *Two minutes*, I tell myself. *You can do anything for two minutes.* With seventy pairs of eyes on me, I'm not so sure.

I've been featured in magazines and on websites, and I'm used to being in the spotlight. Just not a live spotlight, so this is a different type of stage.

Everything Alec gave me to say to Jess streams through my head. They've been best friends for a long time, and he knows her. He knows what she wants to hear.

I do too.

"I can't stand here," I say, gesturing to the horrible spot on the end where I can't see Jess on the other side of Alec and Tara. I walk past Dawson, who's grinning at me like a fool. I swallow, taking strength from him.

"Because I can't see you, Jess." I make it past Tara and

Alec, who've stepped back out of the way. Everyone is silent. Deathly Still with a capital D and S. "I can't stand being at this wedding without you on my arm."

She looks like she's been struck by thunder and then lightning.

"I made a mistake," I blurt out. "I don't want to break-up. I'm—I just wasn't thinking clearly on Sunday. I want to be with you. Can you find any way to forgive me?" I might've missed a couple of things in there, what with all my ADHD and my derailed thoughts.

"Alphabet," Tara coughs out, and I startle.

Jess has started to open her mouth, and I hold up my hand. "Wait."

Her mouth snaps shut, the surprise in those sapphire eyes striking me in the chest. "I think you're articulate, clever, easy to talk to—I miss talking to you so much—and gorgeous. When I got to G, I was afraid to say that, but I'm not anymore. You're *stunningly* gorgeous, and I need you at my side today, tomorrow, and at the agency on Monday."

Callie, who's manning the front of the line of ladies sighs, and her smile encourages me to keep going. "You're interesting, kind, and I'm mad for you. You're open-minded, and an over-achiever, and I love both about you." I have more letters for her that we've gone back and forth with, but I pause to take a breath after the O.

"Okay," she says, reaching up to wipe her eyes. "You can stop."

"You owe me an X and a Z-word," I say anyway, swallowing afterward. "I'm sorry. I'm so sorry."

"You don't have anything to be sorry for," she says, her voice high-pitched and tinny.

"Go kiss him," Tara says, and I'm so grateful for her. Callie too. She steps out of the way, giving Jess free access to get to me. I simply stand there and give Jess a moment. She usually needs one or two or twelve.

I see the instant she's processed everything I've said, and in the next breath, she rushes toward me. I take her into my arms, breathing normally for the first time in seven days. The crowd behind us starts to cheer, led by the bride and groom.

"You don't need to apologize," Jess says, her voice so soft in my ear. "I'm the one who needs to say sorry for not calling you. I'm sorry."

"Kiss me, and we'll agree that we both have some room to improve in our behavior from this past weekend."

Jess grins up at me, and I experience a blitzing, buzzing feeling moving through my whole body. I think it's...*joy*, and I hope I can feel it every single day for the rest of my life. If I have Jess at my side, I'm confident I will.

And when she tips her head back and closes her eyes, waiting for me to kiss her, I'm very aware of *alllll* the eyes.

I kiss her anyway, and Dawson's whoop fills the whole hall and echoes through my soul. I make the same sound internally, because kissing Jess is the single best thing I've ever done.

————

"I'M JUST SAYING," Jess says right before she presses her lips to mine again. "If you apologize again, I'm going to get mad and stop kissing you."

"Mm." I pull her back against my chest. "I'm sorry." I grin at her. "I won't say I'm sorry again." I kiss her, because let's be real. *She* wasn't kissing me. *I'm* kissing her. I should be switching my laundry from the washing machine to the dryer or ordering something for dinner, but the moment Jess walked in, my regular life imploded, and all I could think about was kissing her.

We've been doing that for a while, and I finally take a breath and look around my house. Cha-Cha is lying on the floor in front of the fireplace, looking dejected and forlorn. That's about normal. Everything else seems different. With Jess back in my life, I feel like I can see color again. I hadn't realized how gray and drab every-thing had turned until she'd returned and brightened everything up again.

"Okay," I say, stepping back so she can move away from the front door. That's right. I didn't even let her get out of the doorway before I kissed her. "Dinner? I think you came over for dinner."

"You said you'd cook."

"I lied," I say, giving her a quick smile. "I didn't have time."

"Who called?"

"My momma," I say, leading the way into the kitchen at the back of the house. Chachy jumps to her feet and follows us on her short little legs. "Then Ruth."

Jess doesn't ask if they're badgering me about asking her to marry me. She knows it bothers me, but it's not because they're wondering when I'll ask Jess to be my wife. It's them warning me to take my time.

I can admit I need a little bit more time to get to a place where I'm thinking diamonds and such. Not only that, but I'd saved for three months to buy Hadley's diamond ring, and Jess comes from a far wealthier family than she had.

We haven't talked about gems or gowns yet at all, other than me complaining that my momma wants me to go real slow and make sure I'm very certain before getting down on my knees and popping the question for the third time.

"Are they still sick from Thanksgiving?" Jess gets on the barstool while I open the drawer beside the fridge and pull out the delivery menus.

"Don't seem to be," I say. We'd gone to Thanksgiving dinner with Callie and Dawson, at Callie's parents' place. I'd called Momma, who'd had Ruth and her family down to Florida. Apparently, they'd all gotten sick the night of Thanksgiving, and Ruth is *positive* with a double capital P it's because the stuffing was underdone.

"I don't want to leave the house," I say. If we stay in, I can kiss her more later. "So let's do delivery." I toss the menus on the counter. "You look for a sec. I just remembered I'm waiting for that three-pack of ties, and I got a notification that it was delivered."

She grins at me as I bustle out of the kitchen, then hurry back in to give her a kiss. "You'll help me match them with my shirts, right? You should've seen me last week. It was so pathetic."

"You didn't even go to work last week," she murmurs against my lips, and since I don't want to revisit last week ever again—even if I spent it in sunny Florida with my folks—I just kiss her again.

She lets me for a second, and then she giggles and pushes me away. "Go get your mail. Hurry up so we can order. I'm hungry."

"Yes, ma'am," I tell her. I dash outside and get my mail, then jog back inside. Jess still sits at the counter, and she looks up at me when I enter the house.

"Xerothermic," she says.

I throw the rest of the envelopes and junk on the table just inside the door, retaining the package of ties. "What?" I have no idea what restaurant she's just chosen, and I frown as I walk toward her.

"That's your X-word," she says, grinning at me from that barstool. "It means dry and hot."

I blink, then start laughing.

"Because your sense of humor is so dry," she explains,

as if I need her to. "And you're seriously the hottest man I've ever met."

I appreciate the compliment, but I just finish chuckling and shake my head. I rip open the flap on the package and pull out the bundle of ties.

"Lance," she says, jumping to her feet.

"Hmm?" I look up as she picks up the ties.

Her eyes widen, and she meets my gaze. "These are Burt Carol ties."

I look at them and then her. That obviously means something in the fashion world. Kira nor Tim has called her since she left New York, and she's putting on a really brave face about all of it. I know the rejection stings, though, and while I haven't brought up her sketches or heard much more about her time in the city, she and I still have time to talk about so many things.

"Yes," I say as if I knew all along what kind of tie I was buying. "My dad says they're the best." I take the package from her and start to peel off yet another layer of plastic.

"Your dad," she says, folding her arms.

"Who's—what did you say? Whatever X-word you used for dry and hot. That. Who's that now?"

"Xerothermic."

"That." I grin at her as the last of the crinkly plastic comes off. I drop it on the floor for Cha-Cha, who likes to roll around with it for some reason. Maybe the noise it makes. "You're being very xerothermic right now."

"I don't believe your dad told you about these ties."

"Dawson then," I say, peeling back a blue one from the roll.

"Lance."

"I don't know where I saw them," I finally admit. "Okay? Who is this guy?"

"He's only the very best pattern designer in the world," she says, still plenty of xerothermic qualities in her voice. "He makes the most beautiful fabrics, and then you can construct the most beautiful garments ever."

"Okay," I say. "Well, I did like his ties." I hold up the blue one to my neck. "Yeah?"

"It's a bright one," she says. "I love the little moons on it." She smiles, and everything that's ever been tilted in the world straightens.

I order the Chinese food she wants, and she goes through my closet and matches my new ties to some dress shirts. The doorbell rings, and she's already in the living room with Cha-Cha on her lap while I'm washing out the dog bowl in the kitchen.

"I got it," she says, and I let her open the door and take the Chinese food.

I finish feeding and watering Cha-Cha, who now seems to like Jess more than me, and turn to help Jess with the food. She's already put it on the counter, and she's holding a small package.

"What's that?" I take out the first container of Chinese food, the scent of sweet and sour sauce hitting me in the face.

"It was on the floor by the front door," she says, her voice somewhat awed. "You maybe dropped it when you brought in the mail?" She looks up at me, and my mind kicks at me that something is happening here.

I pause in the unpacking of ham fried rice and watch as she holds up the package. "It's got a return address on it," she says. "It's from Hadley Brown."

All of my muscles go dormant, and the only reason I stay standing is because of the counter in front of me. I somehow reach for the package, though my brain has been disconnected from the rest of my body. I take the package from Jess, and it's small enough for me not to have noticed it in my haste to get the ties.

There doesn't seem to be a box inside, but something stiff like cardboard.

"She's your ex-girlfriend, right?" Jess asks.

"Fiancée," I tell her, but she knows. Everyone knows.

I rip open the package, my heartbeat drowning out the sound of the paper tearing. Between two pieces of cardboard sits a small envelope. I didn't even know someone made envelopes this small. It's not sealed, and I can reach two fingers inside.

I touch metal, and I suck in a breath. I know what this is. I can't get my fingers around the ring, but it comes out when I pull my hand back.

The diamond ring I bought for Hadley tumbles to the countertop, and both Jess and I scramble to make sure it doesn't fall on the floor. Once it's settled and still, we both just stare at it.

"Is there a note?" Jess asks, her voice made only of whispers.

"No." There's nothing but the packaging, the cardboard, and the teeny tiny envelope. This is bizarre, and I'm not sure what to think. I need some time to wrap my head around this strange occurrence.

Jess reaches out and picks up the ring. "Wow, Lance," she says. "This is really nice." She looks at me, which breaks the spell I've fallen under.

"Yeah," I say. "Three months' salary."

Jess admires the ring, seemingly scrutinizing every facet of the gem. "Are you going to get me a ring like this?"

I swallow, not sure what to say. I haven't told her I love her. She hasn't said those three words to me. "I mean, not like that one," I say.

She meets my gaze. "No?"

"This isn't a ring you'd like," I say, gently taking it from her. I drop it back into the envelope and press it between the cardboard again. "It's too...fussy."

"Was Hadley fussy?"

"Hadley was extremely fussy," I say, smiling as I do.

Jess steps around the corner of the island and runs her hands up my chest. "What kind of ring would you buy for me?"

With my hands on her waist and the two of us swaying to silent music in my kitchen, I say, "I don't know. Something unique. Dang, that should've been my U-word for you." I grin down at her and lean forward to kiss her quickly. "Something...classic. Sophisticated."

"Oh, don't go too far," she says. "But I do like a princess-cut diamond, and then yes, go with classic and unique."

I clear my throat. "I'll keep that in mind."

Jess steps out of my arms and picks up one of the containers of Chinese food. "I'm not in a hurry, Lance. Besides, you still need to figure out a Y-word, and I've given you a whole week before I bounced the ball back into your court."

She gives me a look that I better get this letter right, or she might turn me into a frog with one of her withering stares.

I have a feeling I'm going to be ribbiting soon, because I've done Internet searches, and there are no adjectives that start with Y. At least none I'm going to say to the woman I'm almost in love with.

There's always yummy, I think. Then I dismiss it, hopefully for the last time. *She's not a dessert...*

CHAPTER TWENTY-EIGHT

JESSIE

Lance eases Mammoth to a stop in front of the cream-colored mansion, and neither one of us get out. The whole estate bears lights that are just starting to twinkle on this December-near-dusk.

"Ready?" he asks.

I can't nod or shake my head. I'm neutral. I think of the past six months, then twelve. So much has changed since I left Beaufort, left this little community of Ashford, left the first part of my life behind.

"I can't think of a Y-word," he says, and that draws my attention from the pine wreath with the giant red bow on the front door. He keeps his gaze on it as I watch the frustration roll through him. "There's nothing good. I can't say some of them, because they're rude. The ones that aren't are stupid."

He sighs. "I mean, I can't say you're *yummy*, even though I seriously want to taste your lips every second of every day. I can't say you're *youthful*, because we just had a conversation about skin cream on the way down here and I have a feeling you'll think I didn't try." He looks at me, pure energy blazing in those eyes. "I would say *year-long*, because I want to spend years and years with you. But that's idiotic. It's not even an adjective. It's something you say when you're like, battling cancer or something. 'A yearlong battle with cancer.'"

He blows out his breath, shakes his head, and looks at the front of the house again. "Y is a stupid letter."

"How about there's a Y in there somewhere?" I suggest.

He yanks his attention back to me. "Just a Y in the word? Why didn't you tell me that?"

I reach for the door handle, a laugh already starting in his chest. "Because I didn't know you were going to go to *yearlong*." I open the door and slide to the ground. Lance joins me at the corner of the hood, taking his hand in mine.

"Have you tried to find a Y-word?" he asks.

"I have," I say. "They're all *yucky*."

That breaks his moody-mood, and I grin up at him. The gesture falters quickly. "I need you today."

"I'm right here," he assures me, and we face the mansion together. I'm not sure if Amelia or Jonathan will be here, but my guess is yes. If not now, then they'll arrive later. Mama has never been one to not plan a party if there's an opportunity for one.

Lance and I are halfway up the stairs to the yawning front porch when the front door opens. Daddy steps out, and he looks older than I remember. Tears fill my eyes, and I fly up the rest of the steps and into his arms.

"Hey, sugar-doll," he says quietly, holding me so tight.

I can't say anything. The only sounds I hear are my own heartbeat and the footfalls of my boyfriend. I step back and wipe my tears real quick. Lance is a TUB—the ultimate boyfriend—because he's tall, handsome, employed, and smiling at my father like he's genuinely glad to meet him.

"Daddy," I say, all Southern-proper-like. "This is my boyfriend, Lance Byers. Lance, my daddy, Rutherford."

"Pleasure to meet you," Lance says, and he delivers it in his REA voice. The real estate agent in him is surely going to come in handy this weekend.

"The pleasure is mine," Daddy says, and they shake hands.

"Why is this door open?" My mother's voice comes from inside the house. "Rutherford, it's cold outside."

It's nowhere near cold out here, and we all turn toward the doorway as Mama fills it. "Oh." Her eyes round, and her perfectly painted mouth drops open. One hand presses against her heart and then plays with the biggest green gem I've ever seen. "My baby."

"I'm not the Prodigal Son," I say, rolling my eyes

though my heart is rejoicing to see my mama again. I smile at her, because I've learned a thing or two in the offices of Finley & Frank too, thank you very much. I move into her arms, where she holds me and cries into my shoulder.

I wasn't expecting that, though I suppose Daddy and Amy have always been the strong one in our family.

"You knew they-all were comin'," Daddy drawls. "Pull yourself together, Constance."

Mama sniffles as she does that, and I sweep my hand toward Lance. The vein in his throat bobs with his pulse, exactly the way it did at Tara and Alec's wedding. Just like it does when he's nervous. It's the only sign of his nerves I've ever, ever seen, and I realize in that moment how much I love him.

My voice chokes, because I can't just blurt out those three words for the first time in front of my parents. "Mama," I say, a waver in the word. "This is Lance, my boyfriend. Lance-honey, this is my Mama." I beam at him and then her, wondering if love can be conveyed with a simple look or if the words have to be spoken.

As he says how supremely happy he is to have met Mama, I realize that the phrase *I love you* has a Y in it.

He steps back and reaches for me, his love for me right there in his eyes. It's present in the fact that he found a dogsitter for Cha-Cha so we could come to my parents' house this weekend for Mama's holiday parties. It flows between us, because he's right next to me, at my side, supporting me here in Beaufort.

Now I just have to figure out how to say the words out loud, and I wonder if the Z-word I've chosen can help me.

———

MONDAY MORNING ARRIVES, and with it, I bring a platter of cheese, fruit, and wafer crackers into Finley & Frank. Olive meets me at the door, her eyes wide and her hands helpful. "Thanks," I tell her as she holds open the door.

The sun has barely lit the sky, but Lucy got me here just fine. My stomach buzzes, and I wish I could quiet the bees inside. Since I can't—I haven't been able to since arriving at my parents' mansion in Beaufort and realizing I was in love with Lance—I just smile through the wasps and head for my boss's office.

He's never kissed me in there, and I'm about to blow open every barrier he's put between us. In the beginning, I agreed with them, but not anymore. We work together, and I hope to be as good of a real estate agent as he is one day. It's been three weeks since I returned to Charleston from New York, and I haven't heard from any of the contacts I made there.

I haven't emailed anyone either, so I'm probably as much to blame for the silence. Other designers probably send follow-up texts and messages, and I haven't. I'm still trying to decide what I want my fashion sketches to be, because I might not want them to be anything but what they already are. An escape for me. A way to express my creativity and to dream big.

I think of Tara as Olive unlocks Lance's office, the tray of fruit starting to weigh too much for me. Tara goes after her dreams, first with Saucebilities, and then with her cookbook. I know she worked on it for a long time—over a year, I think Alec said—before she did anything with it, and she might not have been able to do much without the help of Dawson's mother.

"Got it," Olive says, and I smile at her before dashing into the office. It's chilly inside this morning, as we didn't come in this weekend. Lance hasn't worked weekends since the open house a while ago, and I'm glad for that. We've been taking more and more weekend excursions, and I like those far better than talking escrows and money and terminology.

He's still teaching me, and I'm still learning a whole lot. I haven't found anything for Sabrina, but I did just start working with another client who I'm excited about. Farrah reminds me a lot of myself, though she's ten years younger than I am. She's new to the city and looking for an apartment or rent-to-own house. She's just my style, and I actually have a few listings to show her today when she drops by.

"Got it?" Olive asks, bringing in the wad of balloons I'd asked her to pick up yesterday. They float above her head, resisting the movement as she strides toward the desk, where I set down the fruit platter and sigh in relief.

"Yes," I say, smiling at the bobbing balloons. "Thank you so much for getting these." I take the balloons from her and set them behind the tray.

"Is it Mister Byers' birthday?" she asks.

"No," I say, grinning at the deep eggplant balloons, interspersed with pale yellow and baby blue. "I just—we have something to celebrate." I grin at her, and Olive nods.

"I'll leave you to it."

"Okay." I'm super early to work, but that's because I knew if I didn't come at seven a.m., I might flee the state. I press my hands together and tell myself to calm down. Lance stepped out of line at Tara and Alec's wedding, and in front of scads of strangers, he said he wanted to be with me.

I can do this.

Lance doesn't usually get to F&F until about nine, and I sit down at my computer and print out the things I need for Farrah. I check my email messages, my throat constricting when I see one from Jason Finch.

For a while there, he acted like he was going to hire Lance, but his email says he wants to work with me. I have no idea what that means, and I narrow my eyes as I open the email. DTAP runs through my head: Don't trust a player, but I wonder if Jason's changed.

He's been professional with me the last few times I've interacted with him, and he was downright gentlemanly at Alec's wedding. He'd shown up with Sabrina Shadows on his arm, and she'd been stunningly gorgeous with her hair down, her makeup more pronounced, and a gown the color of tangerines gripping her curves.

All at once, I realize what Jason wants. It's not me, and it's not necessarily my services. It's Sabrina Shadows. I'm unaware if they've seen each other since the wedding, and I can't remember anything after Lance stepped out of line and kissed me before the ceremony began. But they were there together...

I don't answer his email yet, and I let my eyes scan down the list. I get a lot of junk here at work, but one subject line catches my eye. *Would still love to work with you,* and the sender is Kira Chatwood.

I gasp, then try to breathe normally as I open the email. I think my brain has forgotten what normal is, because my lungs seem non-functional as I scan her two line email.

I enjoyed meeting you in New York. I've been busy, but I'd love to set up a time to chat further.

Her number sits below that, though I did manage to get it before I left the city.

"He's here," Olive hisses over the copier, and I jump to my feet without closing the email. I can't think about this right now. I don't know what to do about it.

I hurry around my desk, trying to get my game face in place. I hear Lance's voice as I duck into his office, which is where he'll expect me to be for our usual Monday morning meeting. MMM, that's what I've dubbed, it and

Lance even uses the acronym when he's texting me about work now.

We'll go over that in our MMM, he says. *I don't want to think about it again this week.*

My heart thunders through my chest as he greets Olive and gets anything she has for him. He then enters his office wearing his long, wool coat, though no one in South Carolina really needs one, December or not.

He's tieless, of course, because I still pick his neckwear every morning, but his slacks are perfectly pressed, and the dress shirt peeking at me from beneath the coat is pale pink. He carries his briefcase bag and a carrier of coffee, one of which is for me.

He pauses, his eyes taking in the tray and the balloons. "What's going on?" he asks slowly, finally committing to entering the office. He toes the door closed behind him, which sometimes happens and sometimes doesn't. After all, there's never been any kissing in here.

Until today, I think, pressing my palms together. He sees that and offers me a smile. "You're nervous."

"I have your Z-word ready," I say. "Put your stuff down first."

He does what I say, laying out four choices for a tie. I pick a brown and navy blue one and step over to him to tie it for him.

"Lance," I say. "You're a creature of habit, which I love about you. I don't quite know what you do at home before you leave for work, but I'm guessing you pick out your clothes the night before."

"Maybe," he says, his voice still wary. He should be, as I've never brought in fruit and cheese and balloons before.

I focus on looping the longer tail of the tie around the shorter one. "Your Z-word is zonal. It means divided into zones. You like things in their compartments. Work at work. Running is running. Home is home. Weekend excursions are weekend excursions."

"Maybe," he says again, but that's really an admission that I'm right.

With trembling hands, I finish his tie and push the knot into place. His hands come up to make sure it's where he wants it, and then our eyes meet.

"I'm in love with you," I say, the words suddenly so easy to say. My voice even sounds normal. "I don't want any more zones between us."

Lance's eyes flicker as he looks back and forth between mine. "There are no zones between us."

"Yes, there are," I say, reaching to fiddle with his tie. I touch the crisp corners of his shirt. "You haven't kissed me in this office. There's a divide here."

Lance slides his hands along my waist, the nearness and warmth of him so close to me making me dizzy and drunk. "Let's get rid of that, shall we?" He touches his lips to my neck, which causes me to lean my head back. His mouth travels up toward my mouth, but stops near my earlobe.

"Because I love you too, Jess."

Delight dances through me, followed quickly by a pinpricking of tears. "Yeah?"

"So much," he says right before he kisses me completely right there in his office. "I love you with a capital I, L, and Y."

"ILY," I say against his lips, and then I kiss him again.

CHAPTER TWENTY-NINE

LANCE

I MEET DAWSON'S EYES AS I PASS HIM, AND HE SIMPLY lifts his drink to his lips. I don't see how he can be so calm. He'd gone with me to return Hadley's diamond ring, and while the jeweler wouldn't give me my money back, I'd recruited Tara and Callie to help me pick out a ring for Jess.

I'd done some super-spy moves to get Jess's phone and get her sister's number, and I'd texted Amy to see if the choice I'd then landed on would be something Jess would like. Amy and I have exchanged a few messages since then, with her initial one being an emoji face with hearts for eyes.

I'd taken that as a *yes, Jess will love this engagement ring*.

"Will you calm down?" Dawson asks. "Were you this nervous when you asked Hadley and Diane?"

"I'm not nervous," I say, because I'm not.

"Why are you pacing then?" He finishes his drink and sets it on my desk.

"Because, I don't want her to think I'm not ready." I'd stayed away from the holidays for a proposal. We'd spent a fabulous New Year's Eve together, and while I'd glared when she'd started working with Jason Finch when I thought he was going to be my client, I was secretly happy for her.

January is almost over, and I don't want to be anywhere near Valentine's Day when I ask her to be my wife. I'm Ready with a capital R, and I'm not sure I've been convincing enough for Jess over the past several weeks.

Dawson stands and reaches for his suit coat. "Okay, well, it's been fun. I have to go pick up my wife, and then we're driving to the airport to get my mother."

"Mm," I say, though I know Lila Houser is hard for Dawson to deal with. "Good luck."

He pauses in front of me. "You've got this," he says. "You love her, and she loves you, and she's not like anyone else you've ever dated or been engaged to."

After a man-hug where I say, "Thanks, Dawson," he nods and leaves my office. It's Friday afternoon, almost quitting time, and the offices at Finley & Frank are almost empty. I walk out with Dawson, and when I turn back to return to my office, I see Peter Frank coming out of his office. He's coated and carrying his briefcase, and our eyes meet.

I grin at him, as we own this agency together. "Heading out?"

"Yes," he says, reaching to shake my hand. "Proposing tonight?"

"Yes." I glance down to my open office door. "You're gone all next week?"

"Yes, Michelle and I are going to Grand Cayman."

"Wow, have fun," I say, wondering where Jess wants to go on her honeymoon. *Our* honeymoon.

"Good luck," Pete says, and he strides out of the agency. One more secretary bustles out before I'm left alone in the office. Now, I just have to wait for Jess to get back from her showing with Bernadette.

She's turned into a great real estate agent, and she's helped two clients from beginning to end now, one with an apartment rental and one with a new purchase. If this afternoon's showings go well, she might be able to get another offer in, the third of her career.

I'm insanely proud of her, and I try to kiss her in my office every chance I get. I'm still letting her pick my ties, and I'm still buttoned up too much, but she doesn't seem to mind either.

I don't mind when she shows me her sketches, or the emails she's still getting from Kira Chatwood. Nothing much has come from them except conversation, and Jess says sometimes the fashion world moves fast and sometimes it moves slow. I just do my best to support her and listen when she talks about her designs and her ideas for designs. She's started some sewing classes, because another designer she met in New York City told her a good designer should be able to make their designs too.

I love Jess for how hard she works and how smart she is. I love her because she loves me, and when I return to my office and pick up the deeply dark velvet box, I'm not nervous at all.

"I'm ready," I say out loud.

"Lance!" Jess calls, and I turn back toward my doorway. She comes skidding around the corner, her face lit with joy.

"You got an offer." I stride out of my office, my happiness doubling the closer I get to her.

"Bernadette wants the Salisbury Road place." She shrieks and drops her new briefcase—the one I bought for her at the beginning of the year. In the next moment, she jumps into my arms, laughing so much I have to join her.

"Congrats," I say, because the Salisbury place is one of ours. One of the agents down the hall from Peter is the selling agent for the house, and we often work with our own agents to get properties bought and sold.

Jess calms down and steps back from me, her grin going on for miles. "You're taking me to dinner to celebrate, right?"

"I do have a reservation at The Prime Rib tonight," I say, scanning her navy skirt, which she's paired with a burnt orange blouse. She knows I love Auburn and the blue and orange, and I can't remember the last time she wore anything red.

Her eyes are wide when I bring my gaze back to hers. "You do?" She falls back another step. "Did you know Bernadette was going to put in an offer?"

"How would I know that?" I ask, taking her hand and leading her gently toward my office. "This is the first time you've taken her to look at houses." My stomach only swoops once as I walk into the office, my eyes already sweeping my desk for the ring.

It's not there.

At that moment, I realize I'm still holding it in my hand. I don't have a fruit platter or any balloons. No wine or low lighting, though the sun sets so early in the winter. No roses. I was going to surprise her with the reservation at the steakhouse, but that cat is already out of the bag.

"Jess," I say, and I don't even have the urge to clear my throat. I do remember being so dang nervous to ask Hadley to marry me, but none of that exists with Jess.

She looks at me, her expression open and unassuming.

I hold up the box and drop to my knees.

"Lance Byers," she says, the words a gasp. She covers her mouth with both hands, her eyes never leaving mine.

I grin at her, completely calm. "I'm in love with you," I say. "ILY from now until forever. I want to marry you. Will you marry me?" I don't crack open the box. Hadley hadn't answered until she'd seen the diamond, but Jess is already bouncing on the balls of her feet.

"Yes," she says from behind her hands. They drop, and she giggles. "Yes!" She throws herself at me again, and since I'm not super stable on my knees—who is?—we both topple toward my desk.

I laugh, dropping the ring box and holding onto her as we tip sideways. We end up on the floor together, and I push her curls back off her face. "You're my favorite person in the whole world," I say, all the laughter gone. Only love remains, and I find it shining in her eyes too.

"ILY from now until forever too," she whispers. "I can't wait to be your wife." She touches her lips to mine, and this kiss is so sweet and so intimate and so perfect.

"How long do we have to wait?" I ask, sliding my mouth along her jaw. "What will your mama want?"

Jess grins and giggles, leaning into my touch, which makes me feel powerful and important to her. "You know what? I don't much care. I'm living *my* life now, so what do you think?"

"I think you're a spring wedding type of woman," I say.

She giggles and tucks her cheek against my chest. "Yeah, and you've been talking to Amy."

I pull in a breath. "I have not." I can't really lie to her, though, so I chuckle in the next moment. "Fine, I have. She said you've always wanted flowers upon flowers for you wedding, and I figure spring is a great time for that."

"Mm, spring would be fabulous," she says, kissing me again. I don't even care that we're lying on the floor of my real estate office, the diamond ring somewhere around in here, which probably hasn't been cleaned in a week. No one else is at the agency, and I can lose hours of my life kissing my fiancée. So I just keep doing that.

————

Read on for a sneak peek at Sabrina and Jason in **JUST HIS PARTNER.**

SNEAK PEEK! JUST HIS PARTNER
CHAPTER ONE: SABRINA

I GLANCE LEFT AND RIGHT AS I GET OFF THE elevator, trying to decide if the smell on this floor is the same as it was when I left for work. There's definitely a funk in the air, and I wrinkle my nose as I walk.

My new apartment sits near the end of the hall, with one more unit beside mine in the corner. I didn't mind the move, because I don't have a whole lot. I had to get out of that place with the blown-up egg bits everywhere, and no, I didn't get my cleaning deposit back. I'm lucky I didn't get an extra bill to redo texture and paint, in all honesty.

I *may* have not left a forwarding address and deleted my former landlord's contact information from my cell-phone. Since I only answer calls from numbers I know on my personal line, I suppose he could've called looking for me. I just don't know it.

With every step I take toward my new apartment—

where I don't want to be living, mind you—the scent intensifies. I glare at 4I as I pass, my goal 4K, which is where I live. I want a farmhouse in the woods, where Archie—the cat who came with this apartment—can chase mice and birds to his heart's content.

I want to tear out a kitchen and put in a new one. I want to soak in a really old tub, and then replace it with something new. I'm not sure why, as I've never done much remodeling or renovating. It just sounds fun. Plus, maybe if I tear down old sheetrock and pull out defunct pipes, I'll cleanse myself of the things that need replacing in my life too.

Such a deep metaphor, I know. I am a lawyer, after all.

I reach 4K and fit my key into the lock, the smell as strong as if I'm in the same room with it. Rodizio across the hall must be making his mother's fajitas again. They put off this decaying smell last time he tried, and I cast a look at 4L across the hall from my place as the knob turns.

"M-row," Archie sings, running past my ankles.

"Hey, buddy," I say to him, but he's streaking down the hall. He's kind of a community cat, though he stays in my apartment, sleeps in my bed, and I feed and water him. So he's kind of mine too. The previous renters of this apartment couldn't take him with them, and they'd asked with such sad-kitty eyes if I'd take him that I couldn't say no.

I'm not sure why. I say no to plenty of other things.

Not Jason Finch, I think as I enter the apartment and

leave the front door open a crack so Archie can get back in. I sigh, reminding myself that Jason Finch—a man I work with at my firm—isn't asking me any yes/no questions. Certainly not if I'd like to go to dinner with him.

That would be a yes anyway, not a no.

I exhale and wipe my hand back across my forehead and into my hair as I drop my briefcase and jacket onto the armchair in the living room. The smell has gotten worse, and that takes my attention into the kitchen.

My mind is stuck on Jason, the wedding we attended together over two months ago, and our working relationship. That at least is working now, so it's probably best that he doesn't ask me out. In this day and age, I can probably ask him, but again, things are going so well at the firm that I don't dare jinx anything.

Not only that, but perhaps he didn't enjoy himself at his cousin's wedding as much as I did. Or maybe he decided it wasn't a date and that we'd simply gone together so he didn't have to go alone. Perhaps I'm just his partner, and that's just how he wants it. No matter what, I feel like I failed some sort of test I hadn't known I was taking.

And I'm a really good test-taker, so familiar frustration fills me as I enter my kitchen.

My eyes land on the slow cooker, and the world narrows to that appliance. The smell intensifies, as if I've been cooking squirrels—or human hands—on low for the past eight hours. Horror fills me, and I dash over to the counter and lift the lid on my "no-fail beef stew."

Oh, I've failed. Big time.

I gag as the full brunt of the scent hits me square in the face, wondering how in the world I ruined a dish that only has six ingredients. Six! Total.

Carrots, potatoes, broth, salt, pepper, and cubed beef.

"More like cubed barf," I say, slamming the lid down on the cooker. I have to get rid of this, stat. How am I the worst cook in America?

"Because you're Sabrina Shadows," I mutter to myself, lifting the heavy stoneware piece out of the cooking element. I look at the sink, which has a disposal, and veto that idea. Knowing me, the stew—and I use that term loosely—will get stuck in the drain and this smell will never go away.

The trash is also out, and I simply head for the door. This whole thing is going straight in the Dumpster behind the building, and I feel like a criminal dragging out a dead body as I enter the elevator, relieved I'm the only one inside the car on the way down.

I dash outside and heave the crock over the top lip of the Dumpster, my heart beating so fast. I just know crazy Mrs. Littleton is watching through her back window, and I glance up to the third floor where she lives. I swear the curtain in the third pane over flutters, and I tell myself I did nothing wrong.

Well, besides the crime against carrots, of course.

I'm going to have to move again. I *want* to move again, and I pull my phone out of my pocket as I march back toward the building entrance. Jessica Dunaway's line rings only twice before she chirps, "Hey, Sabrina."

"Jess," I practically shout. "Any progress on the house hunting?"

"Didn't you get my message?" she asks, causing my brow to furrow.

"No," I say.

"Hmm, strange," she says, and it sounds like she's distracted with something else. I know, because I sound like this all the time, and I'm constantly doing five hundred and eleven different things.

My phone makes a weird *bloopety-bloop* at me, and I pull it from my ear as Jess says she sent over some new listings for me to look at.

Jason Finch sits on the screen, his call coming in over Jess's. I drop my phone, my surprise too great to keep holding it. The device splats against the asphalt, and a terrible cracking noise fills the sky.

The phone tumbles away from me, and I go scampering after it. When I reach it and lift it up, I see a diagonal fissure running from the bottom left corner to the top right. "Great," I say, because the screen is completely black too.

No call connected to Jess. No line ringing in from Jason.

"Just great."

————

LATER THAT NIGHT, I pull into the parking lot at my building, my ire near its breaking point. I hadn't made it to the cell phone store before they'd closed. I can't get a new phone until tomorrow, and I seriously feel like Archie has gnawed off my arm and won't give it back.

I start to pull into my marked, covered, reserved spot and find a car already there. "Are you freaking kidding me?" I ask, wanting to go Fried Green Tomatoes on the fancy-pants SUV in my spot and floor the accelerator. See how they like their luxury vehicle then.

Instead of doing something that can get me arrested, I put my car in reverse and straighten out so I can swing into an unmarked, uncovered, and available parking space. Where that guy should've parked. I tell myself it doesn't snow in Charleston, that I'm not in Montana anymore, and it's fine.

Everything's fine.

I keep the mantra running through my head all the way to the fourth floor, where I step off the elevator, the hint of my beef stew fiasco still lingering in the air. Something else has masked it though, and I cock my head, familiarity running through me.

"Ah, there she is," a man says, and I know that voice.

Worlds collide as I turn toward the voice and my apartment and find Jason Finch himself standing there. He's still in his slacks and tie from work, but he's got

Archie in his arms, stroking the cat as if he's the original owner of him and has been searching for him for many long years.

My heartbeat goes wild, knocking against my ribcage like a crazed fish out of water. "What are you doing here?" I ask, walking toward him. Everything about this scenario is wrong. Jason Finch doesn't exist outside the walls of Farmer, Buhler, and Cason, Attorneys at Law.

And yet, there he stands, that gorgeous smile on his face and that traitorous cat in his arms.

"I called and left several messages," he says, those dark-as-danger eyes firing at me. "Saying I needed to come by so we could go over a case that's been called up in the morning."

"Tomorrow morning?"

"That would be morning," he says.

I glare at him, wishing his face would melt right off. Wait. No, I take that back. He's too handsome for such a thought. "Can you put down my cat?"

Jason looks down at Archie, and the animal is practically asleep, seemingly in complete bliss. I know if Jason held me like that, I would be.

He looks up at me. "Is he yours?"

"Yes," I say, taking Archie from him as I reach him. "How long have you been here?"

"A couple of minutes," he says.

"How did you figure out where I live?" I ask.

"Cheryl," he says, and I nod. She's my secretary, so I

suppose that makes sense. He's here about a case, and he stoops to pick up his briefcase. We've taken two steps down the hall toward my apartment when the elevator dings again, signaling the car has arrived.

I normally don't look to see who it is, but when a voice says, "There he is," in an indignant tone, I do. Mrs. Littleton stands there, pointing her crooked finger in my and Jason's direction. "He's been loitering around here for at least an hour."

Two police officers step off the elevator too, and I can't help but think of the body—er, crock pot—in the Dumpster out back. I blink, imagining a situation where they ask why it smells like death in my apartment and then haul me down to the station to ask me who I killed and then tried to cook slowly into a stew.

When my eyes focus again, the cops are nearly upon us, and one of them frowns at me. "I'm sorry," I say. "Did you say something?"

"He asked if you knew me," Jason says pointedly, to which I blink some more. "Why are you standing there like that?" He sighs and rolls his eyes. "We work together. She's my junior partner."

"Work together," one cop repeats. He's much bigger and beefier than his partner. I can't help but wonder what kind of stew he'd make since he is so beefy. Then my brain catches up to the pun, and I shake my head.

"You don't know him?" the skinnier cop asks. The

three of them stand there staring at me, and Archie goes, "Me-row," before jumping down from my arms.

I watch him do his cat-stalk into the apartment, wondering if he somehow did something to the stew. It was seriously six ingredients, and cats aren't exactly trustworthy.

"Bri," Jason barks at me, and I focus on the more immediate situation.

"Yes," I say to the cops, pulling myself all the way together. It's hard for this late in the day. "I know him. We work together at Farmer, Buhler, and Cason, and we have to go over a case that just got called into court tomorrow morning."

SNEAK PEEK! JUST HIS PARTNER
CHAPTER TWO: JASON

"Took you long enough," I say to Sabrina after the cops have gone, after they've assured the white-haired lady who'd accused me of loitering that I wasn't a stalker, and after we've gone into Bri's apartment and closed the door.

"I was thinking about something else," she says, hurrying into the kitchen to unplug something. It smells like overcooked leather mixed with Brussels sprouts in her apartment, and I really want to go home.

At the same time, the dark-haired beauty across the room holds me captive. I had a fantastic time with her at Tara and Alec's wedding, but I haven't asked her out again. I know how to do it, but I've held back. I want to get things right with Bri for some reason. I don't want her to be another woman in my long list of dates and acquaintances.

I've been trying out a bachelor lifestyle—a true bachelor lifestyle. The kind where I go to work, do a good job, and then go home. Where I don't flirt with every woman I meet, and I don't go out with three or four different women every week. In fact, I haven't gone out with anyone in the past six months, and that started before Tara's wedding.

Seeing her so blissfully happy with Alec changed a lot for me. I want her brand of happiness, and I know it doesn't come from having a different woman on my arm every evening. No matter what, I still go home alone.

I glance around Bri's apartment, taking in the mismatched furniture and the lack of pictures on the wall.

"I just moved in," she says, pulling my attention back to her. I don't see any boxes or anything else to indicate she's in the middle of unpacking, but I don't say anything about it. She opens the fridge and promptly closes it again. "I don't have any food here. Are you hungry?"

"I haven't eaten," I say coolly. "Do you want to get CarryEats or go out?"

She indicates my briefcase with her chin. "We better get CarryEats and get this ironed out." She sounds tired, and boy, do I understand that. Exhaustion pulls though my soul, and no one in law school tells you how tired you'll be some days. They should have an Utter Exhaustion 101 class simply as a way to weed out the strong from the weak.

Right now, I feel like I can't even stand for another second, so I move over to the couch and sit down.

"My phone broke," Bri says, moving to perch on the armrest on the end of the couch. "That's why I didn't get any of your calls or messages."

I look up at her, something quiet and powerful moving between us. I don't know how whatever that is can be both of those things at the same time, but it is. "I'm sorry about your phone."

"I was out trying to get a new one," she says. "You didn't have to wait an hour here."

Embarrassment floods me. That little old lady really sold me out. "It wasn't that long," I say, though it definitely was longer than a few minutes. "We need to go over the case, and I couldn't get in touch with you."

I actually have the case memorized, but Bri and I have been working it together, and I'd love to see her take the lead in court tomorrow. My throat goes dry, because I've never said that to her. Not once.

I pull out my phone and start swiping through the options at CarryEats. "What do you want?"

"Anything but stew," she says, which causes me to look up at her.

She shakes her head, displeasure in her dark eyes. "Don't ask. It's a long story." She pulls the band out of her hair, which causes it to tumble down over her shoulders. Oh, I can't stay here for much longer. Not with her dressing down like that, and not if we share dinner.

I'm going to say something I either mean or don't mean —both are really dangerous right now. I feel fragile, like I'm not sure who I am or what I'm doing. The truth is, I don't. I'm in a state of flux right now, and that is really bad news for me.

"No stew," I say, my voice only slightly pinched. "Not Your Momma's Noodles?"

"Sure," she says. "I like the firehouse mac and cheese there."

"You got it," I say, keeping my focus on the phone and not her. I have to. If I don't...well, I don't even want to think about what will happen if I don't.

She's just your partner, I tell myself. *You don't want to do anything to jeopardize your job.*

I've told myself these things before over the past couple of months. There's no rule at Farmer, Buhler, and Cason that would prevent Bri and I from seeing one another. There's a folder of paperwork though, and the relationship won't be kept secret if I start it.

I'm fairly certain I'm going to have to be the one to start it, as Bri hasn't said a single word about the wedding. She's so different from other women I'm usually attracted to, because she doesn't seem to like me. And that only makes me like her more, crazy as that sounds.

I finish with the order and look up again, sighing this time. "Twenty-four to thirty-four minutes."

She smiles at me and slips down onto the couch. "All right," she says. "Just enough time to lay everything out in order and then go over it while we eat." She pulls the coffee table closer to our knees.

"I want you to take lead," I blurt out, forgetting all of the tactful ways I was going to bring this up with her.

Her eyes widen. "You want me to do what?"

"You heard me." I reach for my briefcase. "So *you're* going to lay this out, and then you're going to present it to me while *I* eat."

"I haven't eaten either," she says, folding her arms and glaring at me. Seriously, that is so annoyingly-attractive, and I can't help grinning at her.

"You can eat when you get the case right."

"You're not my mother, Jason," she says, reaching for the first sheaf of papers I extract from my briefcase.

"Thank goodness for that," I mutter, because it would be super weird if her mother had the same feelings for Bri that I do. I've already fantasized about kissing her, and yeah. Super weird.

"What?" she asks.

"Nothing," I say, speaking up. "Now, that top paper is the list of witnesses the defense is going to call..."

————

BRI EXCHANGES A GLANCE with me while we sit at the prosecutor's table. I barely move my chin, and she pushes to her feet. "Mister Davenport," she says without leaving her spot at the table. "You were driving, correct?"

"Yes," the man in the witness chair says. People think court is so exciting, and it's really not. There's no flashy lights or big-name actors here. This isn't even truly court, but a grand jury to simply determine if we can take the case to court. It's a great way for Bri to get some experience with a witness, and she can consult with me any time she needs to.

"Driving your car, correct?" she asks, moving to the end of the table and leaning one hip into it. It was her idea to explore this idea of who the car and the weapon truly belong to, and honestly, it's a shot in the dark. There are so many witnesses, and so many perpetrators, and every single one of them has a different story.

We've combed over every police report and read every witness declaration, and even I don't know who was really the mastermind behind the United Methodist School robbery several months ago. Bri had the idea to question Derrick Davenport and see what he said about the gun and the car.

Right now, he glances toward the empty defense table and then to me. "Yes," he says.

"Who held your gun to your ribs?" Bri reaches down and shuffles some papers on the table, but I can tell she's not looking at them. She just doesn't want Mister Davenport to feel like she's studying him. There's no judge present today. No defendant is allowed to present his case.

The prosecution lays out the case, their evidence, and can question witnesses, and the members of the grand jury vote in secret as to whether there is enough to proceed with the case. With how convoluted everything in this particular case is, we'll be batting a thousand if we get it past the grand jury.

"Thomas," Mister Davenport says, and Bri lifts her head.

"Thomas Rowberry?" she asks.

Mister Davenport licks his lips. "I mean Teddy. Teddy Christopher."

"Was it Thomas Rowberry or Teddy Christopher?" Bri asks, taking a step toward the podium. She can't go past that, and I told her not to even use it. She stops after a single step, and I mentally cheer for her. She can be an intimidating woman, and Derrick Davenport certainly seems to be shaking in his boots right now.

"Teddy Christopher," he says.

Bri nods and turns back to the table. "And you drove your own car, with your own gun pressed to your ribs, into the river. Is that right?"

"Yes," he says. "Thomas said I had to. Then there'd be no prints."

Bri picks up the folder I slide forward on the table. "Yes, the prints." She holds up the folder. "Evidence for the United Methodist School," she says crisply. "Only Mister Davenport's prints were found on the gun and inside the car. He claims to have worn gloves, but no other DNA evidence was found either."

"Because the car went into the river," Mister Davenport says.

Bri hands the folder containing the print and DNA evidence—or lack thereof to the lead juror in the grand jury. There's twenty-one people here today, and Bri continues with, "You can speak freely, Mister Davenport. The purpose of this session is that you don't have to be afraid of anyone." She faces him again, and I see the fierceness on her face before she does.

"There's not going to be any retaliation from what you say," she says. "No one will know. Grand jury testimony is sealed." She migrates back to the table while Mister Davenport squirms and then coughs.

My word, she was right. He's the guilty party here, and we may have charged the wrong individual with being the mastermind behind the crime.

Our eyes meet, and I hope she gets the message I feel blazing in mine. *Ask him. Ask him now.* "Didn't you simply plan and carry out this robbery by yourself?" Bri asks, taking that step forward again.

Mister Davenport turns a shade of gray I haven't even seen on the sidewalk. "I—" He glances over to the jury.

"A yes or no," Bri prompts.

"No," he says. "It was Teddy Christopher."

"Not Thomas Rowberry?" she asks as if she doesn't really care. She's *good.*

"Teddy held the gun in the car. Thomas masterminded the whole thing."

"So Teddy is the same man who held your own gun to you and commanded you drive your car into the river," Bri says. "And whose prints were not found on either."

Mister Davenport clears his throat. "Right."

"Because Thomas told you both to." She sounds like my very disappointed fourth grade teacher, using a voice that indicates she doesn't believe Mister Davenport at all.

"Yes," he says.

"Very well," she says airily as if she's satisfied with the witness's testimony. She sits down next to me, and I keep my gaze on the notes in front of me while she closes with the evidence we do have, and how we'll be pursuing all leads to make sure the right person is charged and brought to justice in the robbing of a prestigious private school in the city.

"Even if that person is Mister Derrick Davenport," Bri says. "Thank you." We collect our things and prepare to leave the court-like conference room. Mister Davenport glares knives into Bri's face, but she acts like she doesn't even notice.

Out in the hallway, I finally take a breath that doesn't feel like oatmeal in my lungs. "That was great," I say, exhaling most of the words out.

Bri looks at me with hope in those pretty eyes. "Yeah? Really? I felt so...off. I really thought he was going to say he did it alone." She shakes her head, clearly disappointed.

"I think he did," I say. "And I've never thought that before you said it last night."

"I guess we'll see what the grand jury says. I really want to take this to trial. There's something not right with this case." She plops her bag down on a bench and rifles through it.

"You're going to read the brief again right now?"

"How long does the grand jury take?"

"Depends," I say. "Could be a while if they don't agree. Could be hours or tomorrow. Could be fast."

"Mister Finch?"

I turn toward the sound of Deputy Jones's voice. My eyebrows fly toward the sky. "They're back?" I ask, striding toward him. He hands me an envelope, and I flip it open as he returns to the room.

Bri presses in beside me, and I pull out the note. My whole body screams at me about the scent of Bri's perfume, and the way her arm is warming mine. I look up. "We can indict."

Her face splits into a grin, and she laughs. "We did it," she says.

I can't help smiling too, because a happy Bri is so much better than a growly one, and I've seen both. "No," I say. "*You* did it."

She grabs onto me and hugs me, and I try not to close my eyes in bliss. Yeah, that's a try and a fail. "Thank you, Jason," she says, so much sincerity in her voice. Maybe I'm imagining things, but I hear some emotion too.

She pulls back, and our eyes meet. She's maybe five inches from me, and I do what I usually do when a beautiful woman is in my arms. I lean down and touch my lips to hers. Fireworks and the National Anthem and entire choirs of angels sing down from above.

Wow, kissing Sabrina Shadows is *amazing*. Like life-changing-amazing.

She kisses me back, and while she might seem like the uptight, cardigan-wearing lawyer type, the woman has lips made of apples and honey.

My eyes are closed, and the next thing I know, she's ripped her lips away from mine. She says, "No, we're not doing this," and she shoves both palms against my chest.

I stumble backward, my eyes flying open. Surprise and humiliation swirl together in my chest, and all I can do is stand there as Bri marches away from me, collects her briefcase, and heads for the stairs.

"Wait," I say, but she's already gone. I push my hand through my hair and sigh. "Idiot," I tell myself as I collect the indictment paper and my own briefcase. "Stupid, stupid, stupid."

My phone rings, and my cousin's name sits there. How does Tara always know when I've made a complete and utter fool of myself? I won't be able to hide it from her. I'll say one word, and she'll be like, *What happened? Why do you sound like you've sucked down helium?*

If I don't answer, she'll stop by my house with dessert or a pan of lemon chicken and roast potatoes. I decide I better get something delicious out of telling her how I just made the worst mistake possible with my junior partner, and I swipe the call to voicemail.

Then I hurry after Bri, because she drove us over here. Because I have to make sure we're okay before we get back to the seventeenth floor of our office building.

Because she *kissed me back*, and I want to know why she did that if she doesn't want to "do this" with me.

————

She's just his partner, because she's seen the number of women he parades through his life. No amount of charm and good looks is worth being played...until Sabrina witnesses Jason take the blame for someone else at the law office where they both work.

Just His Partner is now available!

BOOKS IN THE SOUTHERN ROOTS SWEET ROMCOM SERIES

Just His Secretary, Book 1: She's just his secretary...until he needs someone on his arm to convince his mother that he can take over the family business. Then Callie becomes Dawson's girlfriend—but just in his text messages...but maybe she'll start to worm her way into his shriveled heart too.

Just His Boss, Book 2: She's just his boss, especially since Tara just barely hired Alec. But when things heat up in the kitchen, Tara will have to decide where Alec is needed more —on her arm or behind the stove.

Just His Assistant, Book 3: She's just his assistant, which is exactly how this Southern belle wants it. No spotlight. Not anymore. But as she struggles to learn her new role in his office—especially because Lance is the surliest boss imaginable—Jessie might just have to open her heart to show him everyone has a past they're running from.

Just His Partner, Book 4: She's just his partner, because she's seen the number of women he parades through his life. No amount of charm and good looks is worth being played...until Sabra witnesses Jason take the blame for someone else at the law office where they both work.

Just His Barista, Book 5: She's just his barista...until she buys into Legacy Brew as a co-owner. Then she's Coy's business partner *and* the source of his five-year-long crush. But after they share a kiss one night,

Macie's seriously considering mixing business and pleasure.

A Very Terrible Text, Book 1: Sometimes the thumbs slip...

She's finally joined the dating app everyone in Cider Cove is raving about...when she accidentally sends a message about wanting to meet up for a first date to her enemy.

A Very Bad Bet, Book 2: *Sometimes a wager only makes things more fun...*

She's got seniority over the obnoxious grump next door, and she's determined to beat him out for the top job in their charming hometown. But a bold bet spins their rivalry into a flirty attraction that could change everything.

ABOUT ELANA

Elana Johnson is a USA Today bestselling and Kindle All-Star author of dozens of clean and wholesome contemporary romance novels. She lives in Utah, where she mothers two fur babies, works with her husband full-time, and eats a lot of veggies while writing. Find her on her website at feelgoodfictionbooks.com.

Printed in Great Britain
by Amazon

45458658R00209